THERE WAS A
LITTLE BOY

THERE WAS A LITTLE BOY

A NOVEL BY

CLAIRE RAINWATER JACOBS

CB

CONTEMPORARY
BOOKS

CHICAGO

Library of Congress Cataloging-in-Publication Data

Jacobs, Claire Rainwater.
   There was a little boy : a novel / Claire Rainwater Jacobs.
     p.   cm.
   ISBN 0-8092-4311-3 : $18.95
   1. Large type books.   I. Title.
PS3560.A2495T4   1990
813'.54—dc20   90-41055
                                       CIP

"How to Eat a Poem" from *A Sky Full of Poems* by Eve Merriam. Copyright © 1964, 1970, 1973 by Eve Merriam. All rights reserved. Reprinted by permission of Marian Reiner for the author.

Published by Contemporary Books, Inc.
180 North Michigan Avenue, Chicago, Illinois 60601
Manufactured in the United States of America
International Standard Book Number: 0-8092-4311-3

For Caroll, Andrew, and Stefan,
and in memory of
Gyongyi and Morris

Acknowledgments

My gratitude to:

Caroll for his belief in me and my writing and for his poem, "Autumn-Tide."

My brilliant agent and friend, Herb Katz, and wonderful Nancy Katz, for their help, inspiration, and encouragement.

Jo Ann Miller for her enthusiastic help and friendship.

Anita Rich for her friendship and moral support.

Andrew Jacobs for his sensitive readings.

Stefan Jacobs for rescuing me from the demon machine.

Cherrill Colson for expert medical advice.

My editor, Stacy Prince, for her hard work, patience, and good humor.

THERE WAS A
LITTLE BOY

Prologue

December 1973

Cheap binoculars focused in on Julie from deep in the shadows behind thick panels of curtain in a room not five feet from where she sat in her apartment rhythmically brushing, brushing her hair. The lens that held her captive was marred by a thread-like crack, partially distorting her face. Trying to focus precisely was useless because the amplification was inadequate, so that the image of Julie sitting sideways at the dressing table in front of the curlicued mirror on the wall perpendicular to the window was ever so slightly blurred. She was brushing a cloud of gold.

The observer could not hear Julie singing softly as she brushed methodically, "Rapunzel, Rapunzel, let down your hair." But the lens lingered longingly on her fair face, and the viewer, scowling at Julie's ambiguous smile, could not have known that Julie was thinking that instant of one of the happier moments with her husband, Les, who called her Rapunzel. And combining fairy tales, he asked her every night, as she let down her hair before going to bed, if she was still spinning flax into gold. She did indeed look like a fairy princess in her long nightgown, brushing her hair.

Suddenly Julie jumped out of the circle of the fractured lens, and gnarled fingers unbent from the binoculars to wait.

• • •

An unseen hand always raised the cracked white window in the morning and lowered it at night. Julie stared across at the

• 1 •

grimy window with the faded red curtains and the ever-present darkness inside, at the hotel room facing her baby's bright, sunny, cheerful room, wondering what poor soul lived there.

You're too softhearted, Les chided her on many occasions when she worried about the residents of the run-down building next door. But his admonition was loving, she thought. And she felt he really understood. "There but for the grace of God go I," he said once, peering nervously at the window with a strange look, barely perceiving a faint shape inside.

The SRO, Single Room Occupancy Hotel, for welfare people stood side by side with their Art Deco building in Manhattan, fronting west on the Hudson. But the impenetrable room faced north on the alley between them, all light unforgivingly blocked by her building, which towered sixteen stories over it.

Julie felt particularly guilty about it, as if it were her fault that the grim room opposite, so close she could almost reach across and touch the crumbling ledge, had no morning sunlight, that its curtain-shrouded windows were identical to those of every other room in the SRO, giving each one that faceless, anonymous quality.

Julie jumped up from the dressing table at the sound of her infant stirring to pick him up even before he uttered a cry. She put her gloomy feeling aside, just as she pushed her other dark thoughts away. The day was too luminous, and her heart lightened at the sight of her baby opening his violet eyes in the handsome antique crib.

"Oh, my little lamb," she crooned, scooping the delicate infant up and pressing his body tenderly to her, his dimpled little fingers playing with her cheek. "What would life be without you?"

• • •

There was a slight odor of ammonia in the room because Esperanza had sprinkled it into the corners to chase away the spirits. Now the large empty basket in the center of the nativity scene was ready, cushioned in expectation.

Esperanza meant hope. And now, for the first time since Marcos, her baby brother, was torn from her, she had hope. Was this why the Virgin had been whispering in her ear all these years? When they sent her away, she never even told them the Virgin spoke to her. They pitied her enough. It was wise to keep it from them. She would never have gotten away. First her voices had led her here, and then God had sent His Messenger to teach her.

The room was dark. Two black candles burned on either side of the basket, casting twisted shadows on the ceiling. They flickered madly against the breeze. Checking across the alley, she shut the window. Then Esperanza raised the binoculars.

She had to have a baby. It was God's will. Esperanza had been cursed at birth, but now God was making amends. She looked down at her hands gripping the binoculars. Ugly, misshapen, like the rest of her body. She squinted into the eyepiece. The baby's face, fresh and innocent, filled the lens. Just like his mother, healthy and blessed with beauty. As soon as she had the infant, Esperanza's disfigurement would magically evaporate. Like last time.

Esperanza rested the binoculars on the bed and hovered over the two fast-melting tapers. The decision was in God's hands, and in a moment she would have His answer. If the right candle burned down first, she would have the baby. If it was the left candle, she was helpless, in spite of her instructions. Esperanza needed God's approval, above all others'.

Today might be her last chance. Which was it to be? She had waited so long.

● ● ●

Julie noticed that the window across the way was closed. It was as if the invisible tenant had waited for her to leave the room so that she would not see who shut the window. She shuddered.

"Time to go, lovey-dovey." Julie whirled the baby around in his pram suit. She had decided to wear her alpaca sweater and skirt, long wool stockings, and her high, laced shoes. She was roasting in the overheated apartment and wondered if she was overdressed.

She turned off the record she had been playing as she dressed the baby for their walk. It was a composition of her husband's that had just been released.

"Aren't you proud of your daddy?" she crooned into her baby's ear. She bent him down to the record jacket, which showed Les, his handsome aesthetic features brooding. "The Les Layton Trio," it read in bold print. "Modern Moods."

She picked up the cover and turned it over to the blurb.

"Listen to this, lambie. 'Brilliant, innovative jazz compositions from the great bass musician, written for his own trio. After a two-year hiatus, the long-awaited . . .' "

Julie stopped reading. "You don't need to hear any more. Enough for you to know your father's a famous genius."

She smoothed the blanket in the crib, feeling the thick velour, loving the white lambs and the clouds on the pale blue background.

"Your legacy from the past," she told her baby, laying him down and raising his head gently to pull his hat over his ears. "Your father slept under that very blanket. Did you know that?

"I wonder what *you* will be when you grow up, my little bright eyes? Musical like your father? A doctor? A lawyer?"

She pushed the carriage toward the elevator, pulling her wool cap from the hall closet at the last moment.

• • •

Esperanza grabbed her coat from the bed as soon as she saw the baby in outer clothes. She raced down ten flights to reach the lobby of Julie's building. The hall would be deserted at this time of day. And the cavernous old marble entranceway had nooks and crannies to hide in. She knew the layout from memory, having worked there for a year cleaning for an old man, who had since died, in the same apartment line as Julie's.

This couldn't be a coincidence, the mother and child living next to her, in that apartment, she realized with joy. For the first time in eighteen years Esperanza felt alive. She had tracked Julie for weeks. Now she knew what she had to do. The right candle had already burned down with a gasp.

• • •

Julie's carriage clattered and echoed in the large entranceway. Passing the stained-glass windows and the old leather couches, the wall sconces and the chandeliers every day felt to

Julie as if she were living in history. A glass bonnet covered the circular driveway, which had been designed for carriages at the turn of the century. There was a fountain on the right for watering horses.

"Faded elegance," Les called it. Today it gave Julie the creeps. The lobby always gave her palpitations, so she hurried outside with her baby into the crisp December day.

"It's chilly," she advised her infant son, pulling up his plaid blanket. His eyes were shining, and he smiled at her. Julie was glad she was wearing her warm clothes as the wind off the river nipped her nose.

"Whee!" she cried, speeding up the carriage to a run. Let's get out of here, she thought, escaping more than merely the December wind.

• • •

It was hard to keep up with Julie. She was young, but Esperanza was strong, and her determination kept her going. She would follow them to the ends of the earth if necessary. But it wasn't necessary. Esperanza knew Julie's routine. And she recognized her colorful wool coat, her matching fringed scarf flying behind her neck as she ran, even as she wound her way through a crowd. By noon they would be back home. And from noon to at least two o'clock the baby would be fast asleep.

• • •

As she maneuvered around the giant mounds of garbage stacked in black plastic bags outside the welfare hotel, Julie tried to concentrate on the party her friend, Bobbie, was throwing that evening. She recognized the growls of Willie English even before she saw him in his usual bizarre outfit, weaving in and out of traffic on Riverside Drive, doffing his feathered hat to the horrified drivers who glimpsed his sleeveless fur jacket, cowboy boots, and the bottle he held in a brown paper bag before they sped by.

Les named him "Our Local Loco," but Julie felt menaced when he came too close to her and hissed into the carriage. Often she heard his growls at night, and they evoked all the schizophrenics who wandered on Broadway talking to nonexistent companions and the pathetic bag ladies who slept in doorways.

She hurried to the bank, crossing Broadway. Why was she so jittery today? She scanned the bank as she waited in line. No crazies. It must be a bank holiday for the deranged, she thought. Tonight at the party she would try to enlist Bobbie's help in alleviating the plight of street women. Bobbie, a teacher like Julie, was also an actress. They had become permanent friends at Catherine Dunbar Junior High School, where Bobbie had taken her under her wing. Julie was running short of volunteers for her causes.

"You love causes," Les had observed when she settled into his apartment after they were married and he realized how much time she devoted to her work outside of teaching.

Julie moved forward in the line.

She remembered the rest of Les's comment. "If I were a simple guy," he had remarked, "you wouldn't have picked me. I'm a challenge," he said laughingly.

Was it true? Sometimes he was too much of a challenge. Something about Les always nagged at Julie. This morning, for example. He was so indecisive, so conflicted. Reflecting on his leaving without breakfast, she realized how troubled he was.

Today, once again, he had been skulking in the back room, his storeroom. Julie remembered Bobbie's remark when she first discovered the room.

"God, Julie! This looks like an old prop shop. What is this appliance morgue, the dark side of Lester Layton?"

Before the baby was born, there were times when she thought she would give up on Lester. There was a secret side to him she couldn't penetrate, a side he would never turn toward her. He was too fragile, too vulnerable. He needed her strong shoulders. Les had few friends, trusted few. Yet she was attracted to him, to his good looks, his shy quality. He was clever and talented. Modest, too.

She could remember the exact moment she fell for him. He looked so poetic, with a profile like Byron or Chopin. She pictured him performing at her college with his band, when she was a naive sophomore in awe of him because he was a famous jazz musician. How her heart had beaten when he picked her out of the adoring crowd to have a drink with him after the show.

Little did she know then that the subculture of a band on the road was totally unlike the aura of glamour that intrigued her when they met. All she saw at the concert was Les, tall, elegant, worldly, his slender fingers plucking the strings of the bass. Later that night all she knew were his eyes, drinking her in, oblivious to the stares of all the other college girls. She had been seduced by the sounds, by the allure of art, by the song of the siren.

"You were so fresh, so open, so young, and yet mature," Les told her when they were married, explaining to her why he chose her that night. "Your eyes sparkled. I could see the world sparkling through your eyes."

She recalled the lines he wrote after they walked through the fallen leaves on the campus the next afternoon.

And turning back the sun burns on
Leaving a blaze of falling leaves.

And when she awoke the next morning, after their first night together, she found the conclusion of the poem, "Autumn-Tide," which he had written to her.

The salt-taste of skin
(Your finger drawn
Across my lips and chin)
Stings imagination
With quintessential delight
of certain savories long
long lost to memory.

How can a man who can write a beautiful poem, play an instrument with such feeling . . .? But the last stanza of his poem finished her thought as she looked lovingly at their baby.

There's a pile of pebbles in the sea
A heap upon the sand
A blue wind swirls the stars
and my arms are full of snowflakes.

The bank line was moving fast, bringing her back to reality. She pushed the carriage up. It was her turn next.

Sometimes Julie was afraid Les didn't want the baby. But when she confided in Bobbie, Bobbie had said that most men don't want the baby at first. Then they get to love them as much as mothers do.

Heading for the exit, Julie imagined Les at the party tonight. Bobbie had arranged for the right people to be there. They would be crowded around him in spite of his reticence. Bobbie always claimed you couldn't succeed on talent alone, that Les didn't know how to get ahead. He was famous but poor. It was because of Bobbie, who had introduced him to his agent, that he had cut the record and Julie was able to quit her job and have a baby.

Les was so well known that he had been listed in the *Encyclopedia of Contemporary Jazz* for years; he was noted for his innovative bass technique and his proficiency with many different instruments. But there were two years conspicuously missing, years Les never discussed. Julie could only guess about that hole in his history.

Julie's thoughts were jarred by the sight of someone dashing around the corner as the bank guard held the door open for them. It was as if she had chased someone away. Just another West Side oddball to contend with, she decided.

Julie moved more rapidly through her errands, and when she looked into the carriage the baby was fast asleep under his blanket, his eyes tightly closed. She nervously pushed the carriage ahead. The baby looked like Les at that moment in that absorbed expression of sleep. Everyone said he resembled her because of his eyes. His hair was straight and dark like Les's; still he favored her. It was silly, but it made her happy. They would be happy, the three of them, she thought.

Suddenly she decided to cut their outing short. It was too cold for a stroll in the park. Automatically she checked behind her and realized she was on edge, looking for an excuse to go home. She had to wash her hair for the party, and she needed an especially long soak in the tub while the baby napped.

That would do it. She pictured the dress she would wear, one that would turn her into the sophisticated woman. It was black, with one shoulder. She would undo the girlish braid she wore down her back and sweep her hair back into a bun and cover it with a glittery net at the base of her neck. She would even wear lipstick for the occasion. She turned back, almost at a run.

The hall echoed, it was so quiet at noon. Julie preferred the bustle of rush hour in the morning, when the tenants streamed out of their apartments and walked briskly through the lobby toward the subway, or the late afternoon, when the elevators were crowded with teenagers and mothers returning from school with their children.

It was eerie. The doorman wasn't on until eight o'clock. She hurried toward the elevator, hearing only muffled sounds of traffic on the Drive. Nothing moved. Did she hear the sound of breathing? She looked down at the baby. Sleeping peacefully. She opened the gate to the elevator and with relief heard the creak as it lurched upward after she pressed the button for the eleventh floor.

• • •

Les retraced his steps down into the Fiftieth Street subway, smelling the foul odor of urine, his disgust extending to the filthy station, the dingy Times Square streets he had just left, and finally to himself. He had just encountered one of his former—what could he call him?—buddies, musicians, in the narrow shop above Sam's Musical Instruments where Les was buying a knife and a sharpening stone for carving his oboe reeds. He was trapped with the guy in the claustrophobic cubicle and had to endure his leering, his attempt at renewing their old connection. And Les had brushed him off.

What a laugh! Did his old "friend" see it? Les was falling apart. He had dashed down the narrow stairs as if he were running from the devil. The train pulled into the station, and Les covered his ears. The screech was god-awful. The train was surprisingly crowded for noon. Graffiti covered the walls and windows, and the light bulbs were dim. Les smelled pot. It could have been midnight.

What's the difference? he thought. It suited his mood. What was he doing back on this train? He should be headed to the

Village, to the music school. For a moment in the shop above the music store when he met the drummer from his past, he had felt a surge of strength and thought he might not go through with it.

But he had deliberately left the back door open, the door to the maid's room, the door with only an inside lock. The maid's room was a room Julie never used. And the train was carrying him inexorably toward that room, out of his control.

He put his face in his hands. Not one of the passengers on the crowded train showed a flicker of interest. Oh Julie, he thought, sweat beading his brow. What am I doing to you?

• • •

Esperanza crept nimbly up the familiar back stairs. She was small and hunched, but she was strong and agile. Hardly tired when she reached the eleventh floor, she positioned herself against the back door. It was thirty feet from the elevator and farther from Julie's front door and entirely hidden from view from the hallway.

Esperanza was totally safe. She knew the household routine. The garbage was set out on the back stairs landing for collection in the morning, and then it was gone. The staircase led to only one apartment on this floor, and it was Julie's. This back door opened into a small room off Julie's kitchen that was designed for a maid in the old days but was rarely used anymore. A stranger visiting the building would not be aware of the back staircase. Esperanza had never been caught going up or down in all the weeks she had been watching, waiting.

Esperanza felt under her coat for the cross that hung from her neck. She had never been anxious before. Why should she be? Julie was just like Esperanza's own mother. Laughing, gay, running around. She would turn out the same way. Her mother had been punished. God was evening the score for Esperanza.

Now she thought she felt vibrations against the door. The front door had slammed shut as the carriage was placed in the foyer of Julie's apartment. It would be silent while the baby slept. Esperanza had watched Julie feeding the baby every afternoon for the past month. This week she started following her.

She knew that after the feeding the baby would sleep, Julie

would bathe, then come into focus in Esperanza's lens again with a towel wrapped around her head, wearing a white bathrobe. Then Julie would disappear. Esperanza had twenty minutes if . . . She had tried the door so many times.

She closed her hand around the glass knob. She turned the knob slowly, slowly. Miraculously, the door gave. The door wasn't locked!

She pushed gently. All was silence. She opened the door barely enough to squeeze through sideways. She was thin and needed only a crack. She eased it shut behind her, praying the click of the door would not give her away.

• • •

As soon as the baby was safely asleep, Julie ran a hot tub. She loved the steamy bathroom, and she scented the water. My afternoon spa, she thought, grateful for the two hours she had every day. "Some newborns sleep through earthquakes," Bobbie had told her when Julie brought her newborn from the hospital. It was certainly true of Les Junior, Julie learned. Bobbie, with two teenagers, had been her mother substitute.

She stepped into the bubbly water, and then she remembered. She stepped out. Paranoia, she told herself, irritated at the watery tracks she was leaving on the wood floor as she tiptoed quickly to the front door. She double-locked the door, feeling foolish but secure. She stepped back into the tub and shut the door. Now she could lie back, relax, and enjoy her bath.

• • •

Esperanza prowled around the maid's room in Julie's apartment. The door had shut soundlessly as she turned the knob in the way she had practiced so many times to still the squeak. She knew the plan of the apartment and the rooms she had to cross to reach the nursery. The kitchen and dining room were back to back with the maid's room. The hall ran alongside it and into the foyer right past the front door. She would have to walk directly in view of the living room, the master bedroom, and the bathroom where Julie was bathing. Those rooms faced the front hall. Then came the nursery, the room farthest from her.

She had seen the baby's room, of course. Many times. Through her binoculars. The baby! *Muy bonito.* Esperanza crouched behind an old refrigerator, absorbed in the jumbled collection of stored junk sheltering her. Huge drums and cymbals were piled on top of a broken TV; an ancient washer and dryer stood amid trunks, under cartons reaching almost to the ceiling. A good place to hide.

Esperanza closed her eyes and pulled the long gold chain with the cross from underneath her coat. The cross had never left her neck from the time her mother gave it to her, that black day when her mother left her in Puerto Rico. She got the cross and lost her baby brother. A lifetime ago.

La Mala was the name she had given Julie and her mother. They were so alike. God had smiled on them both. She never could understand it. This one wore no makeup, or high-heeled shoes, no tight dresses. The bitch! They were the same under the skin.

Her mother with her blue eyes, bleached hair, and white skin. She was so proud of her white skin.

Huddled in her niche, her mind wandering, Esperanza wasn't quite sure which baby she was pining for. *Pobrecito,* Esperanza muttered. She held on to her gold cross, forgetting where she was. It was time for the whispers. Any minute they would come, the whispers in her ear from the Virgin. They always came when she thought of the baby.

Suddenly she leapt up. The baby! The chain of her cross hooked on the handle of the refrigerator and freed itself from her neck. She watched the tiny cross as it rolled on the floor, out of her reach, the instant she felt the tug. But she couldn't stop to pick it up.

Was that her baby crying? Crying for her! Esperanza imagined the cry of her baby brother from the past. The house was silent to other ears.

Heedless of exposure, she ran out into the open. God was with her. The hallway was empty. The bathroom door was shut.

Another cry! She raced to the nursery. *Puta!* Pick up your baby, she thought, staring angrily at the blank door where *La Mala* was hidden. He's crying, you slut.

Esperanza entered the baby's room the way she entered the church. *Madre de Dios,* she murmured faintly, crossing herself. The baby was sleeping like an angel. Tenderly she removed him from the crib. And cradling him in her arms, she wrapped him in the velvety blanket. *Madre de Dios,* she chanted, rocking him as she stole toward the back door.

• • •

The subway plunged dangerously and shrieked to a halt at every platform. Les thought his eardrums would shatter. He was very sensitive to damage to his hearing; he put cotton in his ears when he played the drums. The subway was like an underground nightmare, the graffiti from floor to ceiling, the windows covered with paint. His anxiety increased when he thought about the teaching job that would pull them through the financial crisis Julie wasn't aware of. He had just lost a gig. The economic situation in the country caused by the war and the Nixon scandal was ominous for him.

Julie said he could teach in dry years. But now, with the baby . . . They hadn't planned the baby. Still, things were going well when she was pregnant. Julie had kept him on course, stabilized his life. But as soon as the baby was born some of the old feelings started coming back. There were things Julie didn't know.

The drum and roll of the train on the tracks beat in his head as he thought about money. They couldn't live off his record forever. Before the baby Julie had been his good luck charm. Now it was pressure, pressure, pressure. His head felt like a pressure cooker.

Les looked at his watch. Noon. I still have time, he thought. The baby was just beginning his nap. The next stop was Ninety-Sixth Street. Or he could just ride past.

The train pulled into the station. Les jumped out of the car just as the double doors closed.

• • •

The steamy bathroom with its gardenia scent was soothing and relaxing. From the tub, Julie opened the door a crack to get some air and to check for her baby crying. She was next door to the nursery and could hear his voice if he awoke. Silence. He was fast asleep.

Julie closed the door. Was that a creak? The floorboards? Les?

Julie stood in the tub, grabbed her white bathrobe, wrapped her hair in a towel, and opened the door. There was something wrong. She rushed into the hall. The apartment was quiet. Julie walked toward the nursery.

• • •

Les smelled Julie's fragrance in the lobby. She had recently returned. He pressed for the elevator, feeling queasy. Dizzy. His long leather coat felt like a lead weight. His hands were cold, and he was sweating at the same time as he felt the chill of a draft. At last he heard the drone of the elevator descending. Did he imagine something out of the corner of his eye at the service elevator by the back stairs? His heart pounded erratically. He could run up the stairs. But then the elevator arrived.

• • •

When Julie saw the crib was empty, she screamed, and screamed, and screamed. Her mind stopped working, and she screamed until she had no voice left, only seeing the pattern of the sheet on the crib, the pattern floating before her as if detached.

Julie's back was to the door when she felt the icy hand grab her neck. A searing pain in her heart made her buckle. It was too late when she saw it was Les with a look on his face she would never forget. Then she blacked out.

1

Fall 1987

Julie entered the vault below ground in her bank with a purpose. When the guard led her through the brass gates that rose from floor to ceiling outside the heavy inlaid doors, it could have been the cave of Ali Baba holding shimmering treasures. But the rows of boxes had the permanence of an Egyptian tomb. And Julie knew when the guard helped her unlock her safe-deposit box and slid it from its bed on the wall that she would soon be staring into the remains of her morbid history. For the last time. After years of struggle, Julie felt ready to say good-bye.

Sitting in the private room of the vault, she searched for the gold cross that was lying at the bottom of the box where she had stored the remnants of her secret life. Greg, her husband, had never seen these painful artifacts of her memories. Her previous existence was hidden from him, as were the pictures of her lost baby, a wedding photo, and the wedding ring Les gave her, which had belonged to his mother. Lying among these melancholy reminders in the strongbox was the divorce decree, which had come after Les recovered from his breakdown.

Her attention wandered to a velvet-lined case, and she removed the ring Greg had brought back from his last trip to Italy. It was odd how a jewel of such beauty could cause conflict between them after three years of such happiness. Julie slipped the ring on her finger and admired the delicacy of the design. The small, perfect emerald, an antique, was simply set, and the gold had a rosy cast. Greg had such understated taste. The ring wasn't showy but glowed in a quiet way. Its remarkable quality reminded her of Greg. He was proud of his generosity, and they were fortunate to afford such luxuries. The gift was given from the heart, and that's why Julie felt compelled to wear it. Against her better judgment.

Then something shiny at the bottom of the metal box caught her eye. It was the tiny gold cross. The cross she had tried to forget. She picked it up and held it between her fingers. Julie pictured it gleaming under a layer of dust fourteen years ago, lying on the floor of that creepy back room where Les used to store his drums and other broken and discarded objects he had accumulated over the years.

Leaving that apartment had been a major breakthrough for Julie. It was so much a part of her past—her past with Les. The police had suspected poor Les after he ran away. Julie couldn't believe it. He wouldn't hurt anyone. Especially his wife and his baby son. How unfair that Les had had to bear this double burden. But she had heard the voices of the police echoing in the hallways of the old apartment and the words of the detective— over and over during the years. She heard his voice now, in the quiet of the bank. "Someone close," it accused. The phrase haunted her dreams.

Julie turned the cross over carefully, shrinking from the memory of that apartment where her baby was kidnapped. She hadn't been able to look at the cross in all these years. When she saw it the first time, she imagined it was a family heirloom. Now she must return it to Les. It was the last connection between them.

She scrutinized the cross despite herself. She could barely discern the faded, engraved initials E.L. She dropped the cross abruptly into her bag, postponing her decision. She was reluctant to jolt Les with the latest news about herself. She had to admit she was afraid of his reaction. How could she tell him? It was so easy to get caught up in all the pain again.

Suddenly her anxiety about wearing the emerald ring to the ghetto where she taught seemed so trivial. She had built a wall against the years of memories, to hold them back, to prevent them from flooding and overwhelming her, in order to survive. And it worked. She was transformed from the woman who had collapsed on the floor of her child's nursery fourteen years ago. She had finally stopped searching, endlessly peering into strangers' carriages, had returned to her career in teaching. And she was married to Greg, whom she loved.

Every day she fought off the guilt. She was alive and happy while her baby existed only in the terrifying unknown of her imagination. She closed her mind to the past to begin life anew. She was pregnant! Now her life was complete. But her joy was marred by the thought of Les. How could he share her joy?

Yesterday she had argued with Greg. He wanted her to quit teaching because she was pregnant. He was only trying to protect her from working in a dangerous West Side public school. She had foolishly stopped wearing the ring to class, feeling it crude to sport an emerald around children who wore hand-me-downs and thrift shop clothing. Some of her students were neglected and abused. They came in with rat bites and gunshot wounds. She felt she made a difference in their lives, and being needed had given her life meaning. But she couldn't tell Greg exactly why she didn't want to wear the ring; he would insist that she leave. So she assured him it was safe.

She snapped the lid of the box shut and held the emerald ring to her cheek. She would wear the ring to allay Greg's fears. It would remind her of his concern for her.

When the guard returned the box to its resting place in the wall, she realized with a shudder that the vault reminded her of a morgue, a New York City morgue she had visited during the nightmare of hunting for her baby.

• • •

Esperanza crossed herself as she scurried past the graceful Catholic church on Amsterdam Avenue where she had prayed so many years ago. She always walked with her head down, never forgetting for a moment her deformity, the hump on her back that she stooped to hide. The church reminded her of the white church in Ponce where she had baptized her baby. She remembered how she had walked up all of those steps with the infant in her arms; oh, how easy was the climb, even with the added weight. The steeple was so tall it seemed to sway in the sky. She could stand and look up into the limitless expanse. It was where her voices came from, up in the sky, perhaps from behind the clouds.

The church in New York did not have the whiteness of the Puerto Rican church, but it had the tall steps leading up, and it was vaulted and dark inside, cool and beautiful and quiet. It was filled with spirits, which long ago inhabited the spaces and dark corners. And the spirits had spoken to her. How she missed the comfort of the priest and confession. Especially now when she had such pain.

Esperanza came to realize at that moment that she might never see her church again.

• • •

Julie climbed the stairs from the vault to East Eighty-Fifth Street, the magic eye scanning her ascent. It was a short walk, and she would arrive just in time for her appointment with Dr. Blum, her obstetrician, on Park Avenue.

It was a clear, brisk morning, and Julie walked decisively, her head held high. Her carefully made-up face was still smooth and young at thirty-nine, in spite of all she had been through. Who would guess my past? she thought, furiously shaking off her dread. She loosened the collar of her mink coat as she entered the office from its private entrance on the street.

The office had an antiseptic, sterile quality. She inhaled the sweetish hospital odor and nervously eyed the two women who sat dutifully in the small, quiet waiting room. Each woman raised her head and gazed, pausing a second to note that Julie was a shade prettier, a touch more elegant than she. But that wasn't what arrested their attention. There was a difference, some subtle aura they sensed in Julie, some mystery that separated her from them. Julie felt the difference too and was relieved that the East Side ladies were strangers she could ignore. They nodded politely, and she opened a magazine.

Last week Julie had nearly bumped into two neighbors from her old apartment on the West Side as she checked her coat at the Metropolitan Museum of Art. But her oversized, dark sunglasses and hat, as well as her hair, now dyed auburn, threw them off. She lingered in the coatroom to eavesdrop.

"Doesn't that woman remind you of Julie Layton?" one of them whispered.

"Oh, no." her companion replied. "Never!"

Julie recalled the incident with great satisfaction. No wonder, she thought; I'm a creature from another world, another life, reincarnated. Her face had filled out, and her former sharp contours had been softened by the passing years. The delicate lines etched by her trials and age were now smoothed by the bloom of her pregnancy. She looked down into her lap, at the contour of her pleated silk dress. She was beginning to show, to feel flutterings of life.

Finally ushered into the examining room by the expressionless young receptionist wearing a white coat, Julie realized she was Dr. Blum's last patient. She fastened the paper gown, grateful that Abe Blum was kinder, less businesslike than her old obstetrician. He'd been highly recommended by her newfound friend, Martha. But she would have gone to almost anyone as long as she could avoid the trauma of seeing the doctor who had delivered her first baby. Now she was glad she had chosen dear Dr. Blum.

Julie couldn't help wondering if Dr. Blum was kinder to her because he felt sorry for her. She had had to tell him the truth, of course, about her first baby, swearing him to secrecy, wondering whether he thought she was crazy not to have told her husband she'd had a child before. But what if Greg couldn't handle the burden of that nightmare? Les had broken, had cracked apart. Greg was stronger. Still, telling him seemed riskier than keeping it a secret. She had too many secrets, she thought. One day she would tell Greg. But not yet.

After the exam Julie sat facing the doctor across his desk, reassured. Dr. Blum was a small, middle-aged man, not attractive or particularly distinguished except for his perfectly white, thick head of hair. His voice was unusually resonant and deep, unexpected somehow in a man of his stature. He took her hand when he caught the fear in her eyes. His hand was soft and plump. Julie relaxed.

"Nothing to worry about. Everything is perfect. Your weight is just right; you're both healthy."

Julie smiled happily. "Greg is delirious. It's his first." She saw the doctor's pale gray eyes darken and flinch for an instant. "He's forty-five," she added hurriedly.

"Are you sleeping any better?" he asked.

"Sleeping right through the night. The first time in . . . years." Fourteen, she thought.

"Good," he said.

"Greg says I've stopped grinding my teeth in my sleep."

"Pregnancy seems to suit you. Don't forget your vitamins," he added, showing her to the door.

Julie headed for Madison Avenue. It was a beautiful day. The visit had lightened her heart. Turning into the maternity shop on Eightieth Street, she glanced at her reflection in the window. She hardly recognized herself.

Clutching the parcel containing the maternity dress the solicitous store clerk had helped her choose, Julie realized that at last she was becoming accustomed to the polite treatment, the gentility of the East Side. Here they catered to her idiosyncrasies, treated her as an individual. In the expensive stores, even salespeople seemed to respect a need for a slower pace. The vision of her poor students, hurrying through life, through their childhoods, passed through her mind. Was her son alive to enjoy *any* childhood? She forced the thought back for the thousandth time.

Julie's mind wandered back to the stranger she'd seen reflected in the shop windows. And she remembered that exactly two years ago she had made a decision that transformed her physically, and happily, it had transformed her life. Bobbie and she had always referred to that day as Cinderella Day.

Julie had just sold her big, empty apartment. When the building had gone co-op, she had managed to buy the apartment at the insider's price. With the windfall she received when she sold it, she decided to make a dramatic move. No more reminders, no more crying in rooms filled with baby things, with ghosts of the past. No more familiar fear-filled streets to haunt, pitying faces to meet.

Suddenly the coat she had worn on the day her baby was kidnapped flashed into her mind. Her mother would have approved of the coat. It was heavy wool, French-made, a zipper slanting across the front from shoulder to hem, in a bold plaid, fitted at the waist, flaring gently to the calf. She had loved the coat—it was warm and fashionable yet unpretentious. A young girl should wear bright colors, her mother always said. But in a fit of misery she threw the coat, the scarf, and the jaunty wool cap into a shopping cart and donated them to the poor.

She remembered wheeling the cart past dark, garbage-strewn alleys, dirty basements, past men loitering on corners smoking pot. When she moved to a studio on the East Side, the West Side became to her like the bitter land left behind by the immigrants. She had crossed over to the New World, where the streets were paved with gold.

And on her way to her new life was the beauty salon in Greenwich Village where Bobbie had dragged her. Theatrix catered to poor actresses who ignored the peeling, faded gingham wallpaper, the exposed pipes, and the pink paint on the cupboards and ceiling, long ago abandoned to decay, because it provided good cheer and expertise at low prices. Theatrix was the scene of the turning point in Julie's life, and that day was stamped forever on her memory.

Sitting in the barber chair between Bobbie and Nicola, Bobbie's actress-hairdresser friend, Julie put her new image into their hands. Julie liked the dumpy salon, where the two women eyed her critically before deciding her fate. And almost at once, she trusted Nicola, who was the antithesis of her present Madison Avenue stylist. Quentin charged ten times Nicola's price and embarrassed Julie by treating her like the queen of England.

"She's playing an East Side matron," Bobbie announced. "She has to look totally different. The innocent blond ingenue look has to go."

Julie laughed as they openly discussed her.

"You're my Frankenstein," Bobbie said to Julie, smiling.

"A femme fatale," Bobbie instructed Nicola, a petite, dark wisp of a woman. "But not too fake." Nicola took Julie's chin in her hands, assessing her in the mirror.

"With these bones," Nicola said with a slight Italian accent, "a Garbo!" she dropped her voice two octaves on "Garbo." "A sultry beauty, with those eyes, those full lips."

"Not too dark. We don't want her looking like Bette Davis with a dark wig in a horror flick."

"Chestnut, with a touch of auburn, reddish tints, eh?" she asked Julie. That seemed right to Julie. She stared at her fair skin, her freckles, and her expression in the mirror and for the first time realized she had begun to resemble her mother. Her mother always said that her blond hair did have a hint of red. Nicola ran her fingers through Julie's wild hair, bushed out in ringlets. "Good hair," she said. "Nice weight, but . . ."

"Cut it! Straighten it," announced Julie. "I need a totally new persona."

Nicola glanced at Julie's clothes. "Don't worry," said Bobbie. "We're going to Bloomie's and Saks today. The ethnic jewelry goes, the work boots go, the backpack, the big shirts and skirts. . . ." Bobbie babbled on as Nicola painted on the dark smelly glop on her hair after cutting away Julie's curls, history falling around her shoulders to the floor like stacks of wheat.

"When a child survived a terrible illness in my family in the old days in Russia, her name was changed," Bobbie continued. "Maybe you should change your name too."

"How's Cinderella?" Julie asked.

The hairdresser blew Julie's hair smooth around her neck, twirled her around in the chair, and held a mirror to the back of her head. Her sculpted, sleek hair was a wonder to her. More wondrous were the darkened eyebrows and the chestnut hair. She did look mysteriously, darkly attractive, she thought. Bobbie and Nicola stared at her as she eyed her unfamiliar reflection in the harsh glare of the mirrored wall.

"Do I look ludicrous?" she asked fearfully.

"Divine," said Bobbie.

"Like Sophia Loren," said Nicola appreciatively.

Her head felt light; her whole body felt light when she stood up, exhilarated.

And then it was a whirlwind tour of Fifth Avenue stores to outfit her in tailored suits and silks, gold jewelry, and sedate pearls. They ended the spree with a makeover at Bonwit's.

"You've metamorphosed into a butterfly," Bobbie said, spraying her with French perfume as they sat on the tall stools at the cosmetics counter.

"From a weed into a gilded lily," Julie said, observing her perfectly made up, finished-looking face. A mask? she wondered. Her eyes wandered to her shiny new patent leather pumps and her patterned black stockings.

"I once told my kids this store was a museum," Bobbie said as they stood before F.A.O. Schwarz. Bobbie's stories made Julie laugh. " 'You can look, but don't touch,' I said, and I hustled them out fast," Bobbie admitted.

Julie decided to treat them to tea at the Carlyle to celebrate. They fell into the plush sofas, Julie in one of her new outfits and Bobbie dressed with her trademark theatrical flair.

"Ugh, fish eggs," Bobbie whispered, making a face. And then she made a prediction. "You were made for wealth," she said as she transferred one of her tiny, crustless caviar sandwiches to Julie's English bone china plate. "Caviar, champagne, all the things I hate!" And her prediction had come true.

Two years later, she met Greg. If she hadn't rented that little East Side studio of hers, which was smack up against his town house, she would not be heading home with hope as she was today. She remembered the day they met, when he took her into the library to show her how he was renovating his house, how surprised she was that he wasn't a rude yuppie allowing his workmen to drill and hammer and scream curses at all hours, preventing her from marking papers or having a quiet thought.

She had complained day after day to the workers, never getting a response from the owner. Finally, after lying in wait, in desperation, she saw him enter the house and chased him down.

He was so apologetic. "So you're a teacher!" he exclaimed, filled with admiration. Julie thought he might be a man from Mars.

"I've been out of town," he claimed. "I would never let them disturb you, keep you from marking your papers," he said, inviting her into the house for a drink in atonement.

She remembered the joke he told her as they sat in the living room, when she realized he was keeping her for more than politeness, that he was attracted to her and that he was trying to entertain her.

"Do you know the difference between a yuppie and a pigeon?" he asked her. "A pigeon can make a deposit on a Mercedes."

Julie couldn't help thinking then that he could easily make a cash deposit on a Mercedes.

"I'm a guppie," he added. "A geriatric yuppie. I'm forty-three, and I've been too busy traveling and making money to meet an intelligent young woman like you to settle down with," he said, startling her. Then he told her about his love for French literature, about his favorite writer, Proust, his ten years in Paris as a child, his work in international law, and, before she knew it, they had sipped three drinks, it was past the dinner hour, she was starving, and she knew she wouldn't mark a single paper that night.

Julie smiled. She felt her baby pulse, as if in response to her happy thought. Greg would be totally involved with their baby, protect them all their lives. She pulled her coat tighter against the evening chill. Greg reminded her of her dependable father, in his felt hat and heavy navy blue overcoat. She remembered him braving the wind with her on winter Sundays, her arm linked in his, her fingers wriggling in his silky pocket for warmth on their evening outings to the pastry shop on Broadway in Washington Heights.

Greg didn't read poetry to her or write verses for her the way Les had, but he was quietly cultured. He had read all the books in their prodigious library. She pictured the library in their town house, with its built-in bookshelves holding all the leather-bound volumes lined up in rows, straight as soldiers, hiding great thoughts and bold passions behind their sedate trappings. Just like Greg. And if she hadn't moved to the East Side, her life would still be a gray world of shadowy fears and struggles, with no future to look into, only the horror she glimpsed of the future for her missing son. The recurrent dream she had of her baby floating in gore, his body part of the gore, was so terrible she couldn't admit it to anyone, even her closest friends. It was only after she had met Greg, when the dreams gradually ceased, that she could admit them to herself.

It was getting late, she thought, emerging from her reverie, and she quickened her step toward home.

The cross preyed on Julie's mind when she returned at dusk to her town house. She turned off Lexington Avenue onto Ninety-Second Street as snowflakes began to swirl under the streetlight. The hallway lamp gleamed behind the glass door, and the glow in all the upstairs rooms was shining through the windows. Greg was at home waiting to say good-bye before he left on a business trip to Geneva.

She unlocked the gate, suddenly imagining that she could feel the cross burning through her handbag. When Greg was safely across the Atlantic, she would retrieve it and decide its fate. Julie superstitiously believed that removing the cross after its sleep of many years in her vault was like awakening an evil spirit. She prayed that she was wrong.

Greg had his garment bag, hand luggage, and raincoat waiting downstairs at the door. The company car had just rung up, ready at the curb to drive him to Kennedy Airport.

Greg took Julie into his arms at the top of the stairs.

"I wish you were coming with me," he whispered, brushing his lips across her mouth. Julie felt his mustache tickle her slightly. He continued pressing her close, hugging her to him. Greg was affectionate, cuddly. He liked skin, especially Julie's fragrant skin.

She made no effort to pull away, letting herself be comforted by Greg's warm embrace even while feeling the unspoken conflict between them. She knew how much he would like her to stay at home and wait for him. But if she did, her dark thoughts would crowd in, the memories would creep back, and the horror would come, the horror Greg knew nothing about.

Julie looked at Greg's manly, gentle face, furrows of worry appearing beside his mouth, and she kissed him again.

"I'm so lucky to have you," she whispered. Greg laughed happily at his sometimes unfathomable, pregnant wife.

She watched his broad back, comfortably covered by an English tweed jacket, and his narrow hips, impeccable in gray wool trousers, as he loped down the steep flight of stairs, and a sudden stab of loneliness caught her by surprise. But the moment the door closed in the downstairs hall, she thought about the cross in her handbag.

It would be difficult to compose a letter to Les after so many years of silence. But it was something she had to do tonight, before she changed her mind. She would write to him and return the cross.

2

Morning sunlight awakened Les. When he sat up in bed, he could see the ocean from his window, through the palm trees. Barefoot and still in his pajamas, he walked out onto the balcony. Looking into the clear day, he could see far off into the horizon. There was nothing between ocean and sky at this hour, not even a sailboat. He took the straw broom and swept the leaves the wind left every morning in the corners of the balcony. It was a comforting ritual he performed with pleasure each day before breakfast while inhaling the fresh, warm air of Monterey.

He listened intently to the soothing sounds of the surf. At night lying awake in bed he was unnerved by the crash and ebb in the dark, the shattering against the shore. There was the disturbing suggestion of violence in each crash, a reminder of the vastness of the sea in each ebb and flow. But then followed the reassuring slide of the receding wave. He felt he could get on with his life and his music. His new jazz composition for piano, drums, and bass, which had gotten rave reviews in both L.A. and New York, was influenced by the rhythms of the ocean, by the two conflicting emotions of joy and terror that lived inside him.

Les experienced a sense of freedom stepping out into the breezy sunlight. Nature thrust him outside of himself. He was in command of his mind and body. He knew he was finally cured of his terrible compulsion. He had emerged fit and responsible, restored to his art and reconnected to the real world. Being grateful every morning was a form of worship. The sun in

Monterey became a symbol of his restoration, and he basked in
its rays, literally and figuratively.

Headed for the kitchen, he hurried through the huge whitewashed living room, uplifted by the pinks and blues of the
Indian dhurries on the blue tiled floor and the giant gouaches
hanging high to the ceiling. At sunset he and Eleanore often
relaxed there with a drink, enjoying the azure of the ocean and
the hues of the sunset.

In New York, insulated against the elements, facing dark,
gray days, Les was often depressed. Thoughts matching the
bleak, dirty streets and the clouds that hung over the cold skyscrapers took hold of him. Trepidation and gloom wormed their
way into his moods. Here the sheer beauty, the enormity of the
sea and sky kept his demons in perspective.

Sunlight and Eleanore. Both had helped him back from the
netherworld. He had met Eleanore, the head nurse in the oncol-
ogy unit, when he was in the hospital. She rescued him from
the mental health ward where he would otherwise have spent
years. He was immediately attracted to Eleanore, who was so
impressively wholesome and intelligent, very much the healthy
Californian. She had been living with him for over a year now.

Eleanore had risen early, as usual. Les could hear the whir
of the blender in the kitchen. She would be dressed and ready for
work, neat, sparkling, and—he thought—stunning. She was
preparing her morning concoction for them, orange juice and
lecithin. It was part of their daily regimen, a formula to prevent
cancer.

Les watched her pouring the drinks into juice glasses at the
kitchen counter. She wore a short-sleeved cotton knit top tucked
into a crisp white skirt that revealed the curve of her bottom.
She was muscular yet curvy. Not an ounce of fat. Her long legs,
comfortably flexing in white socks and sneakers, were shaped
and toned by both modern dance and aerobics. She had a
smooth but faint tan, not nearly as brown as Les, who ignored
her warnings about the sun.

Eleanore smiled as Les swallowed the surprisingly delicious
drink. A new strain of music swam in his head as he looked into
Eleanore's freckled, lively face. The melody was definitely up-

beat. In an unusual surge of optimism, Les blurted out, "Nothing, El, is going to ruin this perfect day."

• • •

Eleanore wore a T-shirt and a pair of cotton panties as she sat cross-legged facing Les in the center of their brass double bed. The black night outside was unrelieved by the moon. Les twisted the switch on the three-way lamp on the night table to dim it, and Eleanore gathered up her plans for the health spa she had designed. Their talk had lasted well into the night. It was 3:00 A.M.

He reached over to her, put his finger under her T-shirt, and drew a tentative line across her belly. They were both exhausted, a good exhaustion, with the tip end of energy to spare, to finish their intimate hours together.

She dropped her papers on the bureau. She pulled her shirt over her head, and he helped her wriggle out of her panties. Her naked body aroused him. Watching the languorous stretch of her shoulders, the way she tilted her body toward him, the darkening of her nipples, he began to kiss her belly wildly. She smelled so fresh. He put his head between her breasts and she exhaled. Color rushed to her face. He wet her nipples with his tongue, feeling them stiffen under his lips as he slowly sucked each breast. He stroked her thighs, tickling her tantalizingly, waiting to touch her between her legs, to stroke her gently after parting her, to feel the thin membrane quicken, awaken to him. But she was already kissing him, beginning to move. He felt she was ready for him. She breathed deeply, stretching her body. She was so fast to respond tonight, he thought. She was hardly able to wait. She was thrusting toward him, gripping his shoulders. He entered her with that thud, the rush to his heart.

Inside of her it was ecstasy, uncomplicated, sudden ecstasy. She was breathing loudly, evenly, attuned to him, revealing her rhythmic pleasure. Her sounds sharpened his interest, and he felt himself moving deeper, harder.

Then from nowhere, a sudden flash of what it was like inside of Julie came from beneath his consciousness, from some dark recess of his brain's electric memory. He pounded forward, pushing his passion to excess, to boundless wanting, beyond what he'd ever felt before with Eleanore.

He felt himself falling. He was falling into a bottomless black pit, into depths and more depths. Layers and layers, he repeated to himself, half conscious of the words, losing his sense of reality. Endless. It was endless, until his explosion, until Eleanore, brought on by his intensity, came along with him.

Afterward, as they lay together, a flicker of her eyes told him that she had felt something new. She thought it was because they had been so close, that the excitement of planning the future together accounted for his drawing into her as he had never done before. She thought theirs was a natural coming together after a night of intimacy, their celebration culminating in the enjoyment of their bodies.

But dammit, why was he thinking of Julie now? Was Eleanore right? Was he afraid of being close, afraid of commitment? He pushed Julie's image away, propping himself up on his elbow to watch Eleanore. He was drifting off to sleep, fighting it. He felt wholesome and healthy looking at her. She wasn't shy about nudity. She was young, nubile, and firm. Her skin resonated. Sex with Eleanore was refreshing, like a shower. Lovemaking with Julie had shades and undercurrents. It answered his inner longings. Julie and he merged beyond the tactile, like a symphony that floats beyond the notes, beyond the room, to blend with the atmosphere. When Les forgot he was listening to an instrument, when the sound he was hearing seemed to be its own source, he knew he was listening to a virtuoso. That's the way it had been with Julie. He totally lost himself. It was an escape into the sensual darkness; it drained consciousness, sucked out reality.

To Eleanore sex was bread and water, a physical and emotional necessity. To Julie it was a delicious luxury, like rich chocolate cake, champagne, gilded mirrors and masked balls, colors and electric music. And on the days she was insatiable, he had satisfied her.

With Eleanore he usually took his time making love. He was almost measured in his passion, if that wasn't a contradiction, he thought sleepily. He was getting too tired to think, and his lids weighed heavily. Step one, step two, step three. It was a well-constructed play: act one, climax, denouement. He imagined a cool glass of water, the image of Eleanore replacing Julie. He watched her under closing lids as she stretched out on the sheet, settling her limbs in contentment. It gave him another pulse to see her move her body as if in water. But the milky, thick ooze of sleep overcame him, immobilizing him.

He fell into a deep, deep sleep, and a sparkling stream appeared, reflecting lights thundering over rocks, cascading. And the name in the echo and spray of the waterfall was Julie. "Julie," it whispered.

When Les awoke, Eleanore was gone from bed. It was another beautiful Monterey morning. The elements had not been fickle. Unfailing sunshine greeted each day. Eleanore was up early as usual in spite of their late-night planning and lovemaking. She was full of the energy of her dream for the future. Eleanore hoped to open a health spa, a cancer prevention retreat, using her knowledge of nutrition and exercise. She had salted away her earnings over the years and was ready to take the plunge.

Les had offered to check out real estate possibilities with her, deciding to invest in her project. He had money for the first time in years. He was cutting records and was deluged with gigs. Eleanore had pushed him, correctly predicting the therapeutic effect of his success, and her frugality, happily, had rubbed off on him. He never turned down an offer of work unless he was in a position to choose, and he spent very little of what he earned. Les regarded the spa as a joint venture. He increasingly envisioned the future as including Eleanore.

Hurrying himself into the kitchen a bit later than usual that morning, he started to reach for the glass of shimmering orange liquid Eleanore held out to him, explaining that he had slept through the sound of the blender. Then he saw that in her other hand she held an envelope.

"Good morning," she announced, her voice flatter than usual. "This came Federal Express."

His face darkened immediately.

"It's from Julie," she added quickly, taking a step toward him. Les reached for the cardboard envelope, his hand visibly trembling. An unnameable fear coursed through him.

He looked at Eleanore. Her face reflected empathetic misery. She wanted to stroke him, to comfort him, but the glass in her hand and the outstretched envelope got in the way. She quietly placed the glass on the counter. "Take it. Open it," she said.

"I'm afraid," he murmured, sounding like a small child entering a dark room.

"Oh, Les," she begged, "when will you forgive yourself?"

• • •

Les clutched the heavy, flat envelope protecting Julie's letter and fell into the nearest wicker chair in the living room. As Eleanore's Fiat Spider convertible zipped away, he gulped the lecithin drink to fortify himself.

He ripped it open and removed the letter. Les was moved to tears when he saw his name on the lavender envelope in her familiar, flourished handwriting. Thoughts of their baby and their years together forced him to hold back his emotion so that he could open it.

He was still shaken by the dream. The gardenia scent on the stationery reawakened more vividly that aura of hers, which clung to him from last night. It tore him even more. If he had any faith in ESP, he could believe that thinking about Julie during sex was a psychic phenomenon. He knew deep down that the premonition could only be a bad sign. He had run away from Julie, from New York, from his destroyed life for reasons Julie never knew, that Eleanore and Dr. Wolfson, his psychiatrist in New York, only suspected. Had Julie found out the truth about him?

The letter opener in his hand began to shake so hard he could barely slice the envelope open without mangling it. He finally pulled out the plain, unengraved stationery, which was covered with delicate lettering. He stared at the fanciful script, postponing reading the first word.

Suddenly something fell into his lap. His heart fluttered. He was so susceptible now, so vulnerable, that everything frightened him. Julie had enclosed something in neatly folded tissue paper. He undid the wrapping clumsily and discovered a tiny gold cross. It was simple, with no decoration, and it had a loop for a chain, so it could be worn as a pendant. What did the cross signify? Had Julie in her grief become religious? He read the letter with foreboding.

My dear Les,

It's been many long years. Forgive me for not wanting contact, but memory for me is a source of agony, and I couldn't stand the pain. Even to think about you is painful. I've tried to forget your face. I see our baby's face in your face.

I know you have struggled to get well, how hard you have worked with Dr. Wolfson, and I understand why you fled. I don't blame you. I escaped in my mind, blanking out everything. We all have our ways of surviving.

I write to you because the wound has healed. So much has passed in these long years. I have followed you and your career in music. And when I heard your new composition on the radio, I knew it was time to write, to say good-bye. I'll always have your music.

I'm teaching in the same school where I began after college, with my old friend Bobbie, and I'm happy there, working awfully hard. Helping children has pulled me through the worst years. The school is tough and grueling, just what I needed when the void, the emptiness overtook me. I'm married now and pregnant.

The words stopped his breath. His heart turned over, and he inhaled deeply to quell his emotions. Did he still love her? Is that why he felt such turmoil? He cursed his stupidity. Of course she would remarry. Wasn't she entitled to a life of her own? He had never accepted the finality of the divorce, thinking it was part of their tragedy. And he had never pictured her with another man. Now she was married to someone else. Kiss off the fantasy that Julie would return, he thought bitterly. His sinking heart, his devastation made him recognize the hope he had harbored but never admitted to himself—that Julie would return to him one day. He saw that by dreaming of Julie during sex he distanced Eleanore. This was the death sentence he was afraid of—Julie saying good-bye.

Miserable, he forced himself to keep reading.

Greg knows nothing of my old life. I didn't feel secure enough to tell him. I couldn't afford to lose my new chance, my second chance. Greg is forty-five. He thinks I'm young—I'm only thirty-nine, after all. Sometimes I feel I've lived a whole previous life and that I'm one hundred years old. But I'm trying to be young again, for my husband, my baby, and for myself. I wish the same happiness for you, my dearest Les.

I'm enclosing a cross I found under your old drums when I got rid of the apartment. I know you grew up in that apartment and that your parents lived there for many years before. Perhaps it's an heirloom belonging to your mother or grandmother. It must have been lying in the back room for years. There is an inscription on the back. I felt I had to send you this gold cross. It may be an important link to your past, and I couldn't deprive you of it. I hope it brings you the peace you deserve.

With love,
Julie

Les felt incredible confusion. His face grew hot and red. The wind blowing in from the porch had no salutary effect on him; his blood pressure rose, his stomach clenched, and he felt violently ill. Perspiration broke out on his hairline, and his chest and back were running with rivulets of sweat.

He rushed into the bathroom, retching, his body reacting to his loss of control. By the time he had washed his face in cold water his pajamas were drenched by his perspiration. Apprehension and despair, his love for Julie, and a new disturbing element, the cross, combined to destroy his peace of mind, that tranquillity he and Eleanore had worked so hard to achieve together. It was all lost. In a matter of minutes.

He tore off his pajamas, leaving them in a heap on the bathroom floor. He rushed into the bedroom and fell into the unmade bed. He wept at the thought of Julie's tender words to him. And he wept because his world was coming apart again.

He was undeserving of her caring words, he thought, suddenly thrown into a fit of self-hate. He jumped out of bed, unable to endure another minute. The cross! he remembered. He raced to the living room, bumping into the furniture, his anxiety propelling him. He had to examine it again.

He searched for the cross next to the tissue paper and the letter on the coffee table. But it wasn't there. He got down on his hands and knees and located it, gleaming on the carpet where it had rolled when he dropped it while reading the letter. He couldn't quell his racing heart.

He knew the cross wasn't his!

How could Julie have made such a mistake? The initials were E.L., but his grandmother was Jewish and his mother would never have worn a cross. What was it doing on the floor of his back room?

Then the dread and shock hit him full in the face. He picked up the cross and squeezed it so tightly in his palm it cut into his skin. But he felt no pain.

"No," he moaned into the empty house, trying to deny what he knew. "It can't be," he mumbled crazily, "after all these years."

He raced around the house, hurrying from room to room, trying to outrun his anguish. When he was depleted physically and drained mentally, he stood on the porch, stark naked. His sweaty hair stood on end, his face aged and ragged. He opened his bleeding hand and looked at the cross.

A shiver crept from the base of his spine to the nape of his neck. The meaning of the cross gathered like a black cloud. The cross had been dropped by the kidnapper.

• • •

Esperanza Lebron raised the heavy, ancient window in her top-floor apartment, perched her elbows on the window ledge, and leaned too far out. She looked anxiously for a sign from the carved angels that protruded from the wall, adorning the building only twenty feet from her window. She reached out her arms to the angels, which seemed almost within her grasp. Sometimes the wind pushing the clouds past the wings seemed to make them move. The cherubic faces of the twin angels puffed their cheeks, perpetually blowing their fluted horns. If Esperanza stared too intently, she became dizzy, and if she was distressed the voices from the Virgin would rustle with the breeze in her ears.

It was getting late, and again her son wasn't home. She searched the street eighteen stories below with the same cracked binoculars she had been using for years. There was no sign of him. And it was beginning to snow. She felt an ache in her side, and she pulled herself in and closed the window.

Dusk had fallen. Esperanza rocked in her chair in the dark, waiting. She didn't turn on any lights. The white haze of the snow, the lights from the buildings and the street lamps were enough for her. On clear nights the moon and the stars illuminated the rooms, and she paced, sometimes all night, waiting in vain for her son to come home.

Suddenly Esperanza jumped out of her chair. She became crazy with fear. She had seen *La Mala* again that morning, clear as day. She would never forget those fair features. Even though she was wearing a disguise of dyed hair. Maybe God was punishing Esperanza for taking the baby. Maybe she would never see him again.

• • •

Les dressed hurriedly and reached for the phone. He started to punch the buttons for Eleanore's office. His mind suddenly went blank. Panic overtook him, but he tried again slowly, until one by one his fingers remembered. He willed her to be in.

Damn! He slammed the receiver down. The line was busy. His heart pounded. He would call the airlines, fly to New York, call her from there. Action! He had to act. He rushed to the closet, pulled out a suitcase, threw it on the bed, and clicked it open. The thought of filling it with his clothes from the dresser stopped him dead in his tracks. He couldn't decide. He should tell Eleanore. He owed her an explanation.

He picked up the phone and tried her once again. This time, if she was out, he decided, he would have to leave. His palms were wet and sticky, leaving a print on the receiver.

"Please be in," he said. She picked up on the second ring.

"El, thank God! I've got to see you!"

"What's wrong?" Eleanore asked. She was alarmed, but she controlled her voice. The only response to an out-of-control patient was calm.

"The letter. She's married, she's sent a cross. The kidnapper—it's the kidnapper. It's the kidnapper's cross. I've got something that belongs to the kidnapper!"

"I can't leave now, Les." Eleanore looked at the hospice physician who was staring at her from across the desk. "Are you okay enough to drive? There's no one to cover for me. I'm in a meeting with Doctor Czernik right now."

"I'll drive over."

Eleanore flushed. "Don't hang up. Listen. I'll be through by the time you get here. Drive slowly. Be careful."

Eleanore heard a grunt and a click. She returned to her discussion with Dr. Czernik, aware that she had heard her odd conversation. Eleanore wondered about Julie's letter. I knew that letter was trouble, she thought.

Eleanore sat in her office thinking a moment after the doctor left on his rounds. Sipping some cold cranberry juice, she anxiously looked out of her window, waiting for Les. She would be able to see him drive into the lot from where she sat.

Last night had been the culmination of a gradually improving and important relationship between them. The collaboration on her enterprise, which they both knew went far beyond business, and the terrific sex had given her the green light she'd been waiting for. She was ready to move into the next phase of their lives.

Eleanore had been so elated that morning until the letter was delivered. Usually reserved, she had been exhilarated, bubbling over with ideas for her spa. She couldn't wait to tell Les; by the time he had awakened she had decided to expand its scope to include macrobiotic diets, exercise, group therapy, even curative baths. She had begun to realize there was no end to the possibilities. She hadn't been so stimulated and happy in years. All systems go, she thought, daring for once to dream of marriage and a family with Les. Love and work, as Freud pointed out, were the important things in life. It seemed last night that they were all coming together for her. Until the letter, until Les's frenzied, incoherent phone call.

Eleanore heard a car rumble over pebbles. It was Les, driving his car erratically into the lot. He was attempting to park between Dr. Czernik's car and hers when Eleanore heard a clunk. Les had hit her back bumper trying to get in. But she didn't have time to watch the rest. Her light flashed an emergency on the floor. She ran out of her office, wondering how she would get through the day—one that had started out so brightly.

• • •

Les hurried toward the commotion in room 106. When he got there, he realized with a shock that Mr. Felman, the leukemia patient who had so enjoyed Les's concert in the auditorium last month, had died.

Les felt he was entering a foreign country, an alien world, whenever he came through the doors of the hospice. It disturbed him in spite of the cheerful nurses dispensing doses of touching and caring and in spite of Eleanore, who had made something positive of a nightmare.

Les found Eleanore in the room next to the one that had been Mr. Felman's. Aided by another nurse, she was struggling to lift a large, elderly woman off the floor and back on to her bed. Medicated and oblivious to her surroundings, the woman continued moaning after she was laid on the bed. In distress, Les waited as they settled her comfortably. They patted her long, wild, white hair, which was splayed on the pillow. Les noticed it had patches of lemon color, like a yellowing newspaper. Eleanore left the young nurse to pull up the bars on the bed and led Les to the empty lounge, an area decorated as a living room.

Eleanore chose a small, square table, deliberately avoiding the couch, and motioned for him to sit across from her. She knew he needed objectivity over hand-holding just now. His face was distraught, his hair uncombed, his shirt not tucked completely into his trousers, and he hadn't shaved. Before she could speak, he jumped up, searching his pocket.

"Look at this!" he cried, pulling the cross out. He held it too close to her face. His voice was high-pitched. He shook the object under her nose. She backed away, offended.

"It's the kidnapper's. I know you won't believe me. It was dropped in the back room!"

"Why did Julie send it?" she asked, trying to calm him.

"She thinks it belongs to me. The initials on the cross. E.L.! Don't you see?" he shouted. "She thought it was mine. But it's *not*. It's the kidnapper's! Do you understand? It's a woman's cross."

"So?"

"My baby may be alive. This is the first lead I've had."

"Lead? What are you talking about? You're not making sense."

"I've got to try tracing this cross."

"Les . . . please . . . don't do this."

"Why can't you understand?"

Eleanore smoothed his temples and looked into his sad, sea green eyes. "What will you do?" she whispered, afraid of his answer.

"I'm going to New York. To find my son."

3

It was past dark, and he wasn't home yet. Esperanza felt she had lost control over him for good. Still, she waited for him, hoping. The apartment overlooking Broadway, which her brother Marcos had left them when he moved to New Jersey, was too large for the two of them, too lonely.

Esperanza spent much of her life dreaming of the past. Now that her baby was grown and no one needed her, she had no purpose in life.

She thought back on that happy day when she flew to Ponce, her hometown, back to the overgrown, dilapidated house that had served her purpose whenever she wanted to escape New York with her son. It was Christmas Day when the priest baptized him in the same white stone church where she and her brother Marcos were baptized. She named him Jesus.

Now the memory of the day her mother took Marcos from her was fading. Esperanza's childhood, in which she was always hiding, to avoid the gaze of other children, deprived her of love. Who could love a small, hunchbacked, ugly child? Until her brother, Marcos, was born . . .

Her mother had been happy to turn the baby over to Esperanza to care for. Esperanza had taken good care of her father from the age of eight—cooking, cleaning—giving her some excuse for existence. But two years later, when Marcos was born, her life changed. For the first time she had someone who loved her.

Now the black day her mother took six-year-old Marcos to New York, leaving Esperanza to tend her sick father, was but a dim memory. Losing Marcos had been like losing her own baby. She could barely picture her own father, who before his death had consulted with the spiritualist in the town and arranged for her to live in the convent when the time came. She was seventeen when her father finally died, and she had lived with the nuns until her brother, grown to a man, sent for her. God in his wisdom gave her mother, Maritza, a horrible death from cancer.

Esperanza rocked in her chair in the dark, waiting for her boy to come home. She forgot to turn the lights on. The days and nights were running together again. And she feared that her son, now growing up, was ashamed of her as the others had been. She couldn't help that the Virgin whispered to her. What was she to do?

• • •

Les opened his eyes in terror. He couldn't breathe. He wasn't in his own bedroom. Where was he? His hand gripped his throat. And when the electric lights shining through the window registered on his brain, he realized that in his dream he was being strangled by a gold chain. It was the sound of his own scream, emitted from his throat as a staccato grunt, that had awakened him from his dream.

The number on the illuminated panel of the clock on the bureau moved to 4:30 A.M. It was his first night in his friend Russell Long's apartment. It was too cold to get out of bed, so he pulled the covers up to his neck and stretched himself out, unknotting himself with relief at being alive. The nightmare had catapulted him into feeling endangered and alone. And the night terrors came upon him with the realization that there was no escape. One day he would die.

• • •

Marcos and Carmen Lebron had been awakened by a crash at two o'clock in the morning. In the town of Edison, New Jersey, there were absolutely no noises past ten o'clock—no ghetto blasters, screaming junkies, garbage trucks, ambulance sirens, none of the quality-of-life destroyers they had been plagued with in their Manhattan apartment. The Lebrons were always amazed at how the noise was actually funneled up to their eighteenth-floor apartment on upper Broadway, the din amplified rather than diminished with distance. When their second child was born and Marcos's TV repair shop on Amsterdam Avenue boomed, he decided to bring up his daughters in the suburbs, to smell grass and flowers instead of marijuana and garbage. So they moved to a town with good schools where their girls would live a civilized existence.

When they heard the crash two nights ago, they were jarred and attacked by the decibel invasion they had not been accustomed to for more than ten years. Marcos awoke instantly, and bounding out of bed, he rushed downstairs to the picture window of his two-family house. Parting the lace curtains, he saw that his car had been pushed away from the curb and turned around in the middle of the road, demolished. As luck would have it, his wife's car was sitting in the garage, awaiting a new battery and minor repairs, which he himself planned to do that weekend.

Marcos waited at home with his wife to monitor the insurance adjuster's inspection. Their three daughters had left for school and Marcos and Carmen sat in the kitchen, enjoying the opportunity to linger over coffee on a cold morning. The pleasure of his wife's breakfast and the smell of bacon and eggs still in his nostrils were disturbed by a sudden thought. He slammed the table in irritation.

"I forgot. Yesterday was Open School Day, and I was supposed to go with Esperanza." He shook his head and frowned. "Another disaster."

Carmen got up and clattered the dirty dishes. She knew this was going to be another fruitless discussion about crazy Esperanza, which is what her girls called her as if crazy were her first name.

"You have your own life." She knew she shouldn't have said it as soon as it came out.

Marcos caught the flash of disgust in Carmen's eyes. "She may be strange, but she's still my sister. She brought me up 'til I was six. Was it fair leaving her behind, treating her like a slave?"

"You sent for her, paid her fare. Then she had that baby in Puerto Rico." Carmen shook her head. "And she had to name the baby *Jesus!*"

Marcos laughed. "It's a common Spanish name! She's a religious nut. You know it's a sign of respect in our culture to name a kid Jesus. Are you prejudiced against your own now that you're an American?"

"It's so . . ." Carmen was at a loss for words.

"Isn't your mother's name Mary? The Americans name their girls *Virginia!* All names have meanings."

"Yeah, but I never would name a kid Jesus or Angel." Carmen gave up the argument. "Your *sister* and that baby," she said with a sigh.

"She needed a family of her own. When we got married and had Lydia, she felt left out again."

"It's only natural. We have to live our lives."

"I had to do something. The kid was running wild in P.R. He didn't go to school."

"You gave her our apartment, the furniture. You pay her rent. And now the old house in P.R.? You have your own family."

"The money from the house. I'm putting it in the boy's name when he comes old enough for his education. I feel I owe it to her."

"Education! He'll be lucky if he's not in jail. What does he do with the money he's always hitting you up for?"

"I been lucky, I was just a TV repairman on Amsterdam Avenue. Now I have a house, a business, you and the girls. They're still my family. And I can sleep at night."

Carmen said nothing. A family I would like to forget, she thought. A crazy woman and a delinquent son.

"I would take him in, but the girls . . ."

Carmen's heart sank. She tried to change the subject. "Don't you wonder who the father was?"

Marcos rolled his eyes and uttered a Spanish curse under his breath. Carmen laughed. "Did you ever ask her?"

Marcos rolled his eyes again. "You jokin'?"

"Don't tell me, God sent the baby. Or . . ."

"Some Anglo took advantage," Marcos said, trying to sound hard.

"Good thing you told the girls she was married and the father's living back in P.R.," Carmen consoled him.

But Marcos was in a funk. He had wanted the new year to start out better, and he felt the situation slipping out of his grasp.

• • •

Les ventured out of bed, his feet hitting the cold floor. Typical of New York, he scowled. You roasted at night and then, after leaving the windows open, froze in the morning. The chill had probably caused his nightmare, he thought. Then the heat came banging through the radiator. He dashed into the bathroom, but the icy water on his teeth made the morning even more unsavory. After a long, hot shower, warmth slowly and mercifully snaked back into his fingers.

He made the bed, thinking he could cope with bunking out in Rus's apartment in spite of the schizoid behavior of the heating system. He was lucky to have a place like this. A hotel would be a terrible expense in New York.

Rus, the piano player in his trio, had maintained the same rent-controlled apartment he first occupied when he was a Juilliard student, back when Juilliard was located uptown near Columbia before the days of Lincoln Center. Rus's large, round bed was a remnant of their lifestyle in the sixties.

Unable to think about breakfast, Les walked into the living room. The grand piano with its neatly piled stacks of music was surrounded by folk art from Rus's travels. He raised the piano lid and ran his fingers compulsively over the keyboard, instinctively picking out phrases from his latest piece. The chords he added were jangled and atonal, reflecting his tension. He rambled over the notes, his eyes roaming restlessly about the room, finally settling on a framed photograph of a younger, smiling Rus amid his family. The picture, mirroring Rus's handsome black features, didn't pick up the stunning quality that caused women's heads to turn in the street when he passed, and young girls to blush.

With Rus skiing in Vermont, Les had the apartment to himself. Whenever the trio had a gig on the coast, Rus would stay over in Monterey. He was the perfect guest, never interfering in Les and Eleanore's routines, affable, soft-spoken, and low-keyed, seemingly unaware of his own good looks. Eleanore, who was usually leery of jazz musicians, encouraged his visits.

Les closed the piano and stared at the telephone on the desk. But the thought of speaking to Julie after twelve years caused an instantaneous assault of nerves in the pit of his stomach. He whirled around on the piano stool and searched through his pockets. The primitive, disturbing masks Rus had brought back from his travels to South America and New Guinea, at eye level on the wall opposite, grinned menacingly at him. He extracted Julie's wrinkled, worn letter, which he had read a dozen times on the plane, and read it once more.

• • •

Marcos impatiently counted the rings. Eight, nine, ten. He drummed his fingers on the counter of his repair shop. It was still early. The adjuster had arrived on time and had dropped him off. The "closed" sign was turned out on the door.

He allowed the phone to ring because he knew Esperanza often ignored its sound. Finally she picked up.

"Did you go to Open School?" he asked her irritably, anticipating her answer.

"No! It's cursed!" she snapped. "I don't want him going there."

"Listen, Esperanza. If you take him out of this school, I'm washing my hands of you. This kid needs some stability."

"There's someone there, Marcos. Someone evil to take him away."

"*Dios mio*," Marcos muttered under his breath. He tried to control himself.

"But Marcos . . ." Esperanza began to cry.

Marcos's heart melted. He knew she was assailed by unknown spirits. She bordered on being delusionary, corroded by superstition. To her these imaginings were real terrors. He waited a minute to continue.

When he spoke again, his voice was softened. "Believe me. It's best for him. If you love him, you do this."
Esperanza didn't respond. He heard sniffling.
"Esperanza?"
Esperanza wouldn't answer. But he knew he had won. At least this battle.

• • •

Les searched the kitchen for a blender and unfolded a recipe neatly written in Eleanore's round, regular letters on ruled notebook paper. The handwriting contrasted with Julie's flamboyant style.

Eleanore's Anti-Cancer Drink
Take on an empty stomach and don't eat for an hour after.
1 T. lecithin
1¼ T. olive oil
4-6 oz. grapefruit or orange juice

He poured six ounces of orange juice into the container, pressed on the cover, and blended the concoction. After downing the drink, he headed for the street.

• • •

Esperanza had no way out. She couldn't take Jesus out of school again. If she defied Marcos, who knows what he might do? She was afraid. She lit two candles to see which one burned down first. If it was the left candle, she would lose her son. If it was the right, she would lose Marcos. Or maybe everything.
She cradled her body in her arms and watched the candles burn. Then she opened the windows wide. The flames were extinguished by the wind. Esperanza would do nothing. For now.

• • •

Stepping out onto Broadway at One Hundred Thirteenth Street, Les was amazed at the changes. The shops near Columbia University had always been cheap and dingy, part and parcel of the surrounding ghetto. Except for the West End Bar, which still hung in there and featured jazz in the evening, and

Mondel's hand-dipped chocolates, a neighborhood institution where he had often bought Julie goodies, everything had changed. Korean fruit markets had replaced the discount clothing stores that used to hawk their sundries in stalls on the sidewalk. And Indian and Japanese restaurants had replaced the dark stores with dummy merchandise in the windows, concealing numbers operations in the rear. A rare-book store occupied a cellar formerly inhabited by a Puerto Rican social club. The intellectual West Side had moved uptown.

He wondered what his old neighborhood looked like. Gathering his courage, he continued south on Broadway. The refuse and debris were still part of the landscape, he noted drearily. He was thankful he had chosen to live on the West Coast, to be free of the ugliness of Manhattan. The wind whipped the litter from the gutter, and he had to brush away a dirty handbill that nearly hit him in the face. Some things never change, he thought.

The side streets, he noticed, had not been much affected by gentrification. Bums and addicts hung out on corners, and the buildings were still crumbling and threatening, their steel doors, broken windows, and unlit corridors forbidding. He peered into one, wondering with a shudder how a child might survive there.

He was approaching Ninety-Sixth Street, his old turf. Gourmet shops and elegant restaurants lined up on Broadway. Huge new buildings had mushroomed into the sky. The empty lot that had hosted junkies and drug dealers was now the Columbia, a high rise with a glitzy lobby, advertising a health club. The old, mean streets had been yuppified.

He was headed toward his old apartment building, hoping he could face it. It was the first step in reconstructing his past. Perhaps it would jog a memory, give him a start, inspire him with a kernel of an idea. If it did, it was worth the trip. The changes in the neighborhood helped him. He was not stepping into the past, back in time. He was the new Les, a different person, removed from the scene and observing. He took heart and walked on, turning onto Ninety-Sixth Street toward West End Avenue.

Even the welfare hotels were now condos, he marveled. He wondered what his old building would look like. He pushed south on Riverside Drive to Ninety-First Street. And then he heard it, the growl that transported him back over the years. It was Willie English, drinking from a paper bag and waving his arms in the air, oblivious to the wind and cold. He was wearing his black felt peaked hat with a feather, as always. His cowboy boots were old and worn, but his unwashed pants were stylishly tucked into them. A short wool coat with a button missing kept him warm. He was the same, but aged. His dark skin was more mottled, and he was thinner. His black hair and mustache were scruffier. But his élan hadn't deserted him. It came from the bottle in the brown paper bag.

Les stood before the dreaded building at last. The grand old thing was quite a beauty, he had to admit. The bricks had been sandblasted; the brass on the doors and on the fountain, which had once watered carriage horses, was polished. And the canopy was new. Shrubs lined the circular driveway, filling furrows that had always been barren in the years he had lived there.

He entered the lobby with trepidation. The stained glass had been cleaned, and light poured through. The marble floor had been scrubbed, and new leather furniture was grouped around the restored fireplace.

There was the pillar! The one that appeared in a recurrent dream, the dream in which he walked into the hallway of this apartment building. In every one of the dreams he returned to the open door on the day of the kidnapping. But before he reached his apartment, a shadow appeared around this corner, elongating toward him, reaching for him. And just as the shadow was about to engulf him, he put out his hand to touch it. Then the shadow shrank and disappeared, and he was covered in the darkness of sleep.

Something tugged at his memory. But he was interrupted by a doorman dressed in uniform, heading toward him from the back. Les turned and left, not willing to answer any questions. If only he could remember what he had seen that day.

$$4$$

It was Friday morning, and everything conspired to make Bobbie more miserable than ever. The snow was dirty, black and yellow. She trudged through the drifts the snowplows had pushed from the streets to the curbs, obstructing her passage from one street to the other. Her sore throat was intensified by the mean gusts of wind as she was forced to wade the rivers of melted ice in the gutters in her rubber boots. Her toes were frozen and she began to feel feverish, but it never occurred to her to remain at home to nurse herself.

She kept her head down as much to avoid seeing into the lives of the poor on this ghetto street where the school was located as to protect herself against the wind. Yesterday a handsome, muscular young man was screaming, enraged at a woman. The two were circled by a tattered group of onlookers. The woman, also young, was thin, haggard, and had several teeth missing. She looked dazed. The young man had run out of a building in the cold in his rolled-up undershirt, and Bobbie could see his bare shoulders and arms bulging from bodybuilding. He faced off with the woman, his anger spinning venomously from his eyes and tongue with such intensity the woman seemed tied to the space between them. She was clearly afraid to run. His words were in English, and in the very instant that Bobbie dared to watch she heard him smack the woman in the face with great force. Bobbie stopped on the edge of the crowd. The woman never flinched. When she started to walk away, he commanded her to come back. Bobbie was ten feet away when she heard the sound of the man's hand when the woman obeyed him. This time the smack came with the full weight of his shoulder behind it, harder than before. The crowd grumbled but did nothing. The law of the jungle. Bobbie had rushed into the school knowing they would vanish by the time the police arrived.

Sometimes the worst scenes took place in the schoolyard, especially in winter when the kids weren't lined up and the teachers waited inside to begin the day. Often Bobbie was emotionally exhausted even before the day began. And today was Friday. Free-for-all day, zoo day. Heartbreak day. Sometimes humor got her through.

"Yo! Bummy," a student called to her affectionately. Baumgarten, her last name, amended student style. She laughed as he threw a handful of snow at her, missing her deliberately. She hoped all the snow would melt. The rocks placed in the snowballs had cracked several skulls that week, keeping the ambulances busy outside the school every lunch hour.

On Fridays half the students cut and the other half wreaked mayhem. After lunch it was a holding action. No one, not even the principal, who was in a world of his own, expected anyone to teach. But Bobbie, knowing it was the worst day of the week in the dead of winter, when school was a drag to even the scholarly and they were all in the grips of the doldrums before December, would never take off. Never mind that the absentee rate among teachers was predictably high because of battle fatigue. Bobbie saved her sick days for auditions, the important ones.

The image of the man beating his mate tormented Bobbie. It preyed on her mind, and she heard the crack of his hand on the subservient woman's thin face as Bobbie pushed the metal slab on the door with her arm, opening the door into the slushy corridor. She climbed up to the fourth floor, gagging on the damp cave odors and pot in the staircase, now concentrating on her problem with the troublemaker she could no longer handle, Jesus Lebron. He was only fourteen, but he was already growing up to be as vicious and barbaric as the man she had just seen in the street. She had made a difficult decision she was loath to carry out: third period she would have the unpleasant task of telling Jesus that she was transferring him from her biology class into Julie's reading class. He would never understand that it was for his own good.

It was courageous and typical of Julie to have volunteered to take him on. Bobbie knew that Julie, more than the other reading teachers, had a knack for working with kids like Jesus. Nevertheless, Bobbie had been nervous, and today her nervousness was escalating into a deeper anxiety.

The image of the bully's hand on the girl's skin outside the school yesterday was growing stronger in her mind. She knew, just knew, this was some sort of omen.

The lunch bell rang, and the hordes began thundering down the steps past Julie's room. Julie wondered where Bobbie was. She usually sprinted from the fourth floor with her students, hardly able to wait to wolf down the diet lunch she kept, along with Julie's, in the fridge in her lab prep room. Sometimes their yogurts mingled with frozen specimens and film from the photography class.

Julie knew the school would erupt at the lunch bell, the students fleeing the school like prisoners liberated from Devil's Island. And in thirty seconds she could climb the stairs without bucking the onslaught. The halls were silent when she locked her door, the shrieks and the roar muffled below in the cafeteria.

She was starved, her stomach aching for her turkey sandwich. But when she opened the door to Bobbie's science room, she lost her appetite. The room was a shambles, and Bobbie, fighting back tears, was in the midst of it, her hair disheveled. Julie could smell a rotten odor coming from the fish tank, and Bobbie was siphoning the murky water into the sink.

"I shouldn't be upset by this," Bobbie said, trying to be casual. "I've been through it before . . ." She gestured hopelessly around the room.

Julie took in the wreckage. All of Bobbie's plants knocked off the sills, the charts slashed or ripped from the wall, and her favorite display, "Designer Genes, The Story of DNA," had an obscenity scribbled on it in red Magic Marker. A lifelike diagram of the human skeleton had a bloody gash through the heart.

Julie pulled the defaced posters from the wall, gathered those on the floor, rolled them up, and threw them into the trash barrel at the door. The room looked grim and bare.

"Who did this?" Julie asked.

Bobbie shook her head. "Round up the usual suspects," she said, trying to laugh.

"But how did they get in?" asked Julie, knowing the room was always locked.

"Last two periods a sub covered for Marge," Bobbie explained. "She probably forgot to lock the door."

"Marge Doyle? The new science teacher? The one whose apartment was robbed?"

Bobbie nodded. "She's been absent a lot, and you know what the kids do to subs. They're cannon fodder."

When Julie finally joined Bobbie at her desk, their lunches spread before them, Julie could hardly swallow her food. Terrible things were happening to people close to her, she thought, as they sat side by side in the midst of the destruction. She gave Bobbie a hug of encouragement, but they sat together silent and dejected, feeling defeated.

• • •

Les climbed onto the Amsterdam Avenue bus. The day was cold and clear, and the new, clean bus filled up with well-dressed people. Amsterdam Avenue, formerly the pits of the avenues, unwalkable in the past because of the crime, now presented him with an eyeful at every stop. On weekdays women in fur coats and businesspeople carrying attaché cases swarmed the streets. Today the yuppies in brightly colored ski jackets shepherded their children to Saturday-morning music lessons. The bus passed Hanratty's, a pioneer watering hole, where he remembered a customer had been gunned down right in front of the door. The lovely Gothic Church of the Holy Name stood on the corner of Ninety-Sixth Street; Les could still envision large wedding parties descending the steps on Saturday afternoons.

Suddenly he had an idea. He grabbed the crumpled letter

from his pocket and jumped off the bus. He hailed a cab and read the driver the address he had gotten from the Federal Express packet. The telephone number he had copied from the Manhattan book was scribbled beneath it.

After the cab crossed the park and delivered him to East Ninety-Second Street, he found himself standing before a handsome brownstone four stories high. Steps leading up to the front door were enclosed by a wrought-iron fence and gate. The tall, draped windows were decorated with curlicued wrought iron. There was a weather vane on the roof. His heart pounded. He pushed the gate, but it rattled, unyielding. It was locked. He looked up. The house, as far as he could tell, was empty. There was no movement, not a single light.

He hurried toward Lexington Avenue like a criminal afraid of being caught in the act. He had done a foolish thing. If Julie's husband had been at home, what would Les have done? Julie would have hated him for showing up. What a way to begin. He pulled his muffler tightly around his neck and secured his hat against the wind. There was a gallery across from her in a brownstone. He would get himself a cup of hot coffee and return when it opened. He would stand in the gallery doorway and wait for her without being seen. The air seemed to get thinner, he felt, but the sun continued to shine through the sharp cold.

• • •

Waiting for her, Les thought about how surprised Julie would be at how he had changed. He had gained weight, had lost the gaunt, haunted look he had before he fled to California. And while he tried to picture exactly how Julie would look, pangs of longing and nostalgia overwhelmed him. Then suddenly there she was, packages in hand, unlocking the gate.

The shock of seeing her was too great. Her hair was dark. And she was heavier. Of course! She was pregnant. She was altogether different from his own Julie. She wore a full-length black mink coat, the kind advertised in sleek, glossy magazines. Her expensive leather boots matched her handbag. A gold bracelet glistened on her wrist as she raised her key to the gate. He realized with full force, her appearance speaking to him even more clearly than the letter, how intrusive his showing up would be. Her fancy town house, her rich husband, her new baby—they were the reality he had to reckon with.

He took out the letter again, crushing it in his hand. I'll never do this again, he promised himself. I've done her enough harm.

• • •

Esperanza heard the door unlocked and pushed open violently, then voices. Jesus and Nilda again. Esperanza ran into her bedroom, her sanctuary, and closed the door quietly. Sometimes when they came home there was laughter, but other times she didn't like the sounds she heard.

Today Jesus's voice was loud, assertive. She didn't like the pitch of his laugh. It was too close to anger. Nilda sounded in good spirits but wary. She too knew his moods. The door to his bedroom slammed shut as he pushed Nilda in, and Esperanza heard Nilda protesting, "Stop. Please."

"I'll get you jewelry," he whispered, "like that new teacher wears."

"What kind of jewelry?"

"You'll see. You'll look nice." He stroked her silken hair. "Your hair . . . your hair is just like hers."

• • •

Whenever Julie unlocked the gate, or any door, the question would rise from the past to plague her. *Did I forget to lock the door that day?*

Countless times she tried to envision leaving the apartment with her baby that morning. She had grabbed her wool cap from the closet before she left. Had she forgotten to lock the door?

She had brought it up in the group again last week, the final meeting of the group for crime victims she had joined. She had met Martha there and was glad to have finally gotten together with others who had suffered as she had. They reminded her once more that the victim always blames herself. Don't blame yourself, they had taught her. Her mother, a spunky woman who took on the world, had also taught her to be brave, especially when Julie's father died, very young, of a heart attack.

I'm trying to be brave, Mother, she said mentally. Her mother had died when Julie was a senior in college, but in times of stress she still imagined her mother's comforting presence. She thought thankfully of her old friend, Bobbie, who had helped her through loneliness on many nights over the empty years, and of her new discovery, Martha. Martha was a solace to her.

Julie climbed the stairs to the front door. Once inside, when she arrived at the main floor after climbing the second steep flight, she realized she was a little winded. She patted her stomach, hung up her coat, and started upstairs to the third-floor bedroom when the phone rang.

She plopped down on the bed near the phone.

"Hello," she said cheerfully, expecting Greg's voice. He would be calling to let her know which flight he was taking home.

She spoke into a void.

"Hello?"

Ominous silence. Julie slammed down the phone.

"Oh, Momma," she cried, "when will it end?"

• • •

Les paced in his friend's apartment and impulsively picked up the phone in the living room. He dialed a number he knew by heart.

"New York Psychiatric Hospital," a switchboard operator answered. "Can I help you?"

"Yes," he responded, encouraged by the routine voice. "I'm a former patient. Is Doctor Samuel Wolfson still there?"

"I'll connect you." Les hung on.

At last he heard the familiar, reassuring voice from the past, so soft and calm, a bit distracted as usual.

"This is Les Layton. Do you remember me, Doctor?"

There was a pause. "Of course I do."

Les was relieved. The doctor sounded tired but certain. "It's been a long time," he added.

"Twelve years," said Les.

"You've been well?"

"Yes, Doctor." The doctor's voice had changed, he realized. It wasn't as resilient.

"Is there a problem now?"

"I need to see you."

The doctor tried to judge how serious it was. "When . . . ?"

"Right away. It's happening again, doctor. I'm afraid. I'm even afraid for Julie."

• • •

Julie had almost missed Greg's call from the airport, she was so terrified of the phone. Naturally she hadn't worried him with her fear that a stupid pervert was tormenting her. Any minute now Martha would arrive to rescue her from her phantoms.

Every window was bolted on all four floors of the house. The kitchen and the dining room on the street level, the living room on the parlor floor, the bedrooms one flight up, and above, the atticlike room that was her private study. She descended the stairs and reached the steep flight leading to the front door. She didn't have the nerve to search behind the stairs alone.

The hallway at dusk was dimly lit, quiet as a tomb. At the top of the stairs she gripped the banister to climb down the narrow flight. She stared into the dark behind the parlor floor landing, her heart racing. Just then the doorbell rang.

Thank God. It was no-nonsense, solid, loving Martha waiting at the curtained glass door. Julie took Martha's hand.

They both held their breath, without meaning to. The darkness under the stairs was empty.

"Now every corner is safe!" said Julie, leading Martha upstairs. "Greg would think I was demented," Julie remarked when they settled in the living room.

"Not if he knew," said Martha.

Julie handed Martha a drink and poured herself a glass of mineral water. Her hand shook for just a second.

"Maybe Greg is right. Maybe I should quit. You know how he feels about my teaching while I'm pregnant. He never approved of my working in a tough school in the first place."

Martha looked at the French clock on the fireplace near where Julie stood. An amateur photographer, Martha wanted to get back into the darkroom to finish the work that had been interrupted by Julie's call.

"Do you want to quit?"

"Yes," blurted Julie.

Overreacting, thought Martha. "What will you do? Search again? You have a new life now."

"I always wonder. Always! Where is he?"

Martha ignored the clock. The darkroom could wait.

"Martha, someone is spying on me, trying to find out if I'm home!"

"Don't jump to conclusions," Martha cautioned her, gulping her drink. She eyed the bar.

Julie swished the ice cubes in her glass, unaware that she was spilling her drink.

"It was a kook on the phone," Martha tried to reassure her. "New York is filled with them. Why don't you stay with me until Greg comes back? It's just me and my darkroom, all alone in my four-bedroom apartment." Martha had taken up photography two years after the terrible day her husband was murdered.

Julie shook her head. "It's only one more night. You and Bobbie will be here for dinner tomorrow, and then Greg will be home.

Martha walked to the bar and stood beside Julie. "Maybe you should tell Greg," she said, making herself a new drink. She led Julie to a chair and sat across from her.

"No! You and Bobbie are the only ones who know—and the group."

"Too many secrets, Julie . . ."

"I want a normal life. I want Greg to feel I'm normal."

"You *are* normal. But if you keep on—"

"I'll tell him soon. I just need a few more months of tranquillity."

Martha didn't object. "You're entitled," she said with a sigh.

• • •

Les walked past Julie's town house. It got dark early in the winter in New York, he was reminded; it was only five o'clock, and gloom had settled over the grayed-out city. When he reached the corner, he crossed and doubled back. Bobbie had just opened the unlocked gate. She was expected. He recognized her at once—her jaunty walk, her theatrical, dyed red hair.

He pulled out a pack of cigarettes, lighting up to give himself more time. It wasn't a good sign that he was reviving bad habits. Just then a tall, attractive older woman, well-tailored, with a determined walk, approached. He had never seen her before. He barely caught sight of Julie opening the door. The two women obscured his view. Ornamental wrought-iron bars secured the tall, elegant windows from the attic room to the first floor. He could see the glint of a crystal chandelier in the first-floor window, and bookcases lining a sedate, wallpapered room on the second floor.

He was nervous about hanging around for too long at the dinner hour, worrying that passersby would notice him. He inhaled the cigarette smoke, coughing as he studied the shapes in the second-floor window before heading for the crosstown bus.

• • •

In her formal dining room Julie served cabbage salad as the first course.

"Not too much wine," said Martha. "Tonight I want you to be alert. It's your first lesson in self-defense."

"Oh, I feel so virtuous eating a vegetarian meal," Bobbie raved, eagerly sampling her first bite. "My God, it's divine."

Julie set out the Swiss chard tart and the pumpkin, bean, and corn stew.

"Do you know what one cannibal said to the other at the dinner table when his friend told him he hated his mother-in-law?" asked Bobbie.

"No," said Martha, twisting her face.

"Just eat your vegetables!" Bobbie roared at her own joke.

"I would never serve this to Greg," said Julie as she cut into the tart. "He's a meat-and-potatoes man. And he has the lowest cholesterol level."

"He's lucky like you, Julie," said Bobbie. "You eat like a

horse and look like a bird. I'm the actress, and I look like a schoolmarm." Bobbie was always fighting a weight problem, always on the edge of chubby, Julie thought, sympathizing. She had lived through many of her friend's crash diets. "My mother always told me to get my teaching license to pay for the groceries while I was looking for a part," Bobbie explained. "I guess I was never meant to play Camille or starve in a garret."

Julie observed Martha, who had been so quiet. Martha was composed as usual, the most stunning middle-aged woman she'd ever met. Her hair was salt-and-pepper gray. Her large red glasses accented her hazel eyes. She was perfectly natural, never afraid to be herself. She and Bobbie colored their hair. Bobbie was always auditioning for commercials and summer stock. Julie had her own reasons.

"Why so serious tonight?" Julie asked Martha.

"I just thought . . . with these phone calls and Bobbie complaining about the thefts in school, I'd teach you some tricks."

"Can we have dessert first?" asked Bobbie hopefully. They all laughed.

"Let's finish in the living room," suggested Julie, bringing out the walnut pie. "Martha, grab the coffee things. Bobbie, the plates and forks."

"All so healthy!" said Bobbie, digging into her pie, which Julie had placed on a plate on the coffee table. "I feel so disciplined I could handle anything now."

"Purses have been disappearing at school," said Julie, on edge. "And Bobbie shares a classroom with a teacher whose apartment was burglarized," she explained to Martha.

"Last week someone vandalized my classroom too," Bobbie said.

"Everyone's nervous. I'm not the only one," Julie explained.

"No one can blame you," said Martha, finishing her coffee.

"Especially now," Bobbie said. "The rapist who was stalking this neighborhood . . . It's so scary. He was so ordinary. Women opened their doors to him. He was even handsome. He had a good job, a wife. No scars, no evil look in his eye. I saw him on TV."

"The man who murdered my husband, Anton, had a wife

and kids," whispered Martha. "Do you remember the warden who spoke to us in group? He called rapists dreary and banal."

"The banality of evil," said Bobbie. "That's how Hannah Arendt described Adolf Eichmann."

Julie knew that Martha's husband had been shot dead trying to save a woman from being robbed. Martha had told the story in their crime victims' group. It was because of their friendship and the support of experts in the group, Julie realized, that she and Martha were able to survive so well.

"I feel evil pursuing me," Julie whispered. "I'm so glad Greg is coming home tonight."

Martha stood up. This was the moment, she thought. "Watch this. A magic cure for the hallway attacker." She reached for her tapestry handbag and pulled out a small pistol. "When Anton was killed, I swore I would never be a victim."

"My God!" screamed Bobbie. "Where did you get that?"

"I have a friend in the jewelry district who travels with diamonds. She has a license. She gave it to me." Martha put it on the table.

Julie stared at it in fascination. It looked too deadly to make her feel protected. But she wished she had something to make her feel she was stacking the odds in her favor.

"This makes me so nervous. What if it goes off?"

"It won't," said Martha. She picked up the gun. "I've relived Anton's death a thousand times. With this! And I'm not a widow anymore. I can't be a hero, like Anton, but I *can* defend myself."

Martha sat down between them on the couch. She displayed the gun in her palm. "Don't worry. I'm taking a course in firearms, right here in Manhattan."

"They're making us victims again," observed Julie. "Of fear."

"Only if you're helpless," warned Martha.

"It's so small," observed Bobbie, her eyes riveted on the gun. "Can I pick it up?"

"Is it loaded?" asked Julie.

"Not yet. Here, hold it." Martha offered it to Bobbie.

"My heart is palpitating just seeing a real gun!" said Bobbie. "In person." She recoiled from it, shaking her head.

Julie took the gun in her hand. "It's so strange. It's actually beautiful." She looked at it closely, hefting it in her palm. "So light."

"Eight ounces," Martha supplied.

"It fits in your hand," said Julie.

"Or purse," added Martha.

"The handle is walnut," Julie observed. "It *looks* like a lady's gun or revolver or whatever you call it."

"It's a pistol. A revolver has a rotating mechanism for bullets. This has a magazine." Martha took the gun and pressed the barrel lever, and the barrel tipped up. She pulled out a metal case. It had eight holes. "I put the bullet in . . ." She took a bullet from her change purse. "And load it." She dropped a tiny yellow, brass-tipped bullet with a black dot on its nose into the magazine. "This tiny bullet expands on contact."

Bobbie and Julie watched without comment. Finally Bobby spoke. "Gross!" she announced with a look of disgust.

"Do all bullets do that?" asked Julie.

"I have a choice. This does more damage than an ordinary bullet."

"It's awful to think of it piercing someone's flesh," Julie said. "That you have the capability of doing so much harm with this finely crafted . . . mechanism."

"You have the same capability with a car," Martha answered. But she didn't pursue it. She closed the barrel, and they heard a click. She cocked the hammer. Julie and Bobbie observed intently as she pushed the catch up with her thumb to engage the safety.

"The safety is on now; I can put it back into my purse." But Martha made no move to return it. "Now it's ready to fire!" she announced, pointing it at the floor. "But I won't, of course." She opened the magazine and removed the bullet. "To fire I push the safety down, cock the hammer, and press the trigger."

She demonstrated after she unloaded and redid the safety. "One," she counted, pushing the safety down with her thumb. "Two." She cocked the hammer. "Three." She clicked the trigger.

The women were silent.

"It is ironic that they make these weapons aesthetic," Martha told them. Julie and Bobbie stared at the compact weapon as

Martha admired it. The trigger was gold, and everything but the wooden grip was dark gray metal. The letters P.B. were carved into the top, in beautiful script. "The initials are for Pietro Beretta, the son of the original producer of the gun," she explained.

It was more than Julie cared to know. "Isn't it illegal to carry a gun in New York?" she asked.

"You need a license. The laws are very strict in this state. But I'd rather take a chance on getting caught by the police than by a mugger on a dark night."

Julie knew she couldn't argue with Martha on this topic.

"I'm scared going home to the Village on the subway. Late at night after a performance, the trains are spooky," admitted Bobbie. "But I'm no Bernie Goetz. I don't want a gun."

Martha put the gun in her purse and dangled her house keys. "You don't need a gun. There are simpler methods to defend yourself." She placed a key between each pair of her knuckles, jabbing her fist in the air.

"*Voilà!* Brass knucks."

Julie breathed deeply and exhaled loudly. Martha was right. She didn't want to be a prisoner in her house when Greg was away. But the little gun that was stashed away in Martha's pocketbook left an ache in the pit of Julie's stomach.

"Can we go up to your bedroom?" Martha asked. "I want to show you something." They filed upstairs, and Martha examined the room. After the inspection she removed a book from one of the night tables beside the mahogany double bed. She replaced it with an alabaster statue from across the room.

"That should bash his brains out!" exclaimed Bobbie, getting the point.

"Don't you remember the lecture in our support group?" Martha asked Julie. "Eighty percent of rapes are committed in the home. So keep a heavy object near your bed."

Julie was stunned into silence. Her baby was going to be born into a world she was not prepared to imagine. Or perhaps she was better prepared than most. She stared at Martha, picturing the gun raised in her hand. Julie wondered whether they had all gone mad. Then she felt the baby kick her hard in her side for the first time.

5

At midnight Julie heard the car, and then came Greg's footsteps clumping up the stairs. He kissed her eagerly, his hands grasping packages around her back. She had kept the fire going in the living room, hoping he would arrive on schedule. The *Concorde* had never been late.

Julie was glad she had tried to stay awake to greet him. When she saw the happy expression on his face as he stood in the living room door, and the excitement in his eyes when he threw his arms around her and they kissed, her fears melted away.

"I'm so happy to see you," he said. "I was sure the two of you would be snoozing at this hour." He rubbed her stomach. "I have a present for you," he announced. "I'll get it from my bag."

The fire was spitting sparks, so Julie replaced the screen while he opened his suitcase. Then she unscrewed the cork from the wine he had brought from France. It was still cold from the winter air. She smiled at the sight of the stick of French bread that had flown with him from Europe and opened the pound of liver pâté. She set them on a plate and started on a bite when Greg walked toward her, carrying a gold-papered box tied with silver ribbons.

He poured the wine, and they clinked glasses as they sat together. He kissed her on the lips as a toast. Julie sipped only a drop of the wine to celebrate his return. She had stopped drinking as soon as she became pregnant. She spread another helping of pâté on a slice of the crusty bread. "You're stuffing me like the goose this came from," she said, savoring the deli-

cacy. "I just served a veggie meal, and look at me, pigging out."
The truth was she had been hungry when he arrived.

"The baby needs some nourishment," he kidded her. "I
know *you're* never hungry."

Julie loved being indulged by Greg but always felt a bit
alien to the luxury. She had never before had luxuries without
planning for them. They weren't part of daily life for her the
way they were for Greg.

Julie was wearing a square-necked silk nightgown, which
felt cozy even in this winter weather because of the heat radiat-
ing from the fireplace. As a matter of fact it was getting too hot.
She tugged the loose shoulder away for air, and Greg bent down
to kiss her shoulder, bending her toward him. "Time for bed,"
she said, feeling the warmth flush her whole body. The baby felt
it too. She thought it twisted ever so slightly.

"Can you wait for the present?" he asked. She stood up, and
he pressed her against him. He was still dressed, and his suit
crushed against her nightgown.

"I need a nice soft bed," she told him after he kissed her very
passionately. "Rugs and chairs are out for the next few months."

Thank God he misses me as much as I miss him, she
thought, leading him into the bedroom.

A wave of comfort, of total contentment, overcame Julie
after they made love. She felt sensitized after sex, lying in Greg's
arms. He held her tightly and she snuggled closer. I'm being
held by Greg, our baby between us protected by our love, she
thought.

Greg was a better lover than Les. She dared make the
comparison now that she had written the letter. Greg was more
experienced, sensitive. He was a lover of women. He explored
her body with the same sense of discovery each time they made
love. He was more attuned to her, prepared her more. Was it
because they were older? In the rush of youth with Les it had
been instant fever. Greg was tender, waited for the exact moment. He was experimental.

Men who loved women were sexy. Sexual. The way he
looked at her . . . the thought sent a tremor through her body.

Sometimes after sex she felt she couldn't get enough, that her body was a mass of response. But she grew sleepy. She closed her eyes happily, the weight of his body against her, his arms around her. She slept feeling safe, so safe.

• • •

Early on Monday morning Les sat in the molded plastic chair opposite Dr. Wolfson's desk. He looked around with a sensation of profound relief. The office was still the same unadorned, institutional gray he remembered. There were no pictures on the walls, nothing to suggest the richness of civilization. You're here to be cured, the office cried out to him. No frills.

"You're looking well," Dr. Wolfson remarked.

Les noted how much the doctor had aged. He guessed him to be close to sixty. His hairline was receding, and he was turning gray. Ten years ago he had been short and trim, sporting a brush mustache. Now he was paunchy and his smooth-shaven skin was puffy.

"Yes. You know why," commented Les.

"You're not an addict anymore," Dr. Wolfson stated.

"Direct as ever," Les said with a laugh. "It's all coming back. If it weren't for you, I would never have kicked my problem."

Dr. Wolfson picked up his pen. Les noticed that the pad, which had been abandoned during the last few months of therapy many years ago, was on the desk in front of the doctor again.

Dr. Wolfson waited for Les to speak.

"Julie's pregnant again."

Dr. Wolfson acknowledged the pain in Les's voice with a nod.

"When we got the divorce, I adjusted. I was even happy for her. I knew she needed a new start. But this! I can't cope with it."

"It must be hard to see Julie having a new baby."

"I was getting my life together with Eleanore. I wrote to you about her. I even got my trio together. I compose."

Dr. Wolfson waited for him to continue.

"I'm afraid I'm losing control again."

"In what way? Are you . . ."

"No. No drugs. I'm clean. Been clean for thirteen years. It's not that. I watch her window. I hang around, hoping to catch a glimpse of her. I know all her friends."

Les stopped speaking. The doctor had begun writing. He looked up from the pad.

"I've even called her on the phone. When I heard her voice, I hung up."

The doctor continued writing without any expression on his face.

Les clenched his teeth and bent forward urgently in his chair. He gripped the desk. "There's something else. Something I never told you."

The doctor looked up, compelled by the anguish in Les's voice.

Then Les cried, "It was my fault my baby was taken."

• • •

Julie woke up before Greg, as usual. Now that she slept through the night, her anxiety arrived at the precise moment her eyes opened. She was eager, almost grateful, to get out of bed in the morning and rush about in preparation for school.

Half asleep, Greg kissed her and reached over and held her tightly, quieting her racing heart. He knew she had the jitters every morning but never knew why. He also knew that as the day progressed she became involved in the complicated day's work and her fear abated.

She remained in bed a moment longer, thinking about how much she had changed. Before the tragedy she had been brave, unafraid. She thought about the kidnapping as a tragedy, the word less distressing somehow.

Years ago when Les was on tour she enjoyed being alone. She had had to remind herself to lock the door. Now minute terrors accosted her. Once she had perceived lightning from her window on Riverside Drive as God's brilliant pyrotechnic display. Now a sudden change in the weather induced shocks of anxiety. The electricity parting the black sky seared her heart. Rain, which she had always associated with growth and flowering and natural nourishment of the earth, was a threat. Instead of enjoying the sound of the rain or the wet whiff of the wind as it blew into a room, she ran around fearfully closing the windows against the storm, obsessively concerned that the wind would dash water into her house, rot her floors, drench her drapes, destroy her furniture.

She was afraid of an invasion, of being engulfed by the elements, by forces beyond her control. Just as that day when her baby was taken from her. And she was inexplicably afraid of people, of strangers, even of some of the kids at school, especially Jesus Lebron, the student Bobbie had asked to have transferred. He cast a pall over her day. There was something about him, the way she caught him staring at her. She dreaded his entering her room. Whenever he sauntered in late, interrupting her class with that cocky, cold-blooded expression on his face, every student in the class stiffened with tension.

She would speak to Bobbie about him soon, because he had begun to frighten her terribly.

6

Julie paced anxiously in the main office of the school on the first floor. She hung her keys up on hook number 45 as she had done for so many years, checked for mail in her wooden cubicle against the wall, and listened to the elephant stampede, as Bobbie called it, thunder down the steps. When the shrieks of delight and the roar of students as they emptied the school subsided, Julie unbuttoned her wool coat. A sudden hush enveloped her.

Bobbie was late, ignoring, as usual, the warning never to stay in her fourth-floor room past three o'clock, after the teachers were gone. Julie particularly wanted to talk to Bobbie today. The lone secretary at one of the desks was smoking heavily, and Julie walked into the corridor for air.

She was tired and hot and irritable. She stared into the staircase, hoping to hear Bobbie's heels clanking down, but the custodian giving instructions to a janitor before heading for the basement produced the only sounds she heard.

A sudden crash, and Julie turned to see Jesus and a group of boys charge past her, practically knocking down the students in their path just as the gate securing the school beyond the office fell from the ceiling to the ground, sealing off that part of the school from intruders.

Dammit, Bobbie! Julie thought, removing her coat and looking up the stairwell. She was sweating, but she couldn't leave her tote bag, loaded with books and papers, in the office because soon it would be locked. "Where the hell are you?" she asked aloud, poking her head into the stairwell, knowing she wouldn't be heard.

Joe Russo changed his work shirt in the supply closet on the fourth floor as soon as the school was quiet. Mr. Mac, Brandon McGuire, the school custodian, had reminded him to rush through the cleanup to help him set up the gym for an after-school program. It always meant a few extra bucks, so he was glad to do it. He tossed his old shirt in the corner, pulled out the pint he kept under the paper towels, and took a little swig to hold him 'til later. Old Nan, the cleaning woman, who dusted the furniture and washed the walls like a shadow all day, saw the bottle but kept her mouth shut about it, just as she did about everything.

He pulled the oversized broom, with its big, soft bristles, into the room on the farthest end of the hall. He would work his way back to the room near the only usable staircase, then down to help Mr. Mac in the basement. The first room was usually the easiest. It was the Home Ec room, where he sometimes took a nap on the bed after a heavy night. Then on to the pigsty across the way. That cute new teacher with the short skirts let the kids rampage through the room all day. He methodically pushed the papers in front of him with the broom, accumulating piles in the corridor.

Julie's emotion was no longer irritation; it was concern. She mounted the stairs, feeling queasy. This particular staircase at the end of the corridor was always grim, with no windows and dim illumination. But the gate prevented her from using the large central staircase. It was her only way up. At least it led directly to Bobbie's room, she thought, saving her some steps when she reached the fourth floor. If a parent or a student was detaining Bobbie, Julie would drag her away.

She started up the stairs. She had never in all these years climbed them without the bustle and the onslaught of laughing teenagers, and now she struggled up the stairs, unconsciously darting her eyes into the next corner, forcing herself to move faster, relieved when she finally reached the second floor.

Before Bobbie had been able to stop them at the sound of the bell, her class had made a break for both the back and the front doors, and Freddie Garcia grabbed the lunch pass she had unlocked from her drawer before he took off. Joe was way down the hall, and she was alone. She stood in the midst of the floor, which was littered with paper and candy wrappers. The kids hadn't put their chairs on the desks, and she was dismayed by the debris. The janitor wouldn't work around the chairs, and if she left it that way that fat bitch of an assistant principal would give her a bad write-up tomorrow. She had it in for Bobbie anyway and was due to observe her first period in the morning. Bobbie couldn't give the woman any more ammunition.

She heard Joe opening the closet halfway down the hall as she reluctantly dropped her bag on the desk, her scarf and gloves on it. The sun was sinking, and the room began to darken. The sudden silence assailed her. She could hear no sounds from Joe. She peeked down the long corridor. Every door was locked; there wasn't a soul to be seen. Joe was working in one of the rooms down at the other end. She hoped.

She grabbed a chair and ended the tension by crashing it on the desk. Then the next, and the next, with nervous fury. She began to think she had made a mistake staying alone. One by one she clattered the seats on the desks, their reverberations a rumble of succeeding echoes in the silence. And then she heard it, the slow sweep, sweep, heading toward her. Sweep, sweep, sweep. Then it disappeared.

Julie shifted her overcoat to her right hand and was tempted to lean against the banister, but she pushed on, trying not to inhale the dank odors of decades of smoking, vomiting, and urinating teenagers, the vapors now absorbed into the walls, chronicling, like cave drawings, the life of students in the twentieth century through their excretions. Julie's stomach would flip over if she allowed it. She could hear her own labored breathing. One more floor to go. Why was she doing this dumb thing? But she felt the urgency to go on. It would be worth it when she found Bobbie.

Now Bobbie knew she was alone. The janitor had skipped

her room. Her heart had never pounded so before, and she realized she *had* made a mistake, that staying one minute alone . . . The door! There was a shadow in the top half, in the opaque glass. Bobbie grabbed her keys from her purse. She headed for the back of the room, knocking over the chairs on the desks as she ran. She heard footsteps in the hall. When she reached the back door, she threw it open, trying to get away. Too late! She was staring into his face. And it was a face she knew.

"What do you want?" she shouted, raising her keys and thinking madly, wildly, of a way to escape, knowing before her question was voiced that she had made the mistake of her life, knowing with certainty that she was trapped. She backed into the room, up against a desk, raising her fist and aiming the keys into the sharp points of light that seemed to reflect the yellow rays of the setting sun burning out of his eyes. He was much stronger. She knew there was no hope. But she fought with her last breath, so hard that she didn't feel the instantaneous bursting of her heart as he plunged the knife into her breast.

At last the top. Julie avoided stepping into a slick substance on the top step. She stopped. It was smudged, a shoe print smearing it. Dark. Blood. She glanced down the steps. Fainter marks, carried by footsteps. A child was hurt. That's what was keeping Bobbie. It happened all the time. Still, where was she? It was almost twenty past. Her heart raced past her mind. She tried to still its pounding. It's nothing, she lied to herself. Then she saw the blood dripping out of Bobbie's room and the door partly open. A foot was sticking out of the door.

Bobbie's body was wedged against the door. Julie knelt down beside her, trying not to step in the blood. There was an enormous amount of blood. Julie's stomach turned over and over. Bobbie's eyes were wide open. She was covered in blood from the neck down.

Julie turned aside and tried to control her convulsions, retching a dry retch. She felt it sacrilegious to throw up, even though she could tell without a doubt that her friend was dead. Dear God! She forced herself to look at her to be sure, to be sure this was real, Bobbie lying dead on her familiar classroom floor. But her body was no longer Bobbie's, even though the feet were in her shoes. Her face was already a mask.

A stitch of pain in Julie's side woke her from her trance. She struggled to get up. The hallway was dark. She stumbled to the front of the room and turned on the light. Chairs were strewn everywhere. Bobbie's gloves and scarf were on the floor. Her closet door was open, and the contents of her pocketbook were spilled on the floor. Her wallet was missing. It finally came to Julie that she must listen for the killer, that he could be near.

Julie listened. Her legs were shaking. She tried to scream, but her mouth was dry. She was too weak, and no sound came. She had to run down those empty stairs again.

She opened the front door and looked out into the hallway. Deserted. She picked up the long ruler from the chalkboard, her hand trembling but gripping tightly, and ran. Down the stairs, down another flight, down, down. She heard voices! She had reached the main floor at last. She raised the ruler above her head and emerged from the staircase.

The normal hum of voices, footsteps, the light. She felt she was reappearing into the real world. She lowered her stick. The custodian stared at her, turning his head toward her as he locked his office across the hall. How could she tell him? She opened her mouth, but she had no words. She fell toward him and gripped his arms.

"*Please, Please,*" she whispered, and burst into hysterical sobs.

Mr. Mac looked down at Julie's disheveled clothes as she clung to him, and then he saw the blood on the hem of her dress. It was five minutes before Julie stopped sobbing and told him what he was afraid he was going to hear.

When he called the police and saw the body, he realized that he hadn't seen anything so horrible since his buddies were slaughtered in the hills of Korea.

7

The crash came like a bomb blast, and her baby jumped inside of her at the moment of impact. Greg charged into the bedroom shouting. Martha grabbed her bag, thinking quickly, testing her nerves. She drew the gun as she moved, quickly releasing the catch without a falter, reaching the bedroom seconds after Greg.

Julie looked up at Greg's distraught expression and at Martha pointing the gun, the tension in their faces suddenly relaxing at the sight of dozens of pieces of blue-gray alabaster on the floor.

"I never really liked that statue," Julie said, trying to make light of the accident.

Martha pushed the catch up with her thumb and lowered the gun to her side.

Greg grabbed Julie and hugged her. "My God, I was scared."

"Sorry," moaned Julie. "I was asleep, and the phone rang. I reached out . . . and knocked the damned statue over."

Greg gaped at the gun in Martha's hand.

"It's all right," Martha said. "Really . . ."

"That damn thing is a menace," Greg said.

"Who *was* that on the phone?" asked Julie.

Greg hesitated, to spare Julie. "Someone hung up when I answered."

Julie flashed Martha a look.

"Has this happened before?" Greg was alarmed.

Julie couldn't talk. "Of course," Martha said quickly. "This is New York, isn't it? The weirdo capital of the world?"

Greg started to remove his overcoat. He had been on his way out. "How can I leave you?" he asked Julie.

"With Annie Oakley here, I think I'm okay."

They all laughed, the tension broken.

"I'll be home early. At five," Greg promised. "I'll just be at the office for a couple of hours," he added guiltily.

"I'm not an invalid," said Julie.

Martha backed out of the room, sensing an argument on an old sore point.

Greg held up his hand. "See you later. Take . . ." He hesitated. ". . . care," he finished, rushing down the stairs.

Through the window Julie heard Greg hailing a taxi. Martha returned with the broom. "The baby jumped," she reported happily. "It hears," she marveled, parting the curtains for light.

Julie stared at the empty street. The waning light, the street lamps still unlit, produced a melancholy mood. Martha left and shut the door. While Martha fixed apple juice for Julie and an early cocktail for herself, Julie thought about the grim day they had experienced.

The state of siege had come full circle now that Bobbie was dead. Julie sat at the edge of the bed and shifted her body, feeling the weight of her baby. The baby squirmed, agitated, Julie feared, by the shock of the crash and Julie's turbulent emotions. Feeling the baby move gave her courage. Frightening as Bobbie's murder was, none of the other teachers could afford to quit their jobs, and Julie wouldn't either, she swore. No matter what Greg had to say. She owed it to Bobbie and to the kids.

Julie had just returned with Greg and Martha from the memorial for Bobbie. During the service in the school's auditorium, the teachers, and for once in their lives the students, had sat dumbstruck in their uncomfortable wooden seats as Julie spoke.

Julie felt lonely and battered now that she had one less ally in the world. She knew she had to be strong enough to resist the psychic blows life dealt her. Pretending all these years that her new world with Greg was secure had been a pipe dream. She was in danger now. Her gut told her.

A tremor passed through Julie's body like a seizure. She saw Jesus again and again in her mind. Over and over he dashed through the hall as the gate fell behind him. Upstairs, Bobbie lay bleeding, brutally stabbed. She saw Jesus and his opaque, cold-as-marble eyes. If eyes mirror the spirit, his made her afraid. They shunned nuance, kept his secrets.

Bobbie had set it up for Julie to save Jesus, had given her a mission. Before Bobbie's murder, the desperation, the pain of rejection that Julie suspected had driven Jesus to wreck Bobbie's room had wrenched Julie's heart, burned into her soul. But today she imagined Bobbie reaching out to her from the grave. Don't desert me, her friend pleaded.

Her darling Bobbie was lying in the dirt, a rotting pile of bones. And now the suspicion, the gnawing, clawing notion that she had put aside to get through the funeral, surfaced along with the picture of her friend decaying in her grave. What if it wasn't a thief who killed Bobbie? She had to find out who had murdered her friend.

• • •

"I tole that punk I'd break 'is fuckin' head open. Did you see 'is face when I axed 'im what he was lookin' at?"

"I wanted to go to the memorial," Nilda told Jesus.

"Fuck that. The kid's locker was no problem." He dumped the contents of the book bag he had stolen onto the floor of his room, where he and Nilda were squatting. They were smoking a joint.

Nilda picked through the raggedy contents and made a face. "No one leaves anything good in a locker anymore," she complained.

"So?" he said. His tone was dangerous. Nilda never crossed him. He stuck his face closer to tell her, without a word, to shut her mouth. He had a light mustache, and his face, usually smooth, had stubble, Nilda noticed.

Nilda had helped him tear Baumgarten's room apart, and now that the teacher was dead Nilda felt guilty. She knew Jesus had liked Bummy. Last week the two of them had had a good laugh. Jesus had told Nilda how he tried to con Bummy by telling her he couldn't do his homework because of his bad home life. "Cut the social-worker crap," Baumgarten had told him.

Then Bummy transferred him to that foxy teacher. Jesus was so pissed he had looked the new teacher up and down like she was a piece of flesh he was going to rip apart with his teeth. Nilda had almost felt sorry for her when she saw how nervous the teacher was when he pinned her to the wall in the hallway, but Nilda didn't like the way he looked at the teacher. Nilda sensed a new edge to his anger and a new, unknown element between her and Jesus.

"My mom would beat the crap outta me if she found out I cut school. But it's all talk. She ain't never home." Nilda sighed.

Jesus jerked his head in the direction of the living room. "She don't care. She don't go out. She'd want me to keep her company." Jesus laughed. "Crazy bitch. Tole me never to go to *that* school. 'It's cursed!' " Jesus and Nilda burst out laughing. "She's in there talkin' to herself, the old witch."

Nilda knew there was pain in the anger. There was a time when Jesus had shopped for his mother and shown a little boy's tenderness for her, when he had tried to shield her from the merciless laughter of the other children. Nilda remembered when she and Jesus ran free together through these rooms when they were kids and her own mother wasn't home. But now it was anger, always anger.

Jesus handed Nilda the combination lock he had stolen off the boy's locker. "Throw this shit out if you don't like it," he yelled. His erratic rage made her heart jump. He swept the books and the clothes out from between them with his fist.

"Is it locked?" he demanded. Nilda nodded. "Now count. It should take me about fifteen seconds to open it. Down from thirty it took me to do Bummy's closet." Jesus laughed, remembering. "I stole that dumb teacher's keys from her pocket, ripped off her apartment, and she didn't even know what hit her."

Nilda began to count. When she reached sixteen, the lock clicked open.

• • •

Esperanza believed that the invisible world surrounding the

visible one was populated by spirits both good and evil. She made the sign of the cross over Jesus as he slept the sleep of the dead from his drinking. Esperanza wondered where he got the money for his depraved habits. Last night he had fallen in a heap on the couch, raving about a teacher who had been murdered right there in that hateful school. Maybe now Marcos would believe her.

It was 3:00 A.M. But Esperanza barely slept. Her pain gave her no peace. She prayed over Jesus and gazed at his face tenderly. Then she began the incantation, begging the Virgin to protect them both from the curse that most appalled her, *invidia*, the envy of others. It was the danger that Consorta, the spiritualist, had warned her to be wary of in Puerto Rico.

Destruction was inching closer to them. Why else was she feeling such pain, now in her back? Why was she unable to eat a morsel of food with pleasure? Why else had *La Mala* been sent to the school?

Esperanza would have to perform the ritual over Jesus all alone, reconstructing from memory how Consorta and her three mediums had conducted their séances in Ponce when Esperanza was a girl, when she and her father had walked in the procession to Consorta's house seeking guidance every Sunday after Esperanza's mother had deserted them and taken Marcos. She and her father would watch Consorta become transformed and possessed before their eyes so that she could heal the ills of the congregation and give them God's blessing. The spirits spoke through Consorta's mouth when she fell into a trance.

Esperanza relived the meeting, hearing the sound of the bell rung by Consorta's cousin, Emilio, who slowly intoned the opening prayer. At the memory of his voice she was transported to Consorta's house, and her heartbeat slowed to the rhythm of Emilio's murmured prayer.

Then she remembered how the change came over Consorta's face as she became possessed. Her tranquil features became contorted, her body twisted, and her arms flung in spasms. Emilio rose from his chair, and he too became possessed. When Consorta became calm and her face expressionless, Emilio, also subdued, delivered the holy water. Consorta stood before Esperanza and sprinkled the pure water on Esperanza, and it felt like blessed rain.

Esperanza wished Consorta were there to rub the healing ice water on Esperanza's back, to remove the pain as she had done in the past, as she had cured the afflictions of so many of the townspeople. But Esperanza would have to eradicate the *trabajo*, the work of *La Mala*, by her own *brujería*, or witchcraft, which she had learned from watching Consorta. She felt she might have the *facultades*, the power, now that she was old.

Esperanza felt the weight of destiny upon her, the same way as when Consorta had come to her power, when a vision came to Consorta revealing to her that she would risk illness or insanity if she did not practice as a spiritualist. Consorta had been visited by "the power" as a child when she prescribed an herbal solution for a blind beggar's eyes and people began to flock to her. Esperanza's father had twice been advised by Consorta in private *consultas*: when Marcos was born, and when her father had begun to drink and his wife stopped being an *alma de la casa*, a wife who stayed home with her family.

Esperanza was not possessed, but sometimes her father spoke to her from the other world. Tonight she laid the dining room table the way it always appeared at séances. The plastic flowers and the green veil, the book and the tall candle were set on the white lace cloth. Esperanza brought a bowl with the ice water and sat on a chair next to Jesus as he slept. She dampened her arms and face with the water, and when she was certain he was deeply sleeping she daintily sprinkled a few drops of the water over him. He stirred without awakening. She removed from her pocket the jet-beaded bracelet she had bought in the *botanica*, the religious store near the church, and, risking the shock of the movement, gently lifted Jesus's right hand and slipped it around his wrist.

This bracelet would ward off the covetous eyes of strangers—*el mal de ojo*, the evil eye. And as long as he wore the amulet, Esperanza knew he would be safe from *La Mala*.

• • •

"Double, double, toil and trouble," Julie quoted, stirring

the soup with a large wooden spoon. Martha stood side by side with her in the narrow, old-fashioned kitchen that Julie had refused to modernize, smelling the comforting aroma of home-made potato soup. The windows were steamy against the darkness.

When the phone on the wall jangled, Julie eyed Martha for a split second, but she grabbed the phone with determination before the second ring.

"Yes?" she shouted aggressively. There was a pause at the other end.

"It's Les." His voice wavered almost apologetically. "I'm in New York."

"Don't call me here!" she cried, checking the clock.

"Sorry," Les said. "I'm sorry about Bobbie. I read about it in the *News*."

The pain screeched through the back of her skull. "What are you doing in New York?"

"I wouldn't call unless, unless I had to see you . . ."

It was exactly five. Greg would be home any minute. "I told you never to call. Greg doesn't know," Julie pleaded frantically.

"Meet me at the West End Bar," he said quickly. "Tomorrow at four?"

"Yes, yes," Julie said. It was two minutes past five. She hung up the phone, listening for Greg.

Julie's temples throbbed. Was it a coincidence that he was here the week Bobbie was murdered? She didn't dare tell Martha that she suspected Les, that the police had hounded Les when her baby was kidnapped, that they never believed him.

"Was that Les?" Martha asked. She turned the soup down when she saw it bubbling over.

Martha had put on her coat and held her bag, ready to leave. Julie covered her eyes to soothe the pounding behind the sockets.

Martha shook her head. "It's time to tell Greg. It's not fair to him. Julie bent her head into her hands. Martha smoothed Julie's hair.

Julie squeezed her eyes closed and pressed her temples.

"Not now! I can't tell Greg until the baby is born."

"Are you sick?" asked Martha.

"My head," she answered. When she opened her eyes, Greg was standing in the doorway.

• • •

Dr. Wolfson rode the elevator up to his office after snacking on a bran muffin and sipping tea in the hospital cafeteria. He had twenty minutes before seeing his last patient, Les Layton, and then he would close up shop for the Thanksgiving holiday.

The hospital was decorated with paper cutouts of turkeys, pathetic attempts at festivity that were more depressing to him than the colorless corridors. He unlocked the door to his office, which he noted needed a paint job to restore its grimy walls to their tasteless aqua. Anticipating the celebrations ahead, he thought about the cocktail parties where he and his wife could read the envy in the eyes of the guests when they learned he was a psychiatrist. Stockbrokers under pressure, lawyers, even other physicians fantasized trading their careers for his.

He arranged his notes on his metal desk and pulled out the file on Les Layton. Dr. Wolfson had kept Les coming to the hospital office, and now Wolfson realized how right he had been; the stark reminder of the mental wards was part of Les's therapy. Wolfson often wondered if the patients in his Fifth Avenue office took their therapy seriously enough or whether the plush surroundings gave them a quick, superficial comfort. The minute a patient began to enjoy analysis Wolfson recognized that it was time to terminate the sessions. He stretched back in his chair, facing the door. Les was due in ten minutes.

Today Wolfson felt that the hour-after-hour pileup of misery would sink him, that he would be pressed into the earth by the weight of human suffering. Even though it was his job to help his patients understand, to help them find a way out, sometimes he was appalled by the savagery of even his own existence, of growing old and watching his own family and friends die.

Only last week he had been so moved by the story of Clem LeMay—a middle-aged businessman who felt he had been transformed overnight from a proverbial youth into a worn-out, gray-haired man with a bad heart—that Wolfson had fought against the urge to break down and cry with him.

"Do you know what he would have said," Wolfson had confided in his wife, Rachel, "if he had seen tears in my eyes? 'You're only crying for your own childhood.' That's what he would have said. He would have played amateur therapist."

His wife had laughed. "Everyone's an analyst," she had responded.

But Wolfson had long ago decided that the day he stopped crying over his patients was the day he took down his shingle. Being a shrink was easy only if you didn't care.

This Thanksgiving he had gotten more midnight calls and suicide threats than he could remember. Patients were usually depressed after the holidays, but this year the stew of anger, jealousy, and loneliness had come to a boiling point even before the holiday had begun.

Les Layton was one of Wolfson's success stories. Or so he thought, until yesterday, when Les walked into his office and almost turned Wolfson's world on its sixty-two-year-old head. Fourteen years ago he had extricated Les from the abyss, had plucked a jazz great from oblivion.

Wolfson still quaked at the shock of Les's confession. The doctor breathed deeply. Any second Les would walk through that door.

• • •

Greg was stunned by Julie's words. "What is it you can't tell me until the baby is born?" he asked her as soon as Martha left.

Julie ran toward him, hugging him. "How madly I love you," she said, laughing. "I've never been happier."

Greg pushed her away to look into her face. Her eyes shone; happiness radiated in her face. That couldn't be faked.

"Is there something else you want to tell me?"

"No."

He knew in his heart she was telling the truth now no matter what he had heard when he came in. He was afraid to push it further.

Julie clung to Greg with unusual tenacity. She seemed

unaware that she hadn't given him a chance to remove his overcoat. She put her head in the crook of his neck like a baby snuggled on her mother's breast. She hated to let go, because she couldn't stop thinking about Les turning up in New York and dreaded her secret meeting with him.

• • •

Les's voice was barely audible as he asked Dr. Wolfson the terrible question. "Could I have wanted to kill my own child?"

After a hush he continued, "I never told you." Then his tone became determined. "I didn't trust anyone. The police thought I did it." Les looked away. "I was afraid you might turn me in."

Had Samuel Wolfson guessed wrong? He had never for a moment thought that Les was capable of . . . It was too inconceivable. But then he wasn't perfect. And it cut to the quick his confidence in his understanding of the mind. His depression deepened as he heard Les Layton disgorge his guilt.

"I was free before the baby came. Suddenly I was trapped. I didn't want the baby. Was that wrong?"

"It was understandable," Dr. Wolfson said.

"I couldn't face the responsibility. I thought I could make it, but I was weak. I went back on drugs. I betrayed Julie, betrayed the baby. Who would want a junkie for a father? For a husband?"

The doctor registered the sadness in Les's voice as he spoke of Julie. He knew Les had loved Julie.

"I was jealous of the baby. When you're on drugs, nothing else matters. I'm guilty!" he cried. "I wanted him out of the way."

The next moment was the most excruciating of Wolfson's career.

"Did you have anything to do with the kidnapping?" he asked. And he held his breath, afraid to interrupt Les even with a sigh and not wanting to hear the answer.

8

My hormones are protecting me from my fears, Julie thought, climbing into bed after a warm shower. Greg loved the gardenia perfume she sprayed on after creaming her body with the scented lotion. She crawled under the silky down quilt and felt a sensuous rapport with her surroundings. She knew it wouldn't last, this tactile awareness. She had to take advantage of every moment of pleasure. This sense of well-being was so close to the euphoric satisfaction she felt after sex, only this was sharper. Her body anticipated, was greedy, wanted more.

Greg slept on his back, in smooth cotton pajamas. His sandy hair was thick and curly and tousled in sleep. She eased over closer to him. She could smell his clean, soapy smell but not the male odor she often detected, which turned her on even more when she was in the mood.

She reached over and touched his chest. His eyes were closed, but it wasn't clear whether he was fast asleep. He had turned off the light not long before she had climbed into bed. She rubbed his chest lightly, knowing he would grab her hand, reach for her, respond.

But he didn't move, and he couldn't be asleep, not so quickly. As she withdrew her hand, he moved out from under it and turned over on his side. Greg's back, like a wall, was facing her. Julie's heart plummeted, synchronizing instantly with her abject misery.

• • •

Mad Dog Dixon was the dean of boys. Julie took heart from

the one amusing sarcasm issued by Jesus this morning when she had threatened to send for M. D. Dixon, or Doc as he was alternately named.

"Get your dog," Jesus had snarled, making Julie feel foolish enough to restrain herself from seeking the dean's aid when Jesus disrupted the class. She was grateful to avoid the confrontation because she knew it was wise to save the dean for hard-core, bottom-line situations. Mad Dog was not nicknamed for nothing. He intimidated Julie as well as the kids.

The name was particularly apt because the dean did indeed resemble a bulldog. Julie pictured his round, fat face, with heavy jowls, an unlit cigar, stuck in his thin, pursed lips, a permanent fixture in his features. He chomped down on the cigar for emphasis only before he was about to act, and this caused most kids to experience a most unpleasant rush of adrenaline. He was known to rough up the toughest ones.

Julie had hall duty at the main entrance during her last period before lunch, but she decided to risk the wrath of the principal by skipping the last fifteen minutes and running down the short flight of steps to the basement office to catch the dean before he disappeared with his macho cop buddies.

Although security had doubled since Bobbie's murder and Mad Dog made a show of force by parading through the school with the local police, teachers on patrol were terrified. There were many moments when the extra security guards, either called to an emergency or merely rotating, left the corridors unprotected.

The basement was one long, blank corridor with only a few music rooms recessed along the left. The music room doors had knobs only on the inside, making the hall look like that of a jail. On the way to Dixon's office there was a huge vault where the musical instruments and video equipment were stored. The cafeteria area beyond that was separated from the hall by a permanent metal grille that heightened the image of animals behind bars when the students lined up for lunch, their shouts blending into a massive roar that was counterpointed by the clash of trays and dishes.

Just now the floor was empty and quiet. The sound of Julie's steps bounced off the walls like balls in a squash court.

She stood for a moment to look around. Suddenly a burst of noise caught her as the door opened out from a music room. It was several minutes to the lunch bell, and the balding music teacher, books in arms, was leading his class out. He blinked at her ashen face as she hurried past him toward Dixon's office.

The dean was sitting at his desk just as Julie had pictured him, his huge, six-foot-two bulk parallel to the desk. He was leaning way back in his chair.

"Good morning, Mr. Dixon," Julie greeted him. No one called him by his first name.

There was no answer.

"I would just like to ask you a few questions about someone you know. Jesus . . ." She looked at him for some response.

He viewed her insolently from lazy, listless eyes, his lack of affect effectively depositing her concern in the trash can. His walk and body movements, Julie realized, mimicked his facial expression.

"I'd just like to get some background on him."

"I'm busy now," he said.

Julie looked around. The office was empty. The desk before him was totally clean. He looked at her arrogantly, and she looked back, not knowing whether to laugh. Was this his sense of humor?

"He used to hang out with a bunch of thugs like himself. A gang called the Marauders," he finally conceded. "Now mostly goes alone with his girl, Nilda. That's all I know."

Julie wished Bobbie were here. Bobbie had had a special interaction with the dean that Julie couldn't duplicate.

"He's a fuckin' piece of garbage," Dixon added flatly.

He loves to shock me with his language, Julie thought. He never could rattle Bobbie. That was why he had liked her.

Unceremoniously, he looked away and picked up the phone, dismissing Julie. She turned to go. He doesn't even say good-bye, she realized, flabbergasted. Then she remembered the name Bobbie had called him, "Big Dick," and it made her laugh.

God, how she missed Bobbie.

• • •

It was finally seventh period. Julie was relieved to see that, in spite of the fact that this was the first day back from Thanksgiving break, Jesus was absent. He had cut all morning.

For the next two weeks Julie could count on civilized behavior, then the Christmas madhouse would rev the kids up again. Today they were glad to be here. School didn't seem so bad compared to abuse, drug-induced highs, or boredom at home.

First- and second-period classes had gone like clockwork. Not one incident, riot, or emergency. Even the squawk box (as Bobbie had dubbed it), which broadcast the voice of the principal, Bernie Frankel—otherwise known as Captain Queeg—was silent. She surveyed her class. Without Jesus, they were quietly reading the photocopied sheet she had prepared. She allowed herself to sit on the edge of her desk, enjoying a rare moment of satisfaction as she observed the children absorbed in the story she had written using their names for the characters. She counted on this lesson to keep their interest. You could hear a pin drop.

Then the door banged open and her heart sank. Jesus had flung it wide.

Julie tried to control her anxiety. She had hoped he would cut her class too, because the instant she laid eyes on him she was gripped by a visceral feeling, a revulsion that consumed her and blocked out every other sensation. She could barely concentrate, the mixture of her emotions so intense that she felt she would lose control of herself and her class.

She had never reacted this way to a student. In his presence the room suddenly changed in every aspect. The atmosphere became suffused with a density that hadn't existed before, as if the room, once two-dimensional, took on its third dimension and then was infused with something totally new. The room became the vessel of Julie's emotions.

But in her warring emotions there existed an inexplicable fascination mixed with the disgust. Jesus's personality, his being, arrested her; there was some mysterious connection she felt, the same mesmerizing attraction she felt when she watched a ferocious jaguar in the zoo or a deadly insect—all God's creatures. Did this unexpected tug of regret that she felt come from the joy of carrying her baby? Or was it a strange sorrow for the child Jesus would never become?

Jesus was bright. *Most* bullies were manipulative and bright. They couldn't stay in power if they didn't use their wits. There were too many toughs eager to move up in the pecking order, to knock Jesus out of the number one spot. Jesus was a dictator. The school was his kingdom.

Julie suppressed her distress. At any moment mayhem might break loose. She avoided his eyes as he marched into the classroom. The timid students bent their chins farther down into their desks, not daring to look up, afraid to be selected by Jesus for victimization. Even Francisco, who was bigger than Jesus and tough, decided to make himself invisible. In seconds, Julie anticipated, the jittery ones would bolt their seats and look for trouble.

Her brightest girl, Crystal, who was usually absent, insulted Francisco and precipitated a verbal battle. Darryl, the wiry class clown, asked to leave the room. Julie watched as little Carmelo Santiago, seeing his chance, crouched down low and sneaked to Jesus's desk, placing the books he had carried for Jesus gingerly in front of him. Carmelo returned obsequiously to his seat, apparently to appease Julie.

The meaning of Carmelo's move began to dawn on Julie. He was the slave Jesus had selected to carry his books. Carmelo would also buy lunch for Jesus and surrender his money on demand. Julie's heart went out to Carmelo. He couldn't report Jesus. He was trapped. Julie wondered what it must be like for Carmelo to get up every morning to come to school knowing what was in store for him.

Jesus sprawled in the corner seat near the window at the rear of the room, removed from the other kids clustered up front. He had a nasty smile on his lips. It wasn't a leer merely calculated to intimidate her. It was true contempt.

Julie noted that Jesus hadn't removed his hat or the expensive, thick, leather bomber jacket he wore incessantly. It was the type of jacket kids got knifed on the subway for. It was zipped open to reveal the heavy gold chain hanging from his neck. His hands were in his pockets.

When he caught Julie looking in his direction, he threw her a kiss, taunting her, crudely sweeping his eyes up and down her body. He smiled broadly at her with such assurance that she boiled with anger. He was taking command of her class.

Julie had to act, but she was afraid to approach him. He would either insult her or curse at her. He obviously enjoyed humiliating her. Two students were already standing, ready for action. She had no time left. The room crackled with tension.

Jesus stared at her fixedly, with hostility, waiting. Her heart beat loudly as she pulled a piece of small white notepaper from her drawer and carefully wrote, "Jesus, please come to my room tomorrow, first period. It's important." She made a mental note to clear it with his teacher. She signed her initials, walked over to his desk, and as casually as she was able, placed the note in front of him.

Without a word, without seeing his reaction to reading the note, she turned and walked to her desk. When she looked, the paper was gone, his face was a blank, and the melee had begun. She twisted her emerald ring nervously. She could only wait for the bell to end the period.

• • •

Les hit the street at three o'clock. The sidewalks were bustling with kids streaming from school, guards directing traffic, and mothers collecting their young children. This combination, along with afternoon shoppers, made the streets lively with movement.

Pushers, Les noticed, were stationed at their corners, taking advantage of the hubbub of schoolchildren who had emptied both the public and the parochial schools. He noticed the preppies from the East Side, with their jackets and loosened ties. All were fair game, he noted with abhorrence.

His rage increased at each corner he crossed. "Smoke, smoke," the teenaged sleaze with glassy, watery eyes whispered to him as he passed. "*Tengo,*" announced a dark, Colombian male, with a nod to Les, only twenty feet farther down the block.

To reach the west side of Broadway Les was forced to cross the traffic island, to walk past men and women in rags who were lying in stupors on the benches, too far gone to deal. He could see the West End. He was very early, but he hurried past a group of pushers, their sweatshirt hoods protecting them from the cold, their hands in their pockets as they moved nervously in and out of their circle. Like maggots on carrion, Les thought, dispersing when they heard the lookout's whistle, then returning to their rotted prey.

"Mesc, hash," a mottled-skinned black teenager in sparkling white Reeboks offered him, shuffling out of the knot. Les repressed the urge to scream, "You dirt bag! Scum!" He kept his eyes to his feet as he pressed on.

As he arrived in front of the West End, he thought of Wolfson. Les had worked up his courage to see Julie, to try to make up for the harm he had done. A fiery-eyed junkie lurched toward him as he stood at the door.

"Get lost," Les hissed, striking out his hand to shove the creep away. But the addict retreated before the blow, and Les finally entered the bar he had played jam sessions in so many times. He sat down toward the back in the nearly empty, cavernous room and ordered a brandy. The effort at control after the encounter took its toll. He faced the door, trying to compose himself.

The cross lay in the pocket of the wool jacket he wore under his raincoat. How much should he tell Julie? He could have rehearsed the right words to get her on his side, to show her how this cross would help them find their son. But his nerves were shot. He had used all his resources calling her, listening to her voice, taking the chance that she was alone. He couldn't expect too much more of himself. Showing up here had been hard enough.

Les imagined he smelled Julie's perfume as the minutes ticked by and the brandy relaxed his brain. He thought about the gauntlet he had walked from Rus's apartment to this table. "Crack," he mumbled aloud. The new kink in the dizzying array of temptations since he had left New York. He thought of Eleanore back in Monterey. And then he heard Wolfson's question. "Why are you still obsessed with Julie?" Les would know the answer soon, when Julie arrived.

• • •

It was three o'clock. Julie headed down the wide central

staircase at the precise sound of the bell, as did every other teacher, unwilling to remain a second past its clang. The rapid procession was purposeful, crowding toward the exits. At 3:05 the school was a silent set of lonely chambers. The footsteps of security guards and the crackling of walkie-talkies replaced the din of thousands of feet. Now teachers and students pushed forward through the open doors toward the darkening day that awaited them. They inhaled the fresh air, relieved to be free of their unspoken fear, their recollection of death.

Julie realized that she had left behind her new briefcase, which she had bought to replace the carryall that had been stained with Bobbie's blood. But she immediately dismissed the thought of returning for it. Most teachers were prisoners in their classrooms, fearful of descending any staircase at all, even during the day, unless absolutely necessary. In spite of the guards, her heart had pounded when she walked from her third-floor room to the main floor to phone Martha that morning. Afterward, she had taken her lunch to the teacher's lounge nearby instead of eating in her room, which she would have to do alone now that Bobbie was gone.

Wisely, Julie had dialed Martha's home on the pay phone to avoid the eager ears of the secretary whose phone she was allowed to use. Martha was out, and Julie had left a message on her tape. "Please don't call me at home today," she warned. "I'm meeting Les at four at the West End, and you're my excuse." She had felt slightly ashamed, even more so because her lie was recorded.

Feeling like a factory worker in an assembly line, Julie punched her card out in the office. There was a short wait because every one filed in at the same time in order to leave promptly. She checked her mail and threw all the notices and notes into her purse before hurrying out.

Julie had more than half an hour to kill before meeting Les. She walked heavyhearted toward Broadway, preparing herself. She was so afraid that Les was falling apart again. Why was he in New York? What did he want from her?

She thought about Greg. How she hated this deception. Terrible things were happening again to mar her happiness, this time with Greg and their new baby. Was Les part of it all?

It's just a coincidence that Les is here, she tried telling herself. He's doing a gig in New York, she rationalized. But I *have* to see you, he had said dramatically on the phone. Let Les be all right, she wished. Let me get through this month, the next few months, so that I can have my baby in peace, she thought.

She pushed the door open to the familiar West End Bar. The typical old-fashioned hot table serving plain, probably unhealthy, food, and the huge circular bar—the tables scattered around almost haphazardly in the gloomy but oddly homey and gigantic room—wafted memories of her youth through her nostrils and her pores. She could understand for a moment how people could believe in ghosts. The room seemed to be crowded with the tangible past.

Then she saw him. He was early. Her heart stopped and she almost cried. He was so handsome, yet vulnerable in the same way that she remembered and loved so much. His expressive green eyes, his straight hair, which he was pushing off his forehead with that familiar movement of his long, elegant fingers. The graying, dark strands looked faded against his tan. He was peering at her quizzically. Didn't he recognize her?

"Hello, Julie," he said softly, rising to greet her. But at her touch he felt the old Les returning. He was crumbling, disintegrating, falling away, and he knew that if he didn't do something about it there would be nothing left of him.

Julie pulled away from Les's embrace. She felt he had held her too long. He seemed lost in a trance, unaware of where he was.

He observed her as they parted before they sat down at the heavy rectangular oak table. She could tell what he was thinking. I'm having another man's baby. The look on his face told her. She remembered the thrill that Les sent through her body, remembered his shy smile, his liquid, green eyes that could drown her heart, that sideways glance that seemed to capture her accidentally. His presence still affected her because her old attraction to him had been heady, lasting until the very end, until his breakdown.

Julie looked at Les across the table. They held hands without speaking; she knew he couldn't speak and she would have to begin. That sharp, sweet look was no longer in his eyes. She searched for the light, but she found something else, something disturbing.

His expression told her that reality, the present, Greg, her baby, the years drawn on her, her experiences without him, were not powerful for him at this moment.

A flash of Jesus's face intervened between them. It was strange that his face should flash into her consciousness now. Was she trying to dispose of Les with her own disturbing reality? Was it guilt? Obligation? Fear? What was this echoing sensation at the edge of her brain?

She searched Les's face again to plumb the surface for meaning. And she had guessed correctly. Les experienced the same rush of feeling seeing her, touching her skin, as he always had. She was as familiar to him as her gardenia scent, which now must have seemed to him a retrieved possession. She would be everlastingly familiar in a million intimate ways. How could he erase these myriad experiences that were a part of him? *She* was a part of him.

But she didn't feel that way. He could tell. One day he would make her see it. They would be together again. When he found their son!

"Les," Julie said with feeling. She looked into his face. "I've been avoiding you for all these years. Do you know how hard it is for me to see you?"

Les looked guiltily at her.

"We've cared about each other, haven't we?" she asked. "Even after you left New York."

"I'm so sorry I didn't come through for you when you needed me," Les said with emotion.

"Is that what you wanted to tell me?" Julie shook her head. "It's all over now."

"Not for me. I'm just coming to terms with it. I'm seeing Wolfson again."

"Is that why you're in New York?"

"Wolfson said that some people need to forget to survive. I need to remember."

"It's too terrible to remember."

"I want to make it up to you."

"Please don't. It's hopeless. It took me fourteen years to stop checking every carriage, every street, all the organizations, the posters. I'll never forget him. My flesh and blood, my baby . . . our baby. But I've closed my mind to any more of it. I have a new life, new hope. For the first time I wake up in the morning without wanting to die."

Julie stopped. She had had a flash of Bobbie.

"Don't I deserve some happiness?" she asked Les. "I can't grieve the rest of my life. It won't bring him back to us."

Les reached into his jacket pocket to show her the cross.

"You have nothing to atone for," Julie said. "You weren't well. You were . . ."

"Cracked. Crazy," Les said loudly, attracting the attention of a young couple nearby.

He let the cross drop back into his pocket, his confidence evaporating.

"And now Bobbie," she said. She didn't want to cry. She rose to leave.

"You've changed," he remarked. Julie noted the coldness in his voice. She had a flash of Jesus's face again. She tried to obliterate it.

"If I hadn't cracked . . ."

"You have to stop this."

"I deserted you."

"The police treated you like an animal. And they asked me if I had a history of mental illness. We were the only ones sure of each other."

Julie reached for her parka. "Did you call me and hang up?" she asked him.

"Yes. When your husband answered . . ."

"He still doesn't know. I beg of you, please don't call."

"Where's your mink?" Les asked sarcastically. "I thought you were rich."

He retreated at Julie's shocked expression.

"We still have a son!" he cried. But he saw the fear in her eyes. "Don't worry," he said. "I won't open old wounds."

I'll call you when I find him, he thought.

● ● ●

Julie took a cab home, not noticing the trees in the park as she traveled east. The people, the rush hour traffic, the Christmas lights on Park Avenue were all blotted out as thoughts of Les occupied the landscape of her mind. Sending Les the letter and the cross had only revived dormant emotions better left unclaimed. Les had seemed unbalanced, inarticulate in the West End.

The taxi stopped in front of Julie's house, and she realized, opening her bag to pay him, that the driver hadn't spoken a word to her. She yanked out her purse, but her compact, her keys, her appointment book all fell into her lap with the emergent thought: how did Les know I own a mink coat? She paid the driver, and as the motor idled while he waited for her to open the gate and climb the stairs, she looked behind her.

• • •

In that twilight of consciousness before sleep descended to overtake her, visions and voices softly blurred, like faded daguerreotypes behind her eyes. She saw Bobbie. In and out of the half light at the edge of her dream state, Bobbie's face floated. Bobbie spoke. The wall of her science room appeared. It was the day Julie had walked in on the devastation of Bobbie's classroom, the week Bobbie was killed. The defaced chart on the wall glared out at Julie, the red heart on the skeleton circled, the blood in red crayon, the red globs dripping down.

Remember this, Julie tried to tell herself, knowing that if she fell asleep nothing of what she imagined would reappear the following morning in her memory. Then she slept, unable to resist.

Julie was young again. Her long braid swayed in the sunlight as she moved among the baby carriages in the park. The daffodils were clustered in patches along the walkways, and Julie felt lightweight, missing something. She was thin and her waist was small. Her legs practically flew off the ground as she stopped to examine each carriage belonging to a woman who, alone or with a friend, pushed her baby along the winding concrete toward the playground.

Julie ran out of mommies with carriages as night approached. It was getting dark, and she was becoming despondent. There would be nowhere to look; the children were all in their homes. Julie wouldn't give up, although it was getting darker and darker and the park was deserted. She walked up the steps and there, before her, was the playground. She was happy to see the familiar sandbox, the swings, the monkey bars. Maybe her baby was here, and she could stop searching and go home.

And sure enough, there was a carriage sitting all by itself with no one to tend it. Hope surged in Julie. She ran toward the carriage with the knowledge that she would find what she was looking for.

Her baby! She reached into the carriage to gather up her infant. And as she reached in, she saw the blue bonnet, the blanket with the white lambs, and the top of the little yellow nightgown peeking out from under the blanket. But there was something wrong. She pushed the carriage hood back. Her baby's face was huge, grotesque, old. Horror overwhelmed her. She struggled to understand. This wasn't a baby. Yet its face resembled her baby's face.

"Somebody help me!" she cried, knowing that no one could help her. Dr. Blum, her obstetrician, appeared. "Thank God you're here," she whispered.

"This child is stunted," he diagnosed. "Your baby is fourteen years old," he told her.

Julie awoke with a start in the dead of night. She had a strange sense of revelation. But the sour taste, the aura of the dream overtook her as she felt her baby moving, turning inside of her. Panic overcame her reason. She realized the meaning of the dream. Her baby would be born deformed. The life inside of her was suddenly suspect. And she imagined the developing fetus within her with fear.

Greg was asleep next to her, and she longed to touch him, but she refused to awaken him. That night her tension had led to a terrible fight. She wished she could snuggle up in his arms and he could comfort her. But she couldn't tell him about her nightmare. The certainty that her child would be born healthy and beautiful had turned to dust.

Julie lay wide-eyed all night in the total blackness of her bedroom, waiting alone for morning.

9

Martha's huge apartment on Central Park West overlooked the reservoir from the twenty-seventh floor. The living room and adjoining dining room, with their palatial ceilings, looked to Julie like the ballroom of Versailles. Martha lived alone in the rent-controlled apartment, paying less for seven rooms than many paid for a studio in a slum.

Julie looked out over the park at the soft glow of twinkling lights in the buildings on the East Side. The view was even more spectacular than during the day.

Julie felt sadness but not pity for Martha. Especially now that Julie was on her own so often—because Greg had to be off on one business trip after another—Julie was projecting her feelings onto Martha.

"Successful lawyers don't veg out at home, hand-holding with their wives," Martha advised. "Greg's a hard-boiled lawyer." Martha relaxed on the white sectional, her legs under her, barefoot. She threw her head back comfortably on the soft cotton pillows.

Julie turned away from the window. "I sometimes feel he's going away a lot more because he's angry with me."

"You can't have it both ways. He's got a heavy-duty job. He won't bring in the megabucks if he's not working. Greg is very good to you. He's in love with you. He knows something's up, but he's not the type to punish you for it. You may have explained it away, but he knows there's *something*. He's just decided to let you tell him the truth in your own time."

Julie looked despondent.

"Life's a series of obstacles, isn't it?" offered Martha.

It was time to take a cab back to her own empty house, Julie thought unhappily. At one time the baby she was carrying had kept her company, its miraculous presence buoying her spirits. Now she harbored the hideous notion that something was awry. She worried about losing Greg. Being pregnant made her feel bereft, more vulnerable to being abandoned. And then there was the burden of her latest discovery.

Martha saw the tortured look on Julie's face.

"What else is bothering you?"

"It's Les!" Julie blurted out. "Martha, I have terrible thoughts about Les. He's been following me!"

Martha looked directly at her.

"Why is he in New York?" Julie asked.

"Beats me," Martha said.

"Martha . . ." Julie confided. "I'm afraid of him. I'm afraid of Les. Look!" She held up her hands. They were shaking.

• • •

The sound of the bells drew Les toward the bell tower above the Gothic church on Amsterdam Avenue and Ninety-Sixth Street. He looked up at it, remembering its toll—six bells every evening as it rang over the rooftops at dinner hour. Then at Christmas there was always the sound of the carols, which he imagined when he was a boy were rung at the whim of a happy priest whenever the spirit moved him.

Les picked out the notes filling the streets, and his humor brightened as it had when he was a child. "Hark the herald angels sing," D GG F# GBBA. "Glory to the new born King," DDD CBAB. The sound rang in his mind long after the quivering notes ceased reverberating.

He took the hundred stairs two at a time. He had counted them as a kid, playing as his mother finished conversing with a neighbor, peeking into the church, at the rose windows warming their colors in the sun. He recalled the brides, their flowing veils, the bridesmaids' colorful gowns, and the wedding guests throwing rice at the bride and groom as they descended the steps.

He remembered the somber day years later when in the

gloomy downpour he had watched policemen in full dress fill the avenue in perfect military rows to pay tribute and hear the bagpipes mourn for an officer slain in the line of duty. He had pitied the mother standing at the coffin and had watched Julie cry when the bishop handed the mother the flag. But today Les's heart sang with the carol ringing. He had a most brilliant idea. He admired the carved wooden doors and the Gothic script above them bearing the inscription "The Church of the Holy Name" as he entered the church. It was an inspiration. Where else would anyone look for the owner of the cross, the kidnapper, but in the largest, most impressive church in the neighborhood?

• • •

The next day, when Julie finally pulled from her purse the notices she had forgotten to read, she was astounded at the poem she found written on a sheet of folded loose-leaf paper.

Roses are Red
Violets are blue (like your eyes)
When I get laid
I'd like to FUCK you.

The handwriting was obvious. It was Carmelo Santiago, who dotted his *i* with a large circle and wrote straight up and down in an unmistakable pattern. Carmelo always handed in his homework, always wrote the required compositions. He was a hard little worker, a student who trudged through the muck of his world always doing the right thing. She couldn't believe Carmelo would do this.

The change bell rang, and her students piled in. Jesus was first. He strode in like a monarch, his entourage behind him. When the students took their seats at the sound of the late bell, Julie took attendance. Jesus smirked at her from the rear. Carmelo's seat was empty. Now she understood.

• • •

As soon as the period was over, Julie sent for Jesus's reading scores. She scanned the computer printout, which listed the date for every test. Jesus had been absent for every test except one. The score for that was absurdly high.

This explained how he had been able to pass from one grade to the next, landing him in the ninth grade. Most teachers were afraid to fail him, and the others, she guessed, were eager to move him ahead, out of their classes. The high score that no one questioned had been attained by copying the answers from one of his terrorized toadies. Julie knew the secret he had managed to keep from everyone. Jesus was illiterate. She would have to teach him to read.

• • •

It was a record-breakingly warm morning. The sun winked off the snow, and by noon there would be rivers running down the gutters.

"Let's go to the park and get high," Nilda urged Jesus. It was 10:00 A.M., and Jesus was up and dressed, which was not usual for him, she noted. Esperanza had answered the door. She never seemed to sleep, Nilda thought.

Nilda had found Jesus combing his hair in front of the mirror of the medicine chest in the bathroom. He slicked his newly washed hair down with his comb. His face was smooth.

"Let's drive to City Island," she suggested when Jesus didn't bother to answer. "I'll get my uncle's car."

"You'll get busted one day, and your uncle will kick your ass."

"No, I wear makeup and my mother's earrings, and I'm cool."

"Try goin' to class. It might be a new experience," he remarked, facing her. He was in a good mood.

"Since when are you so smart?" she asked. "Where are you goin'? To *her* class?" She took another risk when she added: "What are you, a momma's boy?"

Nilda stepped back, half expecting a slap. But she was surprised to see him laugh. He surveyed himself in the mirror again, touching his faint mustache with his fingertips. Then he marched past Esperanza, who was sitting in the kitchen, and Nilda followed him out of the apartment.

Esperanza huddled in the corner near the open window, inhaling the warm air, sugaring her tea at the table, unaware that her lips were moving and that the low rumble of her thoughts was audible in spite of her caution. And she tried to curl up and disappear so that perhaps Jesus wouldn't notice her when he walked by with Nilda. But she was happy because she had spied the jet beads, still on his wrist, protecting him while he was away from her.

• • •

Julie's pulse throbbed in her throat, and she felt a grinding sensation where she imagined her esophagus to be. It was 9:00 A.M., her free period, and she was watching the door waiting for Jesus, not knowing which was worse: his showing up or his blatant disregard of her note—again. She had to learn one way or another whether Jesus was the one who killed Bobbie. She could handle it, whatever the outcome.

She had determined that her strategy was to dispense with all the preliminaries and the pretext that Jesus could read. She would begin with sequencing and matching and copying tasks designed to rule out any disability. Then she would give him a "lock box" of index cards that broke words down into syllables, and then locked back together to form words. She would build on the few letters and words he had undoubtedly managed to memorize. A third-grader would be equal to these tasks.

She arranged the materials on the desk facing hers, where there were two chairs, and decided to reject her desk in favor of sitting next to him when she explained the purpose of the cards.

The door finally opened.

"Hello, fox," Jesus said, looking her over and noting immediately where she was sitting. He shut the door behind him. He removed his jacket as he stood over her.

Julie saw that in spite of his height, and without the bulk of the jacket, he was leaner than she had imagined. His T-shirt with the short sleeves rolled up, she realized, was a ludicrous adolescent display to expose his muscles. They bulged, as he flexed, from his skinny, hard-veined arms. Julie thought the wiry arms and prominent veins were odd in a young boy. They reminded her of her father, who had been reedy and gaunt, and she remembered his Adam's apple like a knot jumping in his throat when he spoke.

"Good morning, Jesus," she said as neutrally as she could muster. "Sit down." He was standing too close to her, making a personal assault using his body, invading her space.

Before she could shove her chair away, he abruptly sat down and put his arm around her shoulder. She could smell his body. Her skin prickled; her stomach lurched. She wanted to jump up, to push him away, to run, to be free of him.

But she didn't. She governed her impulse, masked the expression in her eyes, which would have betrayed a burst of anger and aversion. Slowly, carefully, she removed his arm. There was no judgment, no condemnation or rejection. The action plainly stated "I am the teacher; you are the student."

Nothing was exchanged between them, not a blink. Julie tried to hide her relief. She handed him the cards he was required to sort. "Shall we begin our work?" she asked.

He became absorbed in the cards almost immediately, performing a school problem he was able to do. She sensed that his speeding eyes darting on the pictures, his eagerness to succeed, his urgency to prove himself were designed to impress her. It was a common seduction teachers used in reaching difficult children.

She was sitting very close to him, closer than she cared to, but she didn't dare move. She knew that he was fully aware of her presence and that he had temporarily let down his guard, feeling secure under her gaze.

Julie continued to watch him as he became strangely quiet, almost docile, bent over his work. His hat was pushed back, and his ears were sticking out from under it, just like any other little boy. She could see every hair on his neck and the peak of hair formed at the nape. A tender feeling mixed with her distaste for a moment. After all, he was only a child.

When Julie heard her name on the squawk box, Jesus had one more test left to complete and fifteen minutes before the end of the period. Irritated but resigned to interruptions, she rushed down the hall to see a parent in the English Department office.

As soon as the door closed Jesus cased the room, beginning with Julie's desk. He pulled the top drawer out, assessing its contents. Yanking the deep side drawers free, he determined the small coffeepot and all the odds and ends to be worthless. He knew that her purse and the briefcase she carried were secured behind the combination lock of her personal closet. He shuffled through the papers on her desk, hunting for her keys. Most teachers left them lying around, but she was too smart. She kept school keys in a pocket or wore them on a long leather thong around her neck.

The door opened unexpectedly while he played with her papers. It was Francisco. A note dangled from his fingers. "From the guidance office," he said, hanging on to the piece of paper as he swiftly surveyed the room. His face betrayed the knowledge that the message on the paper was about Jesus. Jesus snatched the note as Francisco, seeing that Julie was gone, backed out of the room. Jesus had acted too fast for Francisco to stop him.

Francisco was in a tough spot. He didn't want to fight over this piece of paper. He chose his confrontations carefully. But he couldn't just back down. He returned to the room and focused on the papers on the teacher's desk.

"I'll give it to her!" Jesus told him, holding up the note. Quickly Francisco took in the situation to see what he could gain. Sequential picture cards were scattered on the teacher's desk, and he turned to see where Jesus had been working. Simple elementary school reading material was in plain view on the desk right in front of the chair where Jesus's jacket hung. Francisco could see the whole picture, and Jesus knew it.

Jesus circled him like a lion looking for the right moment to strike his prey. Jesus lunged, shoving Francisco backward against the desk so that Francisco was leaning in a defenseless position, his legs off balance. The surprise gave Jesus the advantage he needed. But he knew Francisco was strong and mean and would fight. The sound of a switchblade released from its catch made Francisco abandon any decision to use his greater power against Jesus. Although he was larger and heavier, fear replaced Francisco's anger when Jesus pressed the sharp tip of the blade to his throat. "Tell anyone and you're dead meat!" Jesus snarled at him.

Then Jesus saw in Francisco's eyes that someone had come into the room. He hadn't heard the door opening. He retracted the blade instantly and concealed it in his pocket. He let go of Francisco and turned to see Julie. She had overheard his threat. He thought fast. She had to have heard the swoosh and click of the blade's swift retraction, but she couldn't prove it. She wouldn't search him herself, and if she called for the dean Jesus would be out of there.

The crumpled note was still in Jesus's hand when Francisco took off. He smoothed it out and scanned it, recognizing his name as he handed it to Julie. Now she knew what every student knew, in case she had any doubts. Jesus was dangerous. But he wasn't worried. As long as he didn't get caught. He gave her a steely look of defiance.

Now, Julie thought, she had enough evidence against Jesus to warn the dean. She would see him today. And if he ignored her fear that Jesus had stabbed Bobbie, she would go straight to the police.

• • •

Grace Frossard was a perfectionist. She opened the elementary school every morning, arriving with the early-bird staff to set up her experiments, arrange the bulletin board, and review her lesson plans. There weren't enough hours in the day to do a good job, she always said. Ms. Frossard was very strict with and demanding of her students. She had straightened out many a wayward, straying child, and as a result there was a waiting list for her class each year because so many parents requested her.

But Ms. Frossard's high standards, although responsible for her success, were also the bane of her existence. Nothing was ever good enough, even satisfactory. There was always a higher level to attain; never time for rest, only time for evaluation; good, better, best . . .

It was probably this trait that had caused her divorce from Ted after only a year. Marriage just wasn't her cup of tea. Not after living all those years alone, wedded to her independence. She and Ted were still friends—that's why she kept his name. People would be very surprised to know that they were still lovers. Most people couldn't imagine that she had passions. Sometimes when her students were taking a test and the room was silent her mind would wander and she would think about her sex life with Ted. Who would ever imagine that!

Entering the marks into her roll book, she had to squint to align the column of names with the little boxes for the marks. Getting old, she thought, remembering how everything had been effortless when she was young, how she had breezed through report cards and test scores.

She had made a mistake many years ago, starting out in a junior high, where the students were unruly and ignorant administrators tried to govern her. The adolescents she taught were ruled by their hormones; they were beyond the reach of her influence. She had moved to this elementary school more than ten years ago. It had been the right decision. Her students worshiped and feared her, and no one told her what to do. Her small children were yet unmolded; she could touch their lives.

Still she had her periods of depression, when she felt she was not equal to her tasks. But she fought them off. And she had a favorite poem, written by Swinburne, that she reread in times of crisis, when she felt the world was against her.

> From too much love of living,
> From hope and fear set free,
> We thank with brief thanksgiving
> Whatever gods may be
> That no life lives for ever;
> That dead men rise up never;
> That even the weariest river
> Winds somewhere safe to sea.

• • •

Every morning he watched the work crew arrive at precisely 8:00 A.M. They came down the steps and through the backyard entrance before the children lined up, and he could see them working on the roof and balancing on the scaffolding all day. The men had been working for a week, and this being Friday, he thought it might be their last day. They wore short jackets, knit wool hats, gloves, and workboots. One of the custodian's helpers, not the same one each day, he noted, opened one bolted door to let them in. When the whistle blew at 8:25, someone appeared to open all the doors for the kids and the teachers.

The remaining staff used the main entrance, where a desk guard scrutinized each adult, checking IDs and signing visitors into the roster. That way was out of the question. He would slip in with the workers, and it had to be today.

It was eight o'clock, and right on schedule the men arrived. He followed them into the yard, carrying a plastic cup of hot coffee between his thick gloves. As the last man entered the building, he casually joined them, catching the door as it closed, and slipped into the boys' john when the group clumped noisily up the stairs. He waited for that moment of silence when he could make a dash for the second floor, where he knew her classroom was. If someone spotted him, he could pass for a worker. With his down vest and his boots he fit right in.

He mounted the steps quickly—restraining himself from running, from searching the halls—listening for the one person who would notice him, identify him later. He knew from experience that if he felt like he belonged, everyone else believed it. He had passed people right after . . . and they never remembered. Blend in and you could get away with anything, again and again. It was only on TV that the police cleverly tracked down the criminal. He had stopped being surprised at getting away.

The classrooms were still locked, but he heard distant voices and on an instinct broke his rule and made a run down the hall to save time. Her classroom was 218, right smack in the middle. He could see her light was on. She would be sitting at her desk, slaving away, not paying attention to anything but her lousy papers. Teachers were so predictable.

He had only a few minutes, and he took a chance. At any second someone could arrive early on the floor. He looked into the window in the door. She was bent over her work, oblivious to the world, as he had predicted. His plans were working out, he thought happily. He reached for the knife with his right hand, bearing down through the thick glove to feel the weapon's reassuring handle. He eased the brass knob of the door softly with his left hand.

Ms. Frossard was reluctant to look up from her work at the sound of the interruption, at the faint creak of the rusty hinge as the door was gently opened.

The girls showed their passes at the front door. It was Ms. Frossard's handwriting. "Please admit Marnie and Deirdre at 8:15 A.M." Mrs. Cruz didn't bother reading the pass. She let the girls in every day. She knew that they helped to wash the boards and mark papers for the teacher, that they were responsible kids and she didn't have to worry about them running around the school causing problems.

"You're early today," she said. "Go on up."

The girls were bundled up against the cold, and they began peeling their clothing as they raced up the stairs, giggling and poking one another.

"Sshh," said Marnie as they reached the second floor, doubling over with laughter at the thought of Ms. Frossard's disapproval. Marnie put her finger over her lips. "You know she doesn't like noise."

Ms. Frossard was irritated. It was too early for the girls, and she resented inroads into her precious time alone. He was already halfway into the room when she raised her gaze, frowning. Before her brain had the chance to register her shock and send its signal to her heart, he drove the knife into her back with enormous force. Pain splintering the light in electrical sparks charged in her brain like fireworks of white heat. Then there was nothing.

He pulled out the blade when he heard her rattling death gasp, surprised at how deep the knife had gone and how much damage it had done. He had overestimated her girth; she was thin. The blade came out easily when he pulled; there was little flesh on the bone.

Fresh blood seeped from the gash that the shining steel had

made in Ms. Frossard's pinstriped white polyester blouse. The blade had the same startling red smeared all over it. Don't make a mess, he thought as he wiped it clean, using the yellow wool cardigan draped on the back of her chair. But then he heard too clearly the voices of children coming down the hall. There was no time to tidy up, take a purse, make it look like robbery. The knife easily slid into his pocket.

This was a closer call than the last—it was exhilarating. He contemplated prolonging the excitement. The little children would be no match for him. But he slipped out the back door and, seeing the girls, turned his face and walked away slowly, his back toward them. He could hear their laughter as they walked into the open room. At a steady speed he sprang down the steps to the sounds of teachers opening doors, to the school day beginning.

Deirdre's face was still rosy from the cold, her expression eager and bright as she respectfully eased open the door, which was ajar. Marnie pushed her in mischievously. Ms. Frossard was sitting crazily at her desk. The desk caught her from slipping down completely in her chair, and her arms were twisted into odd positions on the desk. Was she drunk?

Deirdre giggled uneasily. Ms. Frossard looked so funny. For part of a second Deirdre thought Ms. Frossard was playing a joke, but she knew that Ms. Frossard had no sense of humor. Then the horror crept into her chest, because seeing the blood, she realized that the unnatural look on Ms. Frossard's face was death.

Marnie, standing behind her, understood at once. Slowly her body caught up with her mind and her insides quaked. She could taste the milk her mother had made her drink that morning come up in her throat, and sweat began to form beads on her face.

Deirdre shrieked and clutched her, distracting Marnie from thinking of the class without Ms. Frossard, from the realization that for Ms. Frossard there was no future. And then the room was filled with children pushing in front of her to see, screaming and crying all around her.

Then one little girl, braver than the rest, rushed forward and pulled Ms. Frossard's arm. The body, still limp and warm, slumped forward. The torso lay on the desk, the bloody wound in her back exposed.

Marnie clamped her ears to shut out the histrionic shrieks and sobs of her sixth-grade classmates as they surrounded her. The room began to close in on her, and she quivered uncontrollably as Ms. Frossard's head turned toward them, hanging off the desk. Her eyes were open, and she was observing their hysteria through moronic, unseeing eyes.

10

Bernie Frankel, the principal of Catherine Dunbar Junior High School, called an emergency faculty meeting at 8:40 A.M. in the library. The death of Ms. Frossard had sparked panic in the schools. Fortunately for the students, who were held outside in the yard to wait until nine o'clock, the weather was mild.

For once the librarian, Nicole Bishop (appropriately named, as her husband was a preacher in Harlem), wasn't standing at the doorway badgering teachers to keep the library clean and return all chairs. Even she was seated with her mouth shut, serious and afraid.

Julie walked into the library, past the empty stacks of multicolored milk crates at the door where students were required to deposit their book bags. She remembered when Nicole had instituted the measure to reduce the thefts of books and equipment, when Julie had thought Nicole crazy to imagine the system would work. Library theft was symptomatic of a deteriorating society in which pilfering grew to stealing in epidemic proportions, she thought. Today every citizen expected to be screened at airports for bombs and weapons. She remembered the day Bobbie had derisively sung the Dixieland jazz lyrics "Check your weapons at the door" as Nicole arranged the crates for the first time.

Andrea Pappas, the art teacher, waved to Julie. She was sitting with her friend, David Carr, a science teacher with whom she was living, and had saved a seat next to them for Julie. The entire faculty was silent in minutes as M. D. Dixon and Frankel stood facing them in front of the circulation desk.

Julie noted how Dixon, uncomfortable doing the principal's bidding in public, handed out the green board of education booklets *Safety in School* like a good monitor. She heard the sound of the stiff pages ripple throughout the library as she opened to the first page, headed, "Daily Precautions."

She found that she was strangely comforted by everyone's fear. She could believe that their collective problem meant she wasn't singled out for violence, that the murderer wasn't stepping out from her past.

"The random nature of the killings suggests that every school should be on the alert," Dixon lectured. "This book tells you what to do for your safety on a daily basis. I want to emphasize a couple of things. First, *never* stay after school or arrive early. Second, *never* remain alone in your room. This is even more important for female teachers. Most rapes and sex crimes occur in classrooms and faculty rooms when the teacher is alone. This applies to students also."

The room was filled with grumbles. "Impossible," said Nicole, who always challenged Dixon.

Dixon held up his hand. "Impossible or not, do it!" The teachers quieted down.

"Ms. Frossard, the second victim, was killed at her desk. Remember, you're a sitting duck in your chair. If an intruder enters your room, get up! There's no way you can defend yourself sitting down, no way you can escape."

A murmur of fear went through the room.

"If you feel you are in grave danger, a knee or almost any instrument can become a weapon. A Bic pen will open a can of soda—or poke out an eye."

Julie's heart raced as she thought of Martha's gun.

"Turn to page eight in your booklet," he instructed. "Study the diagram and note the characteristics the police will be looking for if you've seen a crime committed or you are assaulted."

Julie tried to memorize the description sheet depicting a typical criminal.

"The hat, hair color, cut, are fairly obvious," Dixon

droned. "But the police suggest you try to describe strangers by noting beard, sideburns, mustache, nationality, complexion, shoes, scars, whether he's right- or left-handed, and method of escape. Train yourself to be a witness. It's not as easy as you think."

Dixon looked over to Frankel and continued.

"A reminder. When you hear one single bell, it means 'intruder in the building.' Step outside your door as soon as you hear it."

"What good is that?" bellowed Arnie Davis, the shop teacher. "Who are ya kidding?"

June Boyard, the drama teacher, whom everyone ignored at meetings, stood up. "What sort of protection can the faculty expect from the powers that be?" she asked.

Julie checked her watch. There were ten minutes left, in which the meeting would deteriorate into meaningless suggestions from the principal and futile complaints by the faculty. But she noticed that Mat Siegel, the social studies teacher, was not inking in the squares of the *New York Times* crossword puzzle as he did at every meeting.

Then she read with new interest the regulations from the head of security for suspension and arrest of students. It required no discussion. It was the chancellor's edict concerning weapons in public schools. "Possession of the following weapons will result in an automatic Superintendent's suspension and the summoning of police," it warned.

Julie ran her eyes down the array of dangerous items, from firearms, silencers, and dart guns to explosives; from blackjacks and bludgeons and metal knuckles to switchblade knives, cane swords, and gravity knives. She took a deep breath, snatched up her possessions, and headed for her appointment in Dixon's office to turn Jesus in.

Dixon lumbered out of the room when the meeting ended, trying to fend off hysterical teachers who dogged him as he tried to escape down the hall a jot above a snail's pace to the meeting with Julie. He returned the cigar to his jaw, more comfortable now.

"Is he after women?" asked Mrs. Dobson. "Middle-aged women?"

"There are more middle-aged women in the system," that's all." Mrs. Dobson was middle-aged. Dixon turned around. A trail of teachers hung on his words. He felt like he was holding a press conference, happy in his usual position of pushing people away.

"Was it robbery?" asked Ms. Field, Bobbie's young replacement. Everyone deferred to her for an instant. She deserved consideration.

"Her pocketbook was locked up. We don't know if he didn't have time . . . or it was something else."

"Wasn't Bobbie's . . . a robbery?" asked Andrea Pappas.

"I don't know anything more than what you read in the papers," he said, picturing the police photos his cop buddies had shared with him, which showed the pearl necklace and gold ring intact on Frossard's body. He was saved by the nine o'clock bell; not that he was averse to being rude—he enjoyed torturing the teachers—but he was in a hurry to get rid of Julie and then have his doughnut and coffee. The teachers dispersed to meet their students.

In his heart he knew they had contempt for him. But whenever they were in trouble, whom did they come running for? Julie, who was usually calm, one of the strongest teachers, was lying in wait in his office at this minute. She was a bleeding heart type. Did she know he stood between them and total chaos? The women were respectful but superior. He had known Julie would come running back; they all did. Julie usually managed to keep out of trouble, but now that she was involved with that scum of the earth Jesus, she was in deep shit. He had done his job last time; he had warned her about him. Now she was on her own.

As she waited nervously for Dixon, Julie felt Bobbie was looking over her shoulder. He might not show up at all, Julie thought. He felt no obligation to keep appointments. But in he walked just as she decided he would disregard her note.

Dixon sat down at his desk and put his feet up, looking just as Bobbie had described him: like a bouncer in a topless bar. He observed Julie through half-closed lids, his face totally blank, and when he spoke he barely moved his lips.

Life was unspeakably boring to him, Julie thought, and he was indifferent to the horrors. Was the terrible job—dealing day in and day out with unsolvable problems and petty and vicious crimes, hearing the cries of the victim and the victimizer—too much for him? Or had he been that way to begin with? Was he the type the job required?

"So," he said. He raised his eyes slowly, sarcastically.

"I have reason to believe that Jesus may be the killer," Julie said, choosing her words very carefully, trying to appear calm. "I saw him running down the hall on the first floor just after Bobbie was killed. He had a motive. And I think he has a knife."

His eyes narrowed for a second. He realized she was serious. "He could have," he speculated. "He's capable of murder," he added to frighten her. "But he didn't—this time."

He removed his feet from the desk. "I chased him from the third floor and told him if he didn't leave the building I would kick his ass. That's why he was in a hurry. He was causing trouble, and the boss asked me to take care of it myself."

Julie's muscles seemed to cave in all at once. She hadn't realized how tight she had been until she untensed at Dixon's words. She breathed out in relief. It took her a minute to go on.

"Yesterday he was threatening Francisco," she said, somewhat defused. "I think he had a knife."

"You think?"

"I'm not sure. His back was toward me."

Dixon shrugged his shoulders.

'I heard something. I think it was a switchblade."

"Do you know how many kids carry switchblades?" he asked, the terrible disdain leveled at her.

Julie didn't answer him.

"If you think he's a killer, why are you protecting him?" he accused. "He probably has a record."

"I'm not protecting him!" Julie was incredulous. "I'm reporting him!"

"I hear yours is the only class he goes to—besides Arnie's shop."

Julie looked dazed. She's finally flaking out, Dixon thought, looking at the momentary confusion in her eyes. He had seen it before. Burnout.

"Get rid of that piece of shit! What do you need him for?" He felt he was doing her a favor. Usually he didn't waste his time on bleeding hearts. But Julie had been Bobbie's friend.

"I teach him!" she answered belligerently.

"Please don't tell me you're going to save him. You can't."

He gave her a last piece of advice. "Save yourself a lot of grief. Just stick to being his teacher. Don't try to be his mother. He's not worth it."

"We're talking about a human being," she said.

"You just accused him of murder," he smirked.

Julie got up. "I was wrong. *You* convinced me!" she said, leaving in a fury.

But as she stalked out of his office, she had to admit that Dixon had forced her to explore, in that second when her eyes blazed into his, when she suddenly hated his impassive cynical face, some subtle, unfocused hints beneath the surface of her beliefs. And she had been maneuvered by that boor into acknowledging the irrational connections between her and Jesus. There was a subliminal undercurrent, like ionic particles between them, which was as yet unexplained.

Dixon looked after her as she pounded down the hall, his face registering emotion no one would ever witness. He twisted his face painfully. Grace Frossard had most likely been stabbed with a switchblade. And Jesus *could* have conceivably slipped back up one flight to kill Bobbie after he chased him, because when another problem came up he, Dixon, hadn't bothered to watch Jesus beat it down the stairs, as he had claimed.

11

Esperanza remembered the first time she had met the priest. It was thirteen years ago, and he had been young, inexperienced, with the look of innocence. He probably doesn't know how to shave yet, she had thought. And she had wondered how such a green priest could advise her. But his naive look, his clear eyes had made her feel pure, the way her baby made her feel when she touched his new, fresh skin, when she looked into those trusting, violet eyes that made her think of miracles.

It was winter when Esperanza returned from Puerto Rico, where she had hidden with Jesus. He was not even a year old when Marcos telephoned her from New York, sent her one hundred dollars for the airfare (one of the many trips he paid for), and lured her back for the holidays. Esperanza, who never took notice of the weather, loved winter. She loved the snow and the whiteness and the cold. She loved the muffled silence of the noisy city at first snowfall, and she loved Christmas, even the commercial lights and the Christmas trees.

In 1974, the year she returned, it snowed heavily in December. And she remembered how the snowflakes fell past her window as Jesus lay asleep, how she watched them accumulate on the windowsill, and how she saw a snowflake as it alighted on a snowy mound reveal its crystal star to her in the sunlight.

She remembered how she had bundled Jesus in his snowsuit that afternoon and pushed him in the stroller, intending to walk through the park. It was the day she headed toward Riverside Park, where they could feel the clean breeze from the river, feel the sun on their cheeks and crunch through the new snow, and enjoy the fact that the squirrels and birds survived the cold. It was a place where she and Jesus might have thought about God's creations alone, because the park, she could tell from her window, was snowbanked and untrammeled by human footsteps.

That was the first time she saw La Mala. Esperanza could picture the scene as if it were yesterday. She had seen it a million times over the past years. Right on Broadway, before her very eyes, before she had a moment to gasp or cry out or grab up the baby to protect him, *La Mala* had crossed their paths, had been running to catch a bus, running, looking up, past the carriage, past Esperanza, so close that she almost brushed Esperanza's coat—just before the bus door closed with a thumping sigh no louder than Esperanza's heart.

Usually Esperanza's dreams were dark and unhappy and the gloom of the dream pervaded her night. But the day she saw *La Mala* the same crystal star she had spied in the snowflake on the window ledge appeared, magnified and shimmering in her dream. It was a sign. It rose before her in a mystical vision. The next morning she awoke in the inspired aura of the dream and her voices urged her to do something. Anticipation replaced her depression and longing.

Very early that morning Esperanza dressed and took Jesus to the Church of the Holy Name, the beautiful Gothic church with arches reaching up into the darkness, to change her name to Mary. It was the young priest, Father DiFalco, who persuaded her against it and instead gave her God's message and told her what to do with Jesus. And from that day on she never felt doubt. A clarity and peace overtook her. Until now. It had lasted thirteen years.

• • •

That same year, Father DiFalco had been warned by the monsignor when he had taken the young priest aside to counsel him about his duties. The monsignor was trying to prepare him for his job as pastor in a city ghetto, knowing that DiFalco had grown up in a quiet little upstate town.

"Since the city in its infinite wisdom has directed the

hospitals to send the mental cases to the SROs," he told him frankly, "we're getting our share of cuckoos."

Father DiFalco knew that the bag ladies and the scores of strollers on Broadway who gestured and conversed with imaginary cronies were dumped by the institutions into the hotels on the side streets. But they rarely ventured into his church.

"Some of these borderliners will be having visions and religious experiences," the monsignor explained. "Just try to be patient and comforting."

DiFalco remembered the monsignor's remark about the time Esperanza came into the church. "It's Christmas," he had joked. "We get more business around Christmas. The symbols of the church are universal. That's why lunatics are so fond of using them. They speak to the primal, the basics, like literature or dreams."

But when Esperanza announced in the confessional that she was a virgin and that her baby was Jesus, Father DiFalco rolled his eyes upward. "Why do I always have to get them?" he asked God silently in the darkness of the booth. And when Esperanza asked DiFalco if she could change her name to Mary, he felt so helpless in the face of her need. But he wrote down her name to bring up to the social workers for advice. And in the meantime he assured her that Esperanza was a beautiful name. "God wants you to have the baby," he had told her, "or God wouldn't have given him to you." He told her this because he was fearful that she would abandon or harm her child.

Father DiFalco occasionally took liberties giving advice. But his interpretation seemed to satisfy Esperanza, and he didn't see her again, so he forgot all about her.

• • •

Nilda was lying naked on the bed, her long black hair shining. She had a heart-shaped face, and her Chinese eyes were striking. Several men teachers had told her she could be a model, and whenever they said it she knew they would come on to her.

Jesus was looking into her face, and they were talking, something he usually didn't bother with after sex. The door to his room was open. He pulled on his jeans and toked on the joint still burning in the ashtray where he had left it. Nilda got special satisfaction from keeping him from going to school this morning: he had missed reading. It was the first time he had cut, and Esperanza was conveniently at the clinic, leaving the apartment empty for them.

"Maybe you made a baby today," Nilda told him teasingly. She felt so good. And she could see Jesus felt good too. His complexion was soft; he was all soft. She ran her finger lightly over the hair on his chest.

"You're crazy," he said.

"She's so old," Nilda remarked. Jesus knew he was talking about Esperanza. "You gonna wait 'til you're as old as her? I thought she was your grandmother."

"She's forty-eight. I saw her birth certificate. She looks old."

"Mine is thirty-one. She was sixteen when she had me."

"She had me at thirty-four."

"Old, man! *Could* be your gramma. Who's your father?" she asked tentatively.

"I don't know. Who would want *her?*" Jesus said.

"She ain't no virgin."

"Maybe she is. That's why she named me Jesus."

Nilda grabbed the roach from him, and they laughed and tumbled over one another on the bed like wolf cubs at play.

• • •

When Jesus began running around with Nilda, coming home late, he had discovered Esperanza's secret obsession. And now that she was finally home from the clinic he could hear the snip, snip of her little scissors, the sound driving him mad, because how could he forbid her this seemingly innocent pastime?

Esperanza's delusions were getting worse. Just yesterday he had found a prayer sewn into her pillow.

Saint Claire
Guardian of the cemetery You
who have the power of going into purgatory
give my enemy, *La Mala*
Something to do
so she may
leave me alone.

He couldn't bring himself to throw it away, just as he couldn't smash the makeshift altar she had set into the boarded-up fireplace in the living room. Now, just as soon as she arrived home from the hospital, she had busied herself at the altar. He could smell the oil burning in the crab shell, and he knew that the flame from the wick, floating above the two splinters of bone arranged in a cross, was to protect her from enemies.

But the cuts of the scissors drove him crazy. They reminded him that she would never be sane, that he would never have a normal home. And whenever he believed that Esperanza might be lucid, he would hear the little slash of the scissors, and he would know she was at it again, her little scissors curving around the plump, rosy body of a baby in a magazine, the baby pictures growing, accumulating in her album, the nameless babies multiplying, recorded for posterity behind the plastic sheets, never growing old.

They all had their little secrets, he thought, guiltily slipping his thumb into his mouth. The girls all did it openly, sucking their thumbs in school like babies. But he was careful never to let anyone see him. He looked around to see if he was observed, knowing full well he was alone in his room. And while he was sucking his thumb for comfort he listened to the pages of the magazine turn.

• • •

Even after thirteen years the Christmas preparations weighed on Father DiFalco's mind. Now that he had seniority he could leave the details to the others, but the pressure to have everything ready and perfect for the services caused him to lie in bed long into the night, unable to turn off his mind, to rid it of even the smallest detail.

During the day he was irritable, and increasingly he found it difficult to handle the personal emergencies that mushroomed at Christmas more than at any other holiday. There was too much drinking, too much emotion, along with family conflicts, child abuse, fights, incest. If only they knew what he heard in confession. It was enough to make one think that hell was on earth, an original idea he would credit God with, His sly trick to test His mortals. It certainly tested him.

Today he had a visitor for whom even his experience hadn't prepared him. In spite of the tragic nature of his supplicant's problem he was preoccupied; he had a long-distance call to return.

Les held out the tiny gold cross hopefully, imploringly. Father DiFalco noted with concern how the sweat dripped off Les's fingers even though he had just come in from the cold.

DiFalco took the cross from Les's wet palm and held it to the light, listening with pity to the story of his kidnapped baby. He looked at the cross carefully. No, he had never seen the cross before. He was sure of it.

"This cross isn't the sort usually worn by women in my church. The ones I see are larger, ornate and gold-plated. This looks like real gold."

"What about the initials—E.L.? Do they mean anything to you?" Les asked, disheartened.

"No," the priest said, looking up at his secretary, who was waiting for him.

The tiny rectory they were occupying was noisy with volunteers. The phone rang, and the secretary picked it up and held it out to DiFalco.

"I'm sorry," he said after a moment of thought, wishing he had time to console Les. "I don't remember the cross." He had to be blunt.

"God, what can I do?" Father DiFalco asked silently, the phone in his hand, watching as Les walked slowly away, his tall back bent in disappointment.

• • •

The school was charged with holiday atmosphere; next week was Christmas break. Schoolwork was winding down, and the loose control would spiral into chaos by Wednesday, December 23rd.

Julie's classes were disrupted by rehearsals, assemblies, and mammoth cutting, so she found it easy to suspend her small third-period reading class and have them help her pack up the precious but ancient machines from her reading lab that would have to be stored in the vault; they would never be replaced if they were stolen.

The squawk box competed with the escalating din, which would rise to fever pitch by lunchtime.

"Students are not to wear outer garments during school hours," Bernie Frankel harangued in his nasal whine. "They will be confiscated by the dean," he warned. "If anyone found a flute that was left in the auditorium this morning, a reward is offered. Today is the last day for securing equipment in the vault. The vault is open until eleven-fifteen today. I repeat: eleven-fifteen the vault will close. This is your last chance to store valuable items. I urge you to bring anything of value down to Mr. Aaronson in the basement now."

Julie had asked Jesus to help, not knowing whether he would stay. But he surprised her and was directing the packaging efficiently, ordering everyone around, including Carmelo and Crystal. The girls, as usual, were eager to carry heavy boxes to prove themselves, and Jesus sent all the students downstairs one by one, carrying the most fragile equipment himself.

Julie followed them down the central staircase. The halls were bustling with teachers and students. The classrooms were barely functioning. They had fifteen minutes, plenty of time to load the boxes, which they had labeled with her name and room number, into the vault. She knew that Aaronson had allowed extra time for arranging cartons to avoid last-minute hassles before the 11:40 lunch bell.

The giant metal vault door, with its huge four-bolted wheel that was larger than a ship's wheel, was wide open. Maggio, the visual aids teacher, had just stored all of his equipment by the door, so Jesus was directing the assembly line of his drones to the back of the vault. The space was five feet wide and as deep as a classroom.

As soon as Julie turned to speak to Aaronson, the short, bald woodwinds teacher and chairman of the Music Department, the kids disappeared. Aaronson was involved in a heated discussion with Judy Washington, a member of his department, and he waved Julie aside.

"Do you believe what that asshole said to me? 'This isn't a conservatory,' he says; 'this is a public school. Get rid of the strings.' Do you believe it?" He turned to Julie. "Just check that you have labels, okay?"

Julie walked back to the vault.

"I gotta go," said Washington, looking worried.

"Shut the vault," yelled Aaronson to Julie as he trailed after Washington. "You're the last one."

Julie bent down in the dim light to double-check the labels. It was so petty, all this worrying about details. But she checked anyway to avoid a fight. Everyone's a general, she thought. Power corrupts, she remembered . . .

But she didn't have time to finish the thought, because she heard a loud thunk. It echoed inside and everything went black!

12

Julie's heart clapped in her chest as the ton of metal clunked shut like the stamp of an elephant's foot, squeezing the light out of the vault. In microseconds pitch-black night like an executioner's hood dropped over her head. She was enveloped in dense darkness. And for the first time she knew the face of death.

Her heart's thumping was her only assurance that she was alive. "This is your last chance," she imagined hearing the principal's voice, just twenty minutes earlier. She was doomed. Whoever was after her had finally gotten her. The vault wouldn't be opened again until after the Christmas vacation.

She backed into the vault, groping against the cold wall. I'm finally done for, she thought, and she slipped down to the floor and cried.

But the silence intruded on her misery, magnifying her sounds, mocking her. There was no use screaming; no one would hear her. She stood up and stumbled to the door, knocking over a cello, the sound starting her heart up again. She pushed the door, knowing it was useless, pounding until her knuckles and palms were sore.

If Aaronson went home, she would be here at least over the weekend. Would anyone realize she was missing? Greg wouldn't miss her until evening. Who would dream of looking for her in the vault?

First Bobbie; now her. Someone wanted her dead. Was it the same demon who took her baby? She thought of Bobbie in silence and darkness, like this. I'll suffocate and rot, buried alive, she thought. This was her casket. She laughed like a maniac, the certainty of her fate cutting her short of breath. She tried to catch her breath, to inhale gulps of air, but all she could manage were shallow gasps, not enough to fill her lungs. I can't get air! she screamed in her head, choking on her fear. I'm going to die!

Why were the best flute players the ditziest? Aaronson wondered. Of course that wasn't true. The best musicians were the most disciplined; it was only the flamboyant ones you remembered. He was somewhat distracted and disorganized himself, always struggling to keep on top of the boring crap that he had to do, like keeping track of the instruments and locking them in the vault.

"Do me a favor, Yesenia," he pleaded with his best flautist, reluctantly handing her the flute. "Don't take this home." They were both tugging gently on the flute, which was lying in its case. "You were lucky again. Someone turned it in. If you lose it, you can't be in the spring concert."

Yesenia was a tall, light-skinned black kid with freckles and a roll of hair on either side of her face that ended in two thick, ribboned braids. Her hair was bleached reddish and it complemented her coloring.

"I won't lose it, Mr. Aaronson," she promised.

"Your mother will kill you if you lose it. And I'll kill you."

Yesenia hung her head. She gave him a guilty look.

"Lock it up," he advised. "You know you won't practice over the holidays. You have finals to study for." He let go of the flute. "It's up to you," he said. "I'm going to lunch."

Yesenia wasn't sure she had made the right decision. It might have been better to lock it in the vault, to be relieved of the responsibility.

"Do it for the baby," Julie told herself, leaning against the door for support, flattening her feverish cheek against the cool metal. She clenched her throat closed for several seconds, letting the air out slowly, slowly through her nose. She forced herself to empty her mind, to slow her nervous system down to a halt, yoga style, controlling the panic. Her heartbeat slowed; her mind cleared. Nothing. Nothing. Blank. Blank. She studied the imaginary white dot on the wall until she heard her breath return in easy, even takes. Her heart subsided lightly, faintly, into unobtrusive murmurs.

"Calm yourself for the baby," she said aloud, the sound of her soft, steady voice now reassuring. Use the silence, she ordered her brain. She tried not to think of Greg, of the possibilities, or she would start weeping and never stop. Silence and more silence. Use the silence.

Aaronson picked up the flute, stuck it on top of the box of tools the kids used to carve their oboe reeds, and headed for the vault. Yesenia, running out at the lunch bell, had left her flute in the classroom. Boy, would she get a shock when she came back.

He leaned the cases against the vault on the floor and turned the wheel quickly. He had done it a thousand times. It swung open immediately when he pulled.

What he saw on the floor of the vault made him think he was seeing a ghost. Julie was squatting with her legs crossed under her in the lotus position. Her face was white, her lips gray, and her eyes were blank. When she saw him, she smiled unbelievingly.

"Thank God you came," she said as he helped her to her feet.

Aaronson stammered. "What . . . what are you d-doing . . ." He had a speech problem that emerged when he was nervous. He opened his mouth to pronounce the word *here*, but he couldn't get it out.

"Someone is trying to kill me," Julie said calmly. "I'm next," she said in a voice so detached Aaronson's heart chilled.

Aaronson knew he shouldn't have left the vault even for a minute. But his biggest concern had always been theft; he was afraid of leaving the vault unattended. As a matter of fact, once before, when Aaronson's attention was elsewhere, Rudy Ramirez, the guard, had chased off a couple of wise-assed kids who were poking around in the vault, nosing around the instruments. And Rudy had wisely pushed the door shut. It had never occurred to Aaronson that someone might use the vault for murder. But that was before Bobbie was killed, and now a second teacher fatally stabbed. Suddenly the location of the music rooms, which gave him the freedom to work his band so that they could blast their brains out in the depths of the basement, gave him the creeps. Aaronson searched for Rudy. He wanted to warn him to hang close.

• • •

Les sat in the last row of the orchestra in the comfortable, intimate atmosphere of the small Ninety-Second Street Y concert hall on Lexington Avenue, a stone's throw from Julie's house. He had the sensation of being close to her, feeling it was appropriate he should say good-bye to her with music.

The chamber orchestra, playing in the old-fashioned auditorium with the warm carved wood walls, was as close as the performers could come to the salon atmosphere required for this piece, written for two violins and cello. He listened to the music, thinking only momentarily of his last session with Wolfson, where Les had made the decision about Julie.

He was surprised again by the color and drama of the strings, building up throbbingly the way only Vivaldi could write. It was that sunrise effect that moved him so. The deep vibrance of the cello mirrored his emotion. Good-bye, Julie. Tears gathered in his eyes in the darkened hall where he believed with a full heart that he would never see Julie again.

Les headed home to Rus's apartment after the concert, depressed and lonely. It had turned cold again, and he stepped around derelicts curled up in cartons on the sidewalk. He felt sometimes he was but a hair's breadth away from one of them. He had failed in everything: failed with Julie, failed in finding his son, even with the help of the cross. The holidays were coming, and he had to call Eleanore with nothing to show for his trip to New York.

When he arrived at the apartment, he put on one of Rus's old records of Billie Holiday singing the blues and dialed Eleanore in Monterey. He loved the wailing sound of the horn and Billie's dusky voice, the piano trilling in the background. When he felt down, he played the old-style black artists. When he was up, he listened to the cerebral, atonal sounds of modern jazz, the kind of music he wrote himself.

The phone rang distantly, making him feel lower than ever. He waited on, not wanting to give up. One more ring, he thought. A deep male voice snapped him out of his self-pity. What the fuck are you doing at Eleanore's? he thought angrily, scared.

"Hey man," said Les casually, as cool as he could, recognizing at once his old friend Rus. "What's goin' down?"

• • •

The Cuban kid from Eagle Security was kneeling on the ground testing the new lock he had just installed on Julie's front door. He was very efficient and took pride in his work.

While he finished up, Julie tried to reach Les once more. She had to know where he had been yesterday.

Watching the locksmith as he worked, she thought about Dixon, who had actually displayed a flicker of interest when she had reported being trapped in the vault. He even deigned to check his file and reported Jesus immediately to his chubby sidekick in the police department. But Julie wasn't impressed. She had absolutely no proof and, from her experience, had contempt for the police. And as Bobbie had pointed out in her inimitable way, "The cops fucked up the Kennedy assassination, so what do you, an insect citizen, expect?"

Bobbie was right. If you want to accomplish something, do it yourself. Improving the locks was the first step.

"Do you think this will keep me safe?" she tried joking with Ernesto, the locksmith. He was a handsome, clean-cut young man, wearing a neat uniform, and he inspired confidence.

He saw the look in her eye, but he didn't want to fool her.

"In New York there's no foolproof way to protect yourself—you get a Medeco lock and a plate over it like this so they can't drill it out, they take off your door."

"There's an outer door to get through too," she reminded him, referring to the curtained glass door.

"If someone wants to get in, they get in."

"Then what's the point of all this?" she asked, feeling helpless again.

"Usually a burglar will pick the easiest target, the door with one lock or with a pickable lock. He'll skip the difficult jobs. But if he wants to get into your apartment for some reason, if he knows you have jewelry or paintings or something he wants, forget it. He'll get in."

Julie's heart raced.

"But if you're the average person, and you take the proper precautions . . ." He stopped, seeing the look of fright straining the muscles of her eyes and her mouth. "Don't worry. You're not keeping the crown jewels here. Do you have some famous stamp collection or something? Coins? Something that would single you out, make someone come after you?"

"No. Nothing," she responded, a catch in her throat. Why did someone steal her baby? Why did someone want to kill her?

"There's nothing to worry about," he concluded, standing up, satisfied with her new lock, the plate, and the chain. "Why do you want all this?" he asked, snapping his tool case shut.

"I had a . . ." She hesitated. ". . . robbery once."

"Most locks you can open with a credit card. You did everything you could," he assured her, handing her the bill.

• • •

Martha was wearing the tennis warm-up outfit that Julie had seen her play in many times. Julie raised her arms and stretched as they walked briskly around the reservoir in Central Park. "Oh, this is so wonderful!" she cried, "a Christmas gift from heaven." Then she unzipped her jacket, exposing her thinly clad belly to the sunlight. "See, baby, it's not all bad," she said, admiring the barely visible bulge.

Martha laughed. In the warm afternoon, New York appeared its mythical best. The skyscrapers reflected in the circle of the reservoir; the water glistening around the gliding, dipping ducks; and the promise in the grandness of the architecture, in its sheer size, its diversity, were enough to give a cynic hope. The trees, the sun-sparkling water, and the sky beautifying the starkness of the cityscape uplifted Julie. Man's imagination was not all evil, she thought.

"I needed the light and the air after that claustrophobic horror," Julie said. And when Martha wasn't watching, Julie turned to look behind her. But all she could see were joggers, young and old in all shapes and sizes, fat and skinny, muscular and gaunt, sprinting and huffing, sweating and pounding around the dirt track, pumping themselves forward with the most interesting movements, each jogger with a unique style. No one threatening here. She felt safe out in the open, almost normal.

"I can't see why you suspect Les," Martha said, continuing their morning's phone conversation.

"Explain why he left town suddenly," demanded Julie.

"It's Christmas," Martha answered.

"Why are you protecting him?"

"Because you always defended him and I trust your judgment."

The grotesque baby of her dreams and Jesus both flashed before Julie. "I don't know what to believe anymore."

Julie looked across the water to the twin towers on the West Side, mentally reaching farther north to the psychiatric hospital high on the bluff overlooking the river. "I think I'll call Wolfson. He can give me a hint about Les. Maybe Wolfson's looking for a way to reveal the truth and he doesn't know how."

Martha looked skeptical. But she didn't want to discourage her friend.

They had reached the halfway point in the circle. "Would you help me?" Julie asked, certain of Martha's answer.

• • •

Dixon was waiting for Julie at the time clock at 8:00 A.M. She twisted her ring nervously at the sight of him, and her stomach dropped. She turned the stone in the ring in toward her palm, as if to protect herself. It was Jesus. She knew it, and now she would have to leave the school.

"I tried calling you over the weekend, but you're unlisted," he said almost apologetically. "It was Rudy Ramirez who locked you in. Aaronson found out. He said Rudy saw the door to the vault open and he closed it as he walked by. Guess he didn't see you in there."

Julie almost hugged Dixon, but she restrained herself. He might go into cardiac arrest. "Thank you! Thank you for telling me," she cried instead.

"I suppose you're relieved," he said, understating as usual. He started to walk away.

"And to think I accused Jesus. Twice! How unfair," she reminded Dixon, talking to his back.

Julie forgot to punch in, she was so elated. I'm so glad I didn't tell Greg, she thought. She had gotten a good report from Dr. Blum on Saturday when she went in to make sure her baby was okay after the ordeal. And now everything was doubly fine. If Greg had known, she would have quit today, and it was all a crazy mistake. No one was tracking her, out to get her. She couldn't look at every mishap as a threat to her life, connect it to the kidnapping, to Bobbie's murder. This was a dangerous world in a dangerous time. Everyone was susceptible to random harm. And this school was probably safer than anywhere else now, with all the new security. She had to go on believing that. She couldn't quit now. She wanted to, but she just couldn't.

"Like lightning," she had explained passionately to Greg, "the killer won't strike twice in the same school."

13

Jesus would always remember the wooden ducks whenever he was in pain, even more than the months in the Townshend detention center in the Bronx. He had worked on them all term in woodworking class, the only reason he went. They were the ornaments on a Christmas present for Esperanza—a napkin holder with a duck on each side.

At first, when Mr. Davis, the shop teacher, suggested it, Jesus treated the idea the same as all his suggestions. But then, Jesus thought, he was coming in for reading in the morning, so he might as well stay and make her a Christmas present. She had been looking very bad lately, and he knew how much Christmas meant to her. And she stared at all his other presents to her with suspicion.

Jesus found that he was lost in concentration each day as he became involved in the work of carving and painting the ducks. It was the first time he had ever really made anything, had cared about its outcome. At first it was something to do. Then, as each step was completed, he wanted to embellish the next, thinking up new ways. He was especially proud of thinking of putting the female on one side and the brighter male on the other.

He found a book in the library and chose the duck most appealing to him. It was a harlequin duck, which he hoped to meet up with one day on Long Island. The satisfaction he got from completing the shape of the duck, which he sawed out according to his drawing—the perfection of the shape he had designed and the smoothness it had after he sandpapered it—was particularly deep because of the time he took deciding on the picture, drawing it to exact detail. When it came time to paint it, each day he added something different. He matched the colors from the picture, making subtle changes using delicate strokes of color with his thin paintbrush.

On the day he added the bands of white to the pale blue and earth browns of the feathers and daubed the white spots on the head of the female, he was finished. This present would be one Esperanza could keep, one that they could look at forever, unlike a bottle of perfume or a box of candy, which would soon be gone. But she never saw the present, and the incident solidified his philosophy: Be more brutal than the others. Think of the evil deed before they do.

• • •

The school was on a high, Julie felt. It was the day before Christmas break, and holiday fever gripped the students, making the teachers edgy because there was more excitement, more anticipation, more hope, more lies, more drugs and alcohol, more of everything. And the hopes usually turned to dust.

The guards were patrolling the school just to prevent dire chaos and serious disorder. Kids were roaming through the halls, there was partying in most of the rooms, and Frankel was abusing the squawk box so that no one paid any attention. The false fire alarms and the single bell for "intruder" were rung so often that the bells became background clanging for the Christmas roar. Julie didn't know whether to laugh or cry. She wished Bobbie were here to help make her laugh.

The smell of turkey rose from the depressing cafeteria, and Julie was grateful that Andrea Pappas and David Carr had accepted her invitation to lunch to celebrate their engagement. On their way out they passed the first casualty of the season. The new, young, black guidance counselor's car was overturned like a bug, and the students had turned the water hydrant on to finish off the job. The frantic attempts at frivolity on the last day always ended in destruction, Julie thought. Students were ripped off, fights erupted, and Julie knew that as much as they hated school most of the kids had nothing to look forward to over the holidays.

It was one lunch where she could have used a drink, she thought, returning with her friends from the Chinese restaurant on Broadway. On the other hand, it was best to have her wits about her to face the remaining hours.

At 2:30 the principal rang an early dismissal to end the agony, and Julie's kids ran for their coats and screamed down the stairs without waiting for her, even to say good-bye. Sadly she was gathering her coat and belongings, her shopping bag of plants and books, listening to the waning shrieks of the remaining kids, when Jesus dashed in, grabbed his leather jacket from the wardrobe, and reached for his wooden ducks, which he had stored in the rack above the coats.

The heads on both ducks were broken off. Jesus stared at the pieces of wood for a second and tossed them to the back of the closet. For the barest moment Julie saw the hurt in his eyes, something he wouldn't wish to reveal to anyone, least of all to himself. An instant of emotion clouded his steely violet eyes, giving them a depth of swirling, brilliant color like an exotic plant, and it caught her off guard. It was a memory of a far-off place, like a recurring dream or turning a corner and feeling she'd been there before—the very same way.

Then the flicker disappeared from Jesus's expression. It was quickly replaced by a new look, of resignation. And then an "I don't care" flashed like a Morse code message as he kicked the broken gift farther back into the closet before Julie could utter a word of regret. Then the cold look returned to normal, and that made her the saddest, his rejection of that innermost sacred treasure, his feelings.

He saw the instant of pain in her eyes as he started for the door. She wanted to say something to him, but she couldn't embarrass him, and the catch in her throat prevented her from telling him what was really in her heart. Anyway, he was running past her, but something made him stop, his hand on the doorknob. Maybe it was her expression; maybe it was the empty days yawning ahead of him.

"It's nothing," he told her at the door. "Don't worry about it."

"So long," he said. "*Julie*," his voice totally normal, with a dash of tough. Using her first name was teasing, ironic, and nervy. "Merry Christmas."

Before she could tell him what she felt, which was a confusion of sadnesses, he was gone.

The simplicity and incongruity of his "Merry Christmas," after what he had just experienced, of what she knew his Christmas would be, made her want to cry. And it made her ashamed she was going to the Bahamas with Greg, to sit on the rocks and bask in the sun in a fairy-tale world. Greg would never understand why she couldn't completely enjoy it.

• • •

It was a grim, gray December day in cold Central Park, especially without the relief of green anywhere. Nilda was staying with an aunt, and Jesus was wandering through the paths toward East Harlem, not terribly eager to see Nilda or her cousin. But there was nothing much else to do. He had planned to take the ducks home, but now he found himself passing a playground farther downtown than he usually wandered.

It was a playground just off Fifth Avenue, where the stragglers from private school stopped to find their mothers and their toddler siblings or were lured by the rope that swung over the sand. Outside the gate a fourth-grader, Jesus judged, stood beside a squirming blond cocker spaniel tied up by his leash. The boy waited, bored, dangling a worn book bag. Both blond, Jesus thought, taking in the child's neatly cut golden head of hair, the bangs trimmed expertly on his forehead. Jesus surveyed the ski jacket open at the boy's neck, which revealed a tie askew over a white shirt. The kid's navy blazer stuck out from under the jacket. Jesus stared at the little boy's loafers of polished, bright brown leather, and the closer Jesus got, the more the meaning of the scene escalated in Jesus's brain to unexpected heights of fury. The child's vacant look, his groomed carelessness, his blue eyes and fair skin made Jesus want to gouge at him, to make him scream out in pain.

A shiny watch on the boy's wrist gave Jesus his excuse.

"Gimmie your watch or I'll hurt you," he whispered up close to the boy. He saw how handsome and smooth the boy's face was close up. The boy took a second to register the threat, and a look of fright spread in his eyes.

Jesus yanked the watch from the child's wrist, and tears welled in the boy's eyes at the rough handling, at the watch disappearing. Jesus punched him hard in the chest. A hollow blow registered against Jesus's fist. His left hand gripped the boy's jacket by the zipper, and he raised his right fist to smash the boy in the eye, to see blood, to scar him, to give him something to remember him by. But a group of mothers pushing carriages appeared at the playground entrance, only twenty feet down the concrete walkway. Jesus released the jacket and walked abruptly down the branching path leading deep into the park. He could hear the boy's uncomplicated sobs. And he felt better hearing them as he mounted the steep stone steps into the tangled woods in the vast portion of the park that he knew would be deserted.

Jesus and Nilda took the upper end of the park home. She was pissed that he had gone to school, had missed the all-nighter she had with her cousin. They were winding their way around the ball field that ended at One Hundredth Street and Central Park West, their exit from the park.

"What are you gonna tell your teacher about your father?" Nilda asked.

"What do you mean?" Jesus asked defensively. He knew she meant Julie.

"I know she's been askin' about you. About your mother, your father."

"I don't know who my father is, and my mother don't know either," he answered, laughing, trying to steer her away from the subject.

"Why the big interest in you?" Nilda persisted, sensing a weakness, sensing he was vulnerable that day.

"Maybe she likes me. She's a fox. Even teachers fuck."

"Hey, you're nothin' to her. She's a rich bitch. See that stone on her hand, that green emerald ring she always wears? No one looks like *her*."

"Yeah, I know," Jesus said despondently.

"You're beginning to look like her," Nilda said, pressing her advantage. "The way you stick your chin out when you talk. It's weird. Are you tryin' to imitate her or what?"

Jesus angrily squeezed the stolen watch in his pocket. "Shut the fuck up! You're just a jealous bitch. You know she's way over you," he shouted.

But Nilda knew she had twitched a raw nerve. And she knew how to make Jesus forget all about Miss Nosy, Miss Fancy Ass, Miss Wearer of the Emerald Ring. And she had one other ace in the hole. She had discovered something about his idol. But she wouldn't break it to him until after the vacation. She couldn't take the chance. He might take his anger out on her.

• • •

The jazz clubs in California, Les noticed, were less serious and smoke-filled and weren't haunted by apparitions from another lifetime. Maybe it was his past he was imbuing the New York clubs with, but he couldn't help remembering the hours he had spent in Greenwich Village listening to Miles Davis and the drummers who had made the other dank little clubs on Mac-Dougal Street famous.

Rus, Les had to admit, was one of the best living pianists. He looked good up on the platform—competent, confident, classy, with enough style and sheen to please the casual audience and a large enough talent to earn him a place as a musician's musician. Les's happiness at having him in his jazz group was reaffirmed. What a fool Les had been to worry. New York and its pitfalls and dark tunnels, as Eleanore correctly perceived them, were so far away now that he looked across the table at her healthy, open face. He listened to his friend fill the air with his art, the important part of his being, the thing he most cared about in the world.

Last night with Eleanore, in the release of sex with her in the way he had almost forgotten—so caught up had he been with the tortures of the damned in New York—he had renewed himself. The elation had lasted until tonight, and he basked in his friend's solo performance.

Yesterday, when Les arrived at his Monterey house, Rus was

gone. Eleanore explained that Rus had been there only to pick up an arrangement of a piece Les himself had promised Rus and had completely forgotten. But Les was glad he had taken the first plane out of New York. His future was here in California with Eleanore. Julie was history.

• • •

Jesus, Nilda, her cousin Damaris, and Damaris's boyfriend, William, were tired of roaming through the park. It was getting dark, and Nilda suggested they end up in Jesus's apartment. It was spacious, in a decent building—a place you didn't have to be ashamed of—and Jesus was hoping that Esperanza would be in her room, in her own world, out of the way. He rarely had visitors except for Nilda, who was used to Esperanza's crazy ways.

Quieting the rowdy group had been a mistake, Jesus realized later. If she had known someone was coming maybe she would have hidden or stopped what she was doing. But coming in on her, trying to sneak the gang past her in the living room, on the way to his room, they all saw her. Or at least they heard her. She was wrapped in a shawl, invisible in the dark room, rocking in her chair. "*Coqui, coqui,*" she squeaked, like the frog of the same name that croaks in the swamps of Puerto Rico. They all knew what she was singing, and they could see her cross herself and talk to the ceiling when Jesus turned on the light to stop her. But Esperanza continued, oblivious to them all.

Damaris, who had never seen Esperanza before, edged back into the hallway, pushing William back too.

"*Tu bruta,*" Jesus shouted, standing over Esperanza. "*Stupida, bruta!*" he screamed at her, and Nilda wavered in the doorway, not knowing whether to enter or leave.

"Get out!" Jesus yelled, seeing Esperanza's abject face, unable to control himself.

"*Tu es loca!*" he cried, his voice trembling, watching the tears on Esperanza's cheeks. Jesus was relieved to hear the door slam, because he was ashamed. He knew that his mother would never do anything to hurt him if it were in her power, that her strange behavior was beyond her control. And he felt guilty because he had never before made her cry and because he knew that her sickness did not diminish her love for him.

But her misery fueled his fury; it welled in him, rising in intensity, out of control the way she was. He ripped the jet bracelet from his wrist and shook it in her face. And then he dashed it to the floor, stomping on it first and then grinding the black beads into the wood with the heel of his boot.

• • •

"You have therapeutic hands," Les said, kissing Eleanore all over her softened-after-sex body as she lay sprawled on her back. Her nipples were soft pink; her skin had a tender glow. It was noon, and they were lying on a blanket on the tiled living room floor so they could feel the warmth of the sun on their bodies as they made love.

"Shall we start now?" asked Eleanore, always the practical one, wanting to get business out of the way.

Les was reluctant. It was his last and only hope. One that perhaps should lie dormant. "Don't tempt fate," he replied.

"You're feeling the effects of hormone therapy," Eleanore teased, playing with his penis.

Les laughed and hugged her close to him, pressing her against his cooling skin, which was ready for another temperature rise.

14

Eleanore shuttered the windows and sat near Les as he lay on the blanket, his back, buttocks, and shoulders pressed flat to the floor, his arms straight down alongside his body, his palms up.

Les's obsession with that moment when he entered the lobby of his apartment building on the day of the kidnapping, with the tantalizing shadow at the tip of his memory, would at last reappear or be put to rest forever. Eleanore's relaxation technique, her hypnotherapy, would make him receptive to suggestions and allow him to reenter the hallway back in time.

He spread his legs apart slightly, his toes pointed upward. This was the customary position to begin the process. Eleanore's novel combination of the unorthodox Reikian method and traditional yoga was aimed at relaxing the body and emptying the mind of worldly clutter. Les felt peaceful merely preparing his body for the exercise, listening to Eleanore's even, uninflected, soothing voice.

"Close your eyes," she said softly when his lids fluttered open for a moment. "Think of a pleasant scene. Can you hear a flute playing? It is springtime, and you are walking in a field of flowers." She gave him time to imagine the scene. "You are examining the white petals of the daisies. Choose one pretty flower. Look at each petal, one by one. It's a beautiful, sunny day, and you are feeling ver-ry relaxed.

Your eyes are getting ver-ry tired." She spoke slowly, ever so slowly. "Your eyelids are getting heavy." She paused. "They are getting heavier and heavier," she crooned gently, the way he imagined her voice countless times when he used her self-healing ritual, when he was alone and anxious or had a bout of tension preparing for a gig on the road. "Soon you will be asleep," she said softly. She paused for a moment to let the silence intensify her suggestion. A heaviness and a darkness crowded in upon Les. He experienced total, protecting, deepening blackness.

Her voice was fainter now. "Your whole body is relaxing. From the top of your head to the tip of your toes, you are relaxing." He felt his body sink deeper and deeper into weightlessness, his substance sinking lower and lower into gravity. "Relax your head." She waited for his head to sink. "Relax the muscles of your neck." He could feel his neck loosen, and he followed her words with a physical response to the minutest detail. "Relax your shoulders. Your right shoulder is relaxing. Relax your left shoulder." He could feel the wave of release moving down his body.

"Your chest muscles are relaxing." Her voice was almost a whisper. "Your back is relaxing. Your spine is relaxing, vertebra by vertebra." He allowed his back to respond to her command. "Your buttocks are relaxing," she said quietly. He was feeling so loose. All he could see was a field of daisies. "Your legs are totally relaxed." She spoke more slowly. "Each toe is relaxed." She stopped. He could hear the Pacific Ocean, the waves washing, returning. "Your whole body is relaxed," she told him. "You are getting drowsy; your body is getting heavier." He sank into the dark; his body felt like rubber.

"You are feeling good, a feeling"—she hesitated—"of well-being." Les felt his spirits rise. "When you awaken you will be feeling good. Now you are going into a deep sleep."

He felt he could open his eyes at any time, that he was in control, but he wanted to follow her suggestions, and he continued to obey her.

"You are going back in time, back to the hallway. We are going to find the meaning of the recurrent shadow in your dreams. You are coming through the door."

He pictured himself rushing through the door in his leather coat. He saw the stained-glass windows, dull from grime, the cold hallway, the cracked marble steps leading to the elevator.

"We're going to follow the shadow. Do you see the shadow?"

Yes! The shadow darted behind a pillar. He could see her! An old woman. For an instant he saw her as he had seen her fourteen years ago, a split-second glimpse of an old woman hiding from him in the hallway.

He opened his eyes wide. "I see her!" he cried. "It's an old bent woman!" He was elated. "An old bent woman," he repeated. "The kidnapper!"

• • •

Before leaving for New Jersey for Christmas dinner with Marcos and Carmen, Jesus hurriedly picked up the poor, crushed beads of the bracelet he had destroyed the day before. He felt a momentary pang before pushing Esperanza out the door, seeing her coat hang on her thin body, realizing he had caused her pain. But he hardened his heart against her. He had to survive in this world.

On the long ride to the suburbs Jesus remembered when Esperanza was more in touch with the world around her. The recollection was one of his first memories. It was winter, only a much colder one than now, when he became very ill—so ill he couldn't keep any food down and he had a high fever. Esperanza sat beside him on the bed they slept in, praying all night, shivering in her shawl near that fireplace that never worked. The room they lived in wasn't heated that week, Esperanza told him later, and of course there was no hot water. He remembered how her potions and prayers to the Virgin, when he was too young to understand, were comforting, how her cool lips felt when she kissed his fingers.

When Marcos found out that Jesus was sick and took him to the doctor, Jesus remembered being so weak he could barely stand up in the doctor's office. But Jesus was grateful to the Virgin that time, because she saved him from school; Esperanza followed her advice to go home, and they flew back to Puerto Rico, where Esperanza let him run free.

Jesus thought about their house in Puerto Rico. It was always dark inside and cool, because over the years of neglect the shrubbery had become overgrown in the garden and the trees flourished unchecked, shading the windows from the sun. He loved the old house, where he played in the garden and ran barefoot to the neighbors' children. It was the best part of his childhood. Esperanza told him that when he was an infant she used to put him in a laundry basket filled with pillows and set him out to sleep where the porch caught the sunlight between the trees. He could picture her watching him as she sat happily next to him in the old, withered wicker chair that was probably still weathering out there today.

While Jesus stared out of the car window, conjuring pictures of his childhood, Marcos drove them commandingly through aggressive traffic across the George Washington Bridge in his station wagon, determined not to screw up Carmen's schedule. After ascertaining that Esperanza's and Jesus's health and safety were not in jeopardy, he gave up his attempts at conversation; they were both lost in their own worlds. He had tried futilely to convince Jesus to take Esperanza to Marcos's own doctor, knowing that Jesus couldn't dissuade her from the clinic, where she had been cared for over the years and where she felt safe. The effort of communicating with the two of them drained him, and he finally fell silent, deciding to preserve his energy for driving and the long day ahead.

Esperanza contented herself with reveries of the past as she sat beside Jesus in the back, leaning against his arm, enjoying the roll of the car and the numbing roar of the wheels on the bridge. In the old days in Puerto Rico, and even for some years in New York, she and Jesus had always celebrated *Dia de Los Tres Reyes*, Epiphany, the coming of the three wise men, together. Traditionally, on the eve of January 6th, children filled small boxes with grass for the kings' horses and placed the boxes beneath the bed. While they slept, their parents removed the grass and replaced it with gifts. Every year, from the time Jesus was an infant, Esperanza had endured the pleasant agony of deciding what gift to give him. And on Christmas Day the house was filled with the pungent smell of *lechón asado*, roast pig, and Jesus received a special gift, because Esperanza had decided that December 25th was the day of his birth and she had baptized him that way.

Esperanza's only worry in those days was what the nuns at

home would think when they saw her baby. Would they understand that there was no father? She had been so eager to return
to the town with her infant for the first time, to show the
townspeople that she had been loved. But she had a dilemma.
Then, in the airplane, with her infant in her arms, when she
looked out of the window, a voice came to her from a cloud.
"God is the father," it said, and Esperanza felt purified.

The flash caught Carmen and Marcos and the three girls,
Lydia, Jocelyn, and Amy. Jesus pulled the film from the Polaroid, and they crowded around him until the image emerged.
"Now, Jesus," instructed Marcos, "give the camera to Jocelyn and come over here." Jocelyn relieved him of the camera,
and the girls pushed him between their parents to pose before
the tree. They squeezed together under the fragrant, blue-gray
spruce twinkling with bright light. It was understood that
Esperanza would refuse. She never allowed her picture to be
taken, and she never took pictures of Jesus, even as a baby. Now
Marcos insisted on including Jesus, and she couldn't interfere.
Esperanza hung back as Jocelyn clicked the shutter, the flash
blinding Jesus as he stared at Esperanza. The look on his face
was recorded, his thoughts growing visible with the image on
film. Jesus was as uncomfortable as the three girls, who were
eager to bolt to meet their boyfriends.
Esperanza, although happy in the midst of her family, was
suffering under the unaccustomed strain of socializing. Jesus
saw how frail Esperanza looked, how skinny and small. And
even though he felt choked by the atmosphere—knew how out of
place he was around his Americanized, cheerleader cousins,
aware of how relieved they would be when he finally said they
were ready for Marcos to drive them home—an intuition that he
didn't want to care about, didn't want to torment him, pressed in
on him as he watched Esperanza. He tried to resist it, but it came
anyway.
This is her last Christmas, he thought.

• • •

Julie observed Jesus while he fell into intense concentration
at his desk. His fingernails were bitten down and dirty, and he

wore black leather gloves with the fingers cut off. Julie despised his tough-guy look.

Jesus was riveted to the "lock box," and Julie discovered that he learned in a day what she expected him to do in a week. She couldn't hope for him to work at home, so everything had to be accomplished in her room, behind locked doors, Jesus seated at a desk right in the center of the room to prevent anyone who was looking in the window, front or back, from seeing them laboring together.

She planned her trips to the bathroom or to the office at intervals when he had work he could perform alone, and his tasks were always completed perfectly when she returned. She wasn't surprised. The day he arrived in her class he had filled out his Delaney Card, used to keep track of students' personal information and seating arrangements, with the easy script of a fluent hand. There were no letter reversals, which were a sign of a learning disability, and she had double-checked to rule out hidden and subtle forms of the problem.

Julie couldn't keep her eyes off Jesus. As soon as she looked away, she was pulled to examine him again. But she watched him only while he worked, still avoiding direct eye contact with him the way she avoided dangerous characters on the street. The instinct to face off, the eye-to-eye of the animal world, signaled threat, and staring down your opponent, she remembered from college biology, was a primitive means of establishing dominance. A means still used by Homo sapiens, she thought, watching Jesus. If she looked into his eyes, she instinctively knew, he would regard it as a challenge or a come-on. There was nothing in between for Jesus.

Yet she couldn't keep her mind on anything else while he was with her. She was compelled to take him in, to examine him, explore him, know him, understand him. And she suddenly had an insight about him as he sat absorbed in his task. She followed a long, gray, empty passageway in her mind's eye straight into his future, and she saw that his appetite for violence would increase as he grew older, that he would become even angrier, even greedier. And one day, her presentiment told her, would be a terrible day, because no one would be there to stop him, and the forces that moved him would be unleashed.

She continued to watch him, disturbed by her vision as he puzzled out a word, ignorant of her wrenched emotions. The inner directive was so strong, the urge to capture his essence with her eyes so powerful that she began to doubt her motives. Was it only to help a lost boy because Bobbie had bequeathed the mission to her? Or was she watching him like a hawk, pinning him to her with her gaze for some other reason? Was she boring, with her penetrating eyes, into the heart of a murderer?

• • •

Les held tightly to a small carry-on bag as he boarded the jet back to New York. He wouldn't allow himself to think how good it would have been to indulge himself and stay in Monterey. He felt cleansed of the poisonous vapors that had invaded his body in the Big Apple by losing himself in Eleanore's lifestyle. The apple was an appropriate image for New York, he thought. Red apples were tainted by insecticide, and Eleanore refused to buy them. Every day he felt fitter and more sexual in Eleanore's hands. She had dragged him to the courts to play tennis, they had jogged together at sunrise, and he hadn't had a hamburger in two weeks. She had a loving and compassionate soul hidden beneath her nurse's objectivity.

He buckled up and refused the drink the stewardess offered him. His mind was still fresh and clear, and he wondered how long that would last in New York. Wolfson was still on vacation. It's okay, Les told himself; everything's cool. He stiffened his back against the seat as the plane lifted off, leaving his stomach behind. He grimaced as he inhaled the stale, pressurized air of the cabin when the plane finally cruised peacefully above the clouds. There was much he had to do in the Poisoned Apple.

The old gloom settled over him, forcing him to turn his focus away from Eleanore. He set his jaw tighter, strained against the buckle that harnessed him, then released it with a snap. Flying back to New York was like a modern crossing of the river Styx, from the world of the living into the world of the damned. But he was compelled to go back.

• • •

Martha rushed out of the darkroom to snatch up the phone

in her bedroom before the tape began.

"It's a full moon," Julie began excitedly. "Get your equipment and meet me at One Hundredth and Broadway. It's absolutely incredible—the shot of a lifetime. The moon is hanging between the narrow streets, just suspended between the buildings. The perspective is terrific. I've never seen anything like it."

Martha laughed. "You sound like a shutterbug. As a matter of fact I just finished up in my darkroom. What are you doing on the dangerous West Side after dark, anyway?"

"School play. Come on, I'm exhausted and I need some food. I'll treat you to dinner."

"I'll have to lug my equipment."

"Any sacrifice for art," Julie said sarcastically.

"Okay. You shamed me into it. I'll grab a cab and be there in ten minutes."

• • •

Greg arrived home to a darkened house, expecting a fire in the fireplace, the satisfying sounds of the stereo, and a grand welcome. He slammed his briefcase to the floor and wondered where the hell she could be this late. It was nearly eleven. After a harrowing day, he had decided to change his plans and wait until morning to leave on his business trip.

This was the last straw, he thought, wanting to twist the necks off the roses he had brought. Julie wasn't the same woman he had married. What was she hiding from him? He sat down on the couch and calmed himself. The soothing effect of the quiet darkness brought him back to his senses. He was still sitting in his overcoat, the straining in his chest wall subsiding.

But the doubts still troubled him. And he wondered what she had meant when he overheard her that day talking to Martha in the kitchen. Her words rang in his brain. "I'll tell him after the baby is born."

• • •

Martha arrived with her camera and tripod. They were looking east into the dark.

"It's too good to be true, right?" asked Julie, staring at the moon.

"Did you hang that there just to get me out on a cold night?" Martha pushed her glasses up onto her head and squinted into the camera, adjusting her lens, pleased her friend had thought to call her. She would include this in her show. She snapped the roll, knowing it was going to be the highlight of her exhibit. She could see the negatives swimming in the developing fluid, coming to life in the print. The shots would be stunning in the simple frames she would hang them in.

"There's a big, cheery Mexican place on Broadway with balloons and margaritas. We can talk there, and you can stash your equipment near our table," said Julie, collecting Martha's tripod. They walked together companionably.

A mariachi band was finishing up as the dinner crowd started thinning out. It was a gay, whitewashed, airy restaurant. Just the up Julie needed.

"I'll have a small margarita, no salt, please," Martha told the waitress. "The new me," she said in response to Julie's surprised look.

"I feel self-righteous and smug when other people drink and I don't," confessed Julie.

"So what? You have a baby to protect. I see you're beginning to show a little."

"The girls in school have noticed. They love it, fuss over me. They think I should be home with lots of babies, not working."

"When I was pregnant with Greta and Nina, I looked like a blimp," said Martha nostalgically. Julie knew that Martha's grown daughters were married, that Nina was in California and Greta was in Australia, and knew how much Martha missed them. "It's funny," Martha remarked. "You're pregnant, and I'm having hot flashes."

"Did you have your period early?"

"Yes, why?"

"I think it's a pattern—early onset and early over. I didn't have mine until I was fourteen, and I was in despair because all of my friends had started before me. I felt like an utter baby."

"I know. It was status to have it in those days."

"Now the girls I teach tell me they hate having it. Attitudes have inexplicably changed on that one," Julie said, a puzzled look on her face. "I was shapeless and chubby, and boys never even looked at me," Julie reminisced. " I checked myself every day, hoping against hope."

"It's hard to believe you weren't always gorgeous and sophisticated."

"I was certainly a late developer. The ugly duckling."

"Turned into a swan," said Martha. "I was pretty but flat-chested."

"Wow! Look at you now."

Martha laughed. "I tried to reassure my girls when they were teenagers, but they wouldn't believe me." She leaned toward Julie. "Do you know, most women my age are into heavy cosmetic surgery? Especially my single friends. Maybe because I'm a photographer, I appreciate lines and how time writes on your face."

"What if you don't age well?" asked Julie.

"What's aging well?" Martha laughed. "Theoretically I won't care. In ten years we'll see if I have the courage of my convictions." She stopped to think. "Anton had the courage of his convictions, and look where it got him." She waved away the topic with an impatient gesture. "What were you like as a teenager?" she asked, returning to their conversation. "I was a typical, privileged girl in a comfortable family," she confided to Julie.

"I had a hard life as a child. Maybe because I wasn't pretty and things didn't come easily, I was able to survive, become a fighter."

"I'm sure everyone imagines you as the princess, growing up in the ivory tower. Julie with the beauty and brains, pampered in the castle."

"My apartment building in Washington Heights was like a castle with courtyards and turrets." Julie laughed. She finished off her enchiladas suizas, enjoying for once the luxury of the extra calories of the sour cream.

"I guess being a princess is all in your mind," said Martha,

looking at her watch and trading their plates for the coffee they
had ordered. "We should hit the road before it gets too late," she
suggested.

Julie nodded in agreement. "Would you believe that New
York was safe when I was growing up? You could actually ride
the subway alone at two A.M. When I was in college, Les and I
sat in Riverside Park on holidays and walked hand in hand at
dusk looking at the ginkgoes and the black locust trees, never
worrying about my purse or getting mugged."

"Anton was murdered nearly ten years ago. And it's getting
worse," said Martha. She was sorry she had brought it up again.

"Now you need a bodyguard to use the subway. Women are
raped in subterranean tunnels," Julie said.

Martha patted the handbag on her lap. "This is my bodyguard," she said confidently, feeling the outline of her Beretta.

"Thanks for dinner, your highness," said Martha, taking
note of the twisted smile on Julie's face. She could see something
was wrong.

A horrible thought made the heat rise in Julie until she was
uncomfortably warm, breathless. Beads of sweat burst out on her
brow and her flesh crawled as she thought of Les.

"Are you spinning flax into gold?" Les's voice floated into
the restaurant on wings of the past. Why hadn't it occurred to
her before? The princess in the fairy tale had been in danger of
having her baby kidnapped! Why did Les see her as the princess
whose baby was about to be taken away by Rumpelstiltskin?

"I'm the princess whose baby was stolen," she blurted out in
tears, to Martha's great astonishment. "But I never got my baby
back!" she cried.

15

He recalled with relish the summer evening he had murdered Oxley. He could hear the distant screams of terror as Oxley fell under the wheels and the slogan he himself had uttered aloud at the moment of truth. But the screech of the brakes and the moans of horror of the public witnessing the execution had obliterated his triumphant cry.

The principal of Catherine Dunbar Junior High, Anna Marietta Fontana, the woman who had tried to destroy him, had croaked long before Oxley. When the bitch died in an airplane crash, when a terrorist's bomb blew her sky high, that's when everything had clicked into place. The principal's death was a dream come true, and he hadn't lifted a finger. After a summer vacation in Greece her plane had exploded in flight.

He remembered the thrill of realizing how at last she had paid for her crime, that after years of waiting, justice had been done. In his silent white cell he couldn't stop dwelling on the revenge he would take on the others, on all the teachers who had voted to suspend him at the hearing. The pain of that humiliation, of his downfall, still stung him.

The plan he had devised was so satisfying it had cleared his mind of the debilitating hate that had nowhere to go. He would kill every teacher who had condemned him, beginning with Oxley. And as soon as he decided on murder, the institution had released him, stamped him cured, because he had suddenly become clearheaded. He had found a purpose in life.

Justice delayed is not justice denied, he decided. The explosion provided him with the inspiration for eliminating his enemies. Taking his cue from the tribunal that had condemned the enemies of the French Revolution, he had summarily convicted them. And like traitors, the three he had executed so far had all deserved their fates.

He took a moment to imagine them once again in the one period in history he could relate to, eighteenth-century France after the storming of the Bastille. His own great-great-grandfather had been white, a Frenchman, who left his pure black wife to return to France to fight in the revolution for freedom. It consoled him and tranquilized him to drag his victims back in time, to that setting, in that era, where he could picture them led into the courtyard one by one, kneeling at the stone, laying their heads in the groove under the blade of the raised guillotine. First Oxley, then Baumgarten, then Frossard. The blade fell with a thwump! Their heads rolled to the ground. Blood flowed in rivulets on the pavement.

"*Rivers of blood*," he said, closing his eyes. He rolled the syllables on his tongue, luxuriating in the violent vengeance of his imagery.

• • •

Nilda had always known that Jesus used her as a crutch when he was forced to shop for groceries. She suspected that he needed glasses or that there was something strange about his vision. She heard that sometimes kids saw letters wrong or sideways, and she knew Jesus would never wear glasses. Every year the homeroom teachers checked vision with an eye chart on Health Day, but of course she knew kids in every class who memorized the chart, even backwards when they wanted to pass the test.

She remembered how, when she lived down the block, before her family moved to East Harlem across the park, she and Jesus would go shopping together, and he would take money from the coffee can Esperanza left in the kitchen for them to get food, mostly essentials like milk and juice and breakfast cereal. Then it was fun, an adventure together. But now something bad always happened.

Sure it was exciting to steal. She got a kick out of it too. But sometimes she felt that Jesus pushed it, that they were always on the edge of getting caught, that he was stealing for more than the thrill, for more than the money or the satisfaction of getting over on the store managers. But she couldn't refuse. At the same time that she felt afraid, she felt sorry for him. She still saw the six-year-old who went to the supermarket with her, playing house and laughing, even though he looked almost like a grown man now because he was getting tall and trying to grow a mustache.

Nilda saw how agitated Jesus had been all day. This morning his mother had gone to the clinic because of the pain and because she was losing weight. She had stopped eating. He didn't tell her, but Nilda knew that Jesus wanted to fill the house with food. She would go with him and try to get it over with quickly.

Jesus remembered when Esperanza still cooked meals for him, when the odor of *sofrita,* his favorite spicy dish of bacon, ham, and beans cooked in tomato, garlic, and onions, came from the kitchen. Maybe Nilda would help him make it for her if they shopped for the ingredients.

Nilda helped him at the supermarket when Esperanza forgot to shop, which was often, when he was still a kid. He remembered only too well how sometimes he was hungry because there was no food left in the refrigerator and how he could barely stretch up to the kitchen shelf to reach the can where she would leave the coins to buy some bread.

He had learned to memorize the labels on the boxes and cans in the market for when he shopped alone. Breakfast cereal was easy; the pictures on the boxes told you what was inside. But when the colors or the designs on the cans were changed, he would find that he had bought the wrong thing, or else it was a brand that tasted different.

It took him a long time to get used to Sloan's changing around the locations of products he wanted when the store was remodeled, and for months every time he shopped his frustrations would seethe in his chest.

He remembered the stunned look on Nilda's face once in the Gap, when he mixed up the labels of Levi's with Jordache—not even close. But somehow she never caught on that he couldn't read. Today he needed her help badly. He hoped he wouldn't make a mistake again and have to smash the cart into the freezer because he couldn't stop the charge of anger he had to have to hide his shame.

● · ●

No one had ever discovered his identity. In a sense, neither had he. Now when he decided to strike, he had the weight of history behind him, the moral justification of an enlightened society.

How he had laughed when the police reported on TV that "There is no apparent connection between Grace Frossard's death and the death of Barbara Baumgarten." He remembered the words exactly. He had an excellent memory.

The morons! There were *three* murders. It angered him that they were so stupid, that they hadn't even recognized the fact that he had put three of them to death. Not two! He supposed he should be grateful. Their ignorance gave him the freedom to carry out the next execution.

● · ●

Julie had dialed the psychiatric hospital where she remembered Dr. Wolfson had treated Les. She pictured the hospital, high on the jutting cliffs with a commanding view of the river, as she waited for the switchboard operator to return.

The hospital was located in the old neighborhood in Washington Heights where she had spent her childhood, where she felt at home. But she remembered the feeling of alienation and mystery she had experienced as a child whenever she passed the tall beige building with its Victorian, mesh, open-air pavilions way at the top that reminded her of cages. On warm days on the rare occasions when she found herself in that neck of the woods, walking by with her friends, she would look up at the patients in their pajamas and confused thoughts of dread would creep up on her. She would turn away, embarrassed to be staring, but her mother's description had added to the fearful image. "Insane asylum," she had called it.

"Doctor Wolfson's still on vacation," the young woman informed Julie.

Julie was relieved. She felt the same sense of awkwardness, of prying, she'd felt as a child. She had no right to ask Dr. Wolfson to invade his patient's privacy. But she had no choice; she would risk his wrath and her discomfort. The urgency of her concerns overshadowed etiquette.

"When will he be back?" asked Julie.

"Not until January fifteenth, it says here. Do you want to leave a message?"

Julie considered for a moment. "Can you tell me where Doctor Wolfson's office is located?" she asked.

"Speyser Pavilion, 1053B," the voice responded after a rustle of pages.

"I'll call back again," announced Julie without leaving her name. Why tip my hand? she thought. She had two weeks to think, and the perfect solution was beginning to dawn on her.

• • •

His favorite reverie was remembering how he had tracked his first victim, then murdered him.

Sy Oxley was so ordinary-looking he was hard to pick out in a crowd, especially in the New York City subway. But he kept Oxley in view even through the throngs at rush hour because he knew him so well. Oxley was just slightly taller than average, so he looked for the graying Afro above the crowd as Oxley moved, as his teacher did every evening on the way home from his after-school job, toward the edge of the platform to wait for the train. Everyone ignored the dirty yellow danger line that was painted six inches from the edge. There was no avoiding it with people pushing behind you.

Oxley was ordinary in almost every way, in his height, his weight. Even his brown skin was ordinary, medium brown. His face had pleasant, totally even features; light brown expressive eyes; even, large, but not too large, rather white teeth. Maybe that was why Oxley was so quiet and undemanding, he suddenly thought, watching him being carried in the swelling mob. Maybe Oxley recognized that no one would pay attention to him whatever he did. He always seemed resigned but not depressed. He was a patient man.

Oxley always carried an unobtrusive brown briefcase and a wrinkled *Times*, like today. It was sweltering, but his tie was fully knotted and his suit hung neatly on his squarish body. There was a train delay due to a fire in a nearby station, and, eyeing Oxley, he was aware that people around him were restless, angry. They had been sharing the same steamy space for nearly half an hour, waiting. The crowds were always uncomfortable, standing pressed together in the heat, but today they were becoming mean, ugly, ill-tempered. What choice did he have but to wait?

Oxley was right in his sights as he maneuvered himself just behind him. The mood fit perfectly into his plans. The pushing, shoving crowd was just what he needed, he thought. He stood directly behind Oxley, like a leech on his back, never separating from him no matter how insistently the ranks behind him pushed. At last he heard the distant roar of the train, and he elbowed anyone who tried to come between them with his slight but strong body, finding most gave way to the resistance. When the light shone through the tunnel and the signal sounded, he could feel the crowd gearing up for the onslaught, flexing itself toward the oncoming train.

The cars, almost full, rattled to a halt, and the first phalanx crammed through the open doors. *He* would have shoved himself on and squeezed in, had he been in Oxley's place, but the doors closed, leaving Oxley to stand dumbly in line with the troops in the front row, watching the train depart.

Newcomers closed ranks on them, and before he knew it he heard the blast of a horn and the roar of the next train as it descended on the station. He would have to think fast.

He could feel the eyes of the people around him. They were determined to board this time, focusing ahead of them, fixating on their goal. The heat was intolerable, suffocating. The fumes that wafted from the station fire mixed bitterly in his saliva. He almost lost his balance, the people behind him were pushing so hard in anticipation. He couldn't use his hands, and he had one second. He gave Oxley a terrible blow to the calf muscle, the gastrocnemius, with the hard point of his shoe. Oxley flopped right over like a doll in front of the train as it rolled over him in a flash, coming to an ear-shattering, shrieking halt halfway down the platform.

Looking up from the tracks as Oxley hit, he caught sight of the motorman going by. And he knew from his eyes and from the expression on the poor fucker's face that the man would never forget the sight of Oxley going over just as he was pulling into the platform, of Oxley dying under his speeding wheels, just knowing there was no way he could stop the train from grinding him to bits.

Timing! What timing! People were screaming, shouting. Someone fainted, and that was also in his favor. In the confusion all he had to do was walk away.

16

When the phone rang, Martha set the timer for five minutes and began pedaling.

"I'm sorry I bothered you with my problems the other night," Julie apologized.

"Don't be silly," Martha said.

"Greg was so furious when he came home to an empty house. And I was so angry that he imagined I would be waiting at home. Then when he stormed out and slammed the door without a word. . . ."

"Are you okay?" Martha asked.

"You were right. He doesn't trust me because of my secrets. But he came right back, and we made up!" Julie laughed.

"Aha!" Martha said, pedaling faster, wondering what else Julie had up her sleeve.

"You sound out of breath," Julie remarked.

"I've allowed myself five minutes to talk," Martha said. "I'm pedaling at twenty miles per hour on my exercise bike."

"That's putting gossip to good use."

"Since we stopped playing tennis, I've gained weight. When I was a kid, I was such a bean pole that it's hard for me to realize I have to watch it now. Remember reading for hours and stuffing yourself?"

"What did you read as a kid?" asked Julie. "Heavy tomes?"

Martha laughed. "Are you kidding? More like *Gone with the Wind* and *Little Women*."

"In junior high I read Freud, Ellery Queen, and *God's Little Acre*."

"With the risqué passages underlined, of course."

"Of course. Today those lines wouldn't raise an eyebrow. As a matter of fact, this afternoon the librarian read a book to my teenaged class, and there was a passage about a boy masturbating."

"Did they riot?"

"There wasn't a sound. I wouldn't have the guts to read it aloud. Which brings me to the point of my call."

"Are we going to describe how we lost our virginity now?

"How much more time do you have on your clock?"

"Two minutes," Martha said between breaths, giggling.

"We'll have to save that for later."

"What's up?" asked Martha, tiring.

"Let's meet for a drink—of Perrier," suggested Julie, sounding serious. "Can it be this week? I'm going to ask you to do something . . ." She hesitated.

"Hurry up. Time is running out," Martha said.

"I want you to help me do something illegal," Julie said just as she heard the timer ping.

• • •

Even after the class settled down, Julie found it hard to concentrate on the lesson. After the girls had crowded around her to exchange stories about their baby brothers and sisters, waving photos at her, they quizzed her about her family. "What's your husband's name? What does he do?" they asked, falling in love with her life. Jesus had hung back from the circle, listening. "Greg's a lawyer," she told them, causing a second's silence, of admiration. Jesus had pricked up his ears and was watching her, staring at her dress, which hung loosely about her. It was her first maternity dress and could have been mistaken for designer fashion.

Then Jesus, as if he had been waiting for ages for the opportunity, stuck his hand through the circle of kids, just as the late bell rang and they headed for their seats. He had pulled a Polaroid shot from his back pocket and thrust it at her. She contemplated the picture of Jesus standing awkwardly between his cheerful parents and his wholesome sisters before their

Christmas tree, as her students read their assignments. His cap was off, his hair combed, but his expression was as contorted as ever. He was looking elsewhere, not at the camera. And his convoluted thoughts were almost visualized in the photo.

But a commotion interrupted her examination of Jesus's family, and she dropped the picture on her desk. She heard shocked murmurs as the kids watched in awe because Karl Luscz, without any warning, attacked James Little, a quiet, enigmatic boy whom Julie didn't know too well. Usually during fights her students jumped to cheer, but today they were fixed in their seats.

James sat passively in his chair as Karl got up, walked over to him, and began pounding his head with his fists. Like a prizefighter—bam, bam, bam—he hit James in rapid punches to the temple, with determined blows. James averted his head to protect his face and put his hands to his ears, but he stoically and resignedly took it.

"Stop it!" Julie screamed at Karl, moving toward him. She had never seen anyone punch like that outside a ring. She had seen kids tear at each other in rages; she had seen blood. Even the girls rolled on the ground, their clothes ripped off, their breasts exposed in the heat of the fray, but she had never seen this kind of deliberate, dispassionate harm to an immobilized victim.

She was afraid the poor child's brain would be damaged, the blows were so heavy. But she couldn't intervene; she could only beg them to stop. Karl was six feet tall and powerful. No one ever messed with Karl. She was beginning to believe he was mentally ill.

"Help, please do something," she pleaded. But the class was silent, mesmerized by the event, by the extraordinary sense of seeing a slice of evil. "Send for Dixon," she yelled to Carmelo. "Please," she begged again. She was now convinced that James would be damaged. She imagined his mother in the hospital, her son in a coma.

"Do something!" she shouted, edging closer, risking coming between the blows. Only Jesus stood up. He yanked Karl, who was still leaning over James, methodically beating him.

Jesus broke the spell, interrupting the repetitive thud he actually heard, realizing Karl would continue relentlessly until James fell unconscious.

"Come on, man, yer gonna kill 'im," he said to Karl. He chose his tone to convey friendly, nonthreatening intervention, acknowledging Karl's victory. Deferring to him, he was still Karl's equal.

Jesus dragged James by the arm to wash up, seizing the moment of decision Karl had given him, making further anger anticlimactic. Karl stood up tall, looked Julie in the eye without expression, and slowly strode out of the room. Julie's heart clenched when he looked at her. She was afraid he would hit her.

After he left, Julie and her students, now comrades in the trenches, relaxed. Jesus, for once, was the hero.

Karl never returned. And after that, Julie had order in her class. When she spoke, there was immediate attention. She never had to raise her voice a decibel. Because of Jesus, her word was law.

• • •

Nilda passed Jesus the container of Coke laced with rum and reached into the paper bucket of popcorn. She couldn't concentrate on the vigilante movie blinking and flashing on the screen, and the Dolby stereo was an ocean of noise on her eardrums. The pot smoke was so pungent in the theater you didn't need a joint, but Jesus was happily smoking anyway.

She leaned over to take the cigarette. Might as well get high; everything went wrong today, she thought, and she stepped into a sticky spill underfoot. She grimaced and realized that Jesus was no longer predictable. Today she had told him his teacher was pregnant, and he didn't get upset at all. He just took the picture of his cousins and his aunt and uncle from his pocket and told her that he had passed them off to the teacher as his sisters and his parents.

"This will keep her quiet," he explained nonchalantly. "She won't ask me no questions no more 'bout my family." But Nilda knew giving her the picture was important, that he was involved in something deeper than he could admit, and she felt with foreboding that, whatever it was, it would take him away from her.

• • •

Julie pulled the eraser across the Hobbes quotation she had written hastily on the board during an impromptu lesson, raising the fine chalk dust, noting that James was absent. Jesus had sat in the back of the room, his eyes fixed on her during the entire lesson, mesmerized but not saying a word.

Before the lesson, Julie had chalked on the board the announcement of the citywide exam. She had felt like a monster doing it, because as soon as the words appeared three girls jabbed their thumbs in their mouths and began rocking. But she had no choice; it was a mandated test.

The assistant principal, Julie realized, would have hated her lesson. It hadn't followed any of the rules. Still, the gang of children flocking around her desk attested to its success. She had started out reading an article from the *Times* about blind people attending a circus, intending to ask the class to describe the circus to the audience, but she never got past her first question.

Nancy, a heavyset, solemn girl who rarely spoke, described how an elderly blind man selling scarves on the street near the school had his table overturned and his wares stolen.

"Did you lift anything?" asked Francisco.

"I *helped* him," Nancy protested.

"Yeah, yeah," said Francisco.

"I only took one," admitted Nancy.

"That's rotten," said Akisha.

"Everyone else grabbed as much as they could and ran," said Nancy.

"What would you have done?" Julie asked the class.

There was chaotic debate, but no one volunteered an answer.

"It's survival," explained Carmelo. "They ripped him because you gotta look out for yourself."

Julie wrote the Hobbesian view of man in the middle of the board. "People live in continual fear of violent death. And the life of man is solitary, poor, nasty, brutish and short."

"Do you believe the philosopher, Hobbes, who said this, is correct?" asked Julie.

"I'd steal if I knew I could get away with it," admitted Francisco. The class laughed.

"It's wrong to steal," said Akisha.

"Why didn't Nancy take as many scarves as she could?" asked Julie.

"Chicken," yelled Carmelo.

"Dumb," said Lucy, Nancy's friend, who was sitting next to her. Nancy gave her a poke.

"I felt sorry for him," said Nancy. "A blind man . . ."

Julie wrote *empathy* and *guilt* on the board. "When do you feel guilt?" she asked.

"Nancy felt guilty about ripping this guy off," said Crystal.

"Why don't some people feel guilt or know right from wrong?"

"Upbringing," said Angela. "Their mothers don't teach 'em nothin'."

"A famous philosopher once said that you should guide your actions as if there were a law that everyone else in the world would have to act the way you did," ventured Julie.

"You mean if I steal everyone steals?" asked Carmelo.

"Yes, imagine that! What would the world be like?" Julie asked.

"Fucked up," blurted out Francisco, and the class laughed. But Julie was saved by the first bell.

Jesus, she noted, headed straight for the door, but the girls crowded around her.

"How many kids do you have?" asked Nancy.

"I . . . I . . . don't have any . . ."

"You couldn't have no kids before?" asked Angela.

Julie felt tears come to her eyes.

"She has a career, stupid," said Crystal.

"Maybe she don't want a lotta kids," said Angela, who was one of six.

"Yeah, like your mother," said Akisha.

"Your mother!" said Angela.

"Don't get up in my face . . ." Akisha threatened.

"Akisha, Angela," Julie said.

"How come you're only havin' one? You don't like babies?" persisted Nancy.

"None o' your business," said Akisha. "That's private."

"Miss Keating don't have no kids," said Crystal.

"She isn't married," said Julie without thinking.

There was silence for a second. "You don't need to be married to have a baby," explained Akisha.

"Of course," said Julie. "Some women choose not to have children or wait until they're ready, 'til they finish school . . ." She realized that she had lost their interest, and when the change bell rang she tucked that discussion away for another time. In a year or two many of them would be mothers. It would make good material for a composition. The topic was pregnant with possibilities, she thought, smirking.

• • •

"To think," said Julie in spite of the hour, her hands on her chin. "I had doubts about this man before we were married, I thought he was too distant!" She contemplated the half-eaten carrot cake on Martha's slate coffee table.

Martha groaned. She was spread out on the couch, her head on the soft throw pillow, looking up at the ceiling. Julie was on a high about Greg, and Martha couldn't stop her.

"I'm too tired to object to your sudden enthusiasm. All of this exercising has done me in. Say, what's the cause of this sudden appreciation for your husband Julie? I can't keep up with you."

"He pays attention to my needs; he takes care of me. He even admires my need to take up causes."

Martha sat up and stared at her. "Okay, Julie, let's end this chit-chat and get to the real point of this meeting. What's this all about?"

"We're going to break into Wolfson's office," Julie said.

• • •

It was too bad about Oxley. He didn't like to kill blacks. But sometimes a pawn had to be sacrificed by the Friend of the People, as Robespierre had done.

He would like to kill her as Charlotte Corday had killed

Marat—surprise her in her bath and stab her to death, watch her blood filling the tub, watch her slipping under, naked, unprotected, swimming in her own blood. A bloodbath! It would be poetic justice. But foolhardy.

Robespierre had taken risks. Was she worth the risk? Was seeing her blood spilling, watching her die, worth the danger? His heart raced in anticipation; his blood pressure rose. He caught sight of his face in the mirror. His cocoa-colored skin burned with the thrill of fear, fevered by the throb of joy.

17

"Is this Ernesto . . . ah—Camacho?"

"This is Julie Greenwood." Martha listened nervously to Julie's end of the conversation. "Thank goodness you're in," Julie lied, knowing exactly what his hours were.

Martha smiled, leaning against the open door of the phone booth in the dark corner of the hospital lobby. The last stream of the staff—doctors, nurses, and teachers—had left for the weekend, leaving only a skeleton crew. Julie had counted on this exodus in order to go unnoticed on the floor where Wolfson's office was located. She had staked it out the previous Friday; by 4:30 most workers abandoned the hospital and the offices were dark.

The third floor consisted mostly of nursing staff offices. Wolfson's was the only private office, and it, fortunately, was at the end of the T, off the main hallway. At the other end of the T was an unmarked door behind which were tiny cubicles used by various women who wandered in and out on an irregular basis. When she had peeked in on her last visit, Julie had discovered that the women were nursing supervisors. They made quick phone calls, stored their paperwork, and spent little time at their desks. Julie hoped that the anonymity of the large hospital would protect them when they carried out her brilliant plan to break in.

By 4:30, Julie remembered, the occasional door closing, the measured footfall, the clang of the elevator gate, or a distant voice were the only interruptions in the lifelessness of the windowless floor. The lobby was no better. She was grateful for Martha's presence even though the mental patients were locked away, silent and invisible.

"I need your help," she pleaded with the young locksmith. "I'm in a very tough spot. I locked my keys in the office, and I've got to get in. I'm meeting my husband at the airport, and I've got to get his papers and my luggage—in less than two hours!" Julie tried hard to imagine how helpless she would feel if the story were true. Her voice grew desperate. She didn't dare to look at Martha.

Martha put her ear closer to the receiver. "No problem. I can be there," Camacho responded. "Where are you?"

"I'm in Washington Heights. I know it's far, but I'm willing to pay for your time. You did such a good job on my house on East Ninety-Second Street. Remember?"

"Sure thing. It'll be a hundred dollars plus extra for a tough lock. Okay?"

"I feel like such a jerk," Julie said.

"Don't worry, you'll make your plane. It happens to everyone. I get at least one call a week like yours. And on holidays! I'm out all day." Julie slumped in her seat in relief.

"What if someone sees us?" asked Martha when they reached the third floor.

"I'm Wolfson's wife," said Julie with bravado as they paced the marble hexagons, waiting for the elevator to bring them their unsuspecting burglar.

• • •

Jesus knew he should head for home. The sky was darkening, he heard the boom of distant thunder, and the teenaged lovers had vacated the park benches. Mothers were hustling their children home, and the drizzle was plopping lightly on the sand in the playground. But he remained seated on the wooden slats.

A shaft of light caught a drop as it hung illuminated on the metal rail, and the colors of the rainbow in pale miniature dazzled in the drop for an instant before it fell.

A sweet memory filled him and fled. He tried to capture its essence before it was lost. It was her, Julie. Today she had glowed like the raindrop. Her skin was so smooth, so pink. Her eyes were shiny and clear. An added blush flushed her face from a vacation in the sun. Even her short hair, glossy and sculptured, shone, always perfect, sailing around her neck with every movement of her head.

He could see into her life. She was free of worldly worry, free of daily care. It was a life filled with luxury, with the ease of the rich. And it was her ring, the emerald ring she always wore, that was her symbol, that seemed to represent her essence and connected her to the rain, to his random thoughts. The emerald was her. Other teachers wore diamond engagement rings, but her jewel was different. It was like part of the rainbow, expressing her, the variegated vibrance like the changing flow of the distant waves in the Caribbean, undulating from blue green to sea green, to purple, and finally melting into the color of a plum. When he looked into her eyes, which he had taken to doing when she wasn't aware, a memory beckoned. Perhaps it was only the colors of the ocean from his childhood in Puerto Rico. Perhaps he was mixing her up with pleasant sensations, dimly recollected impressions, reminiscences of infancy, mythical memories that he had heard reached back into the womb.

At home he smoothed the limp homework sheet he had unfolded from his pocket. It was a questionnaire the shop teacher, Arnie Davis, had prepared, explaining that he had assigned it only because the department chairman had demanded it. He hardly expected it back from Jesus. Wet ink caused the letters to run crookedly on the damp paper, but Jesus was able to mentally enunciate the syllables of the longer words and managed to identify the shorter ones from memory.

He took his time, lingering on the pleasure of seeing the letters come to life, remembering how the first word he had read outside of the reading room spelled itself out to him from the supermarket shelf so that he was hardly able to contain himself, feeling elation like Edison, the inventor. C O R N F L A K E S. The letters blended immediately on the box. He had almost shouted it to Nilda.

Jesus took his ballpoint and slowly and carefully filled in the blanks, remembering how he had learned to stuff things from Woolworth's and the supermarket into his coat because it was better than asking for credit at the *bodega*. Taking things gave him a sense of independence, of control over his life.

He was tempted to list it in the blank line under the heading, "Career Education" on the line labeled "Skills Learned in Everyday Life." He almost laughed aloud at the thought of the teacher reading it, along with sewing, cooking, and baby-sitting, when the lists were handed in.

He painstakingly wrote it in. "Stealing," he penned on the line, remembering with pride to put the *a* after the *e* instead of doubling it the way it sounded.

Every time he read something he remembered her. Whether it was a word or a phrase, in the supermarket, on the subway, in a headline, or one day it would be an entire book, throughout his entire lifetime, he knew she would be beside him. It was a gift from her, something of hers he would have forever.

But it wasn't enough. Because the words, the connection, the association only served to hound him, to pursue him. From the second he opened his eyes in the mornings to the nights he lay in bed trying to sleep, he couldn't rid himself of the stamp of her face on his memory. And now on his dreams.

• • •

Camacho, using his tools, picked the lock with ease. He was flanked by Julie in her mink and Martha with her Saks shopping bags. The only man to pass through the hallway peered into the corner where they were huddled, took in the obvious situation, and, apparently satisfied, continued on to the elevator without missing a step.

"It's one of the advantages of looking like respectable middle-aged women," remarked Martha after Julie pressed the hundred dollars on her unwitting accomplice. They entered the unfamiliar office as soon as he was gone.

It was a sorry sight. Suddenly Julie knew what Les had gone through in the two years before he left for California. The office was bare except for a metal desk, the wooden swivel chair behind it, and the greenish, plastic seat in front of it; a huge file cabinet, a metal rack with a black umbrella, two hangers dangling sorrowfully, and a brown metal wastepaper basket completed the scene.

"Who's his decorator?" asked Martha. "The Grim Reaper?"

Julie locked the door and pulled the cords that opened the slats of the metal blinds to capture the remaining light. Beams of headlights and the red taillights of commuter cars crammed the cross streets, beginning the rush hour to and from the West Side Highway.

The desk was totally clear. Martha's heart accelerated as Julie opened the file cabinet. In the top drawer her fingers found "Les Layton" among the alphabetized folders. She placed it on the desk and yanked out the next drawer. The divider was pushed way back, and Julie saw audiotapes piled in narrow shoe boxes next to a recording machine. She had struck gold. There were five tapes labeled with Les's name.

She sat opposite Martha in the twilight-darkened room, plugged in the machine, and popped tape number one in.

"Do you mind the tape?" It was Wolfson's voice.

"I'm used to being recorded. I'm a celebrity. Remember, Doc?" It was Les. Julie's heart sank. She felt instant remorse. She was listening to his diary, an inexcusable transgression. She lowered the sound guiltily.

"My record, *Moods,* is a CD now," Les said, trying to sound conversational, as if he were putting the doctor at ease.

"Of course," replied Wolfson.

"Now, tell me about . . . what you did with your baby. How did you do it?"

Julie's heart skipped a beat.

"I left the door open!"

"Did you know the kidnapper?"

"No! No! I left the door open to get my drugs."

"Did you . . . take the baby?" Wolfson sounded confused.

"Of course not!" Les sounded shocked. "I left the door unlocked and came back to get my drugs in the back room, where I hid them behind the drums. I did it all the time, while Julie was busy with the baby at the other end of the apartment.

I left her and the baby exposed. In a place like New York, where a junkie will kill for a few bucks, I left the door open so I could sneak back for drugs. And my baby was kidnapped!"

"Is that why you feel guilty? Like a murderer?"

There was a long silence.

"Maybe I left the door open because subconsciously I was hoping something bad would happen. I couldn't cope with the responsibility of the baby. I went back on drugs." Les's voice was a whisper. "I've been living with that."

"Did you consciously want to harm your son?"

"Never! Never! I've been tortured by my mistake. Blaming myself, keeping it a secret."

"Maybe it's time to tell Julie. She might forgive you."

There was a thump. Julie imagined Les's face in his hands on the desk as he spoke. "I can't," he cried.

There was a scraping of chairs. Julie hoped that Wolfson was leaning toward Les, putting his hand over Les's clenched fingers, over the white knuckles she had seen stretched taut so many times. Then she heard Wolfson's consoling voice.

"Freud said, 'Sometimes a cigar is only a cigar.' Your only crime was leaving the door open for drugs."

• • •

Julie felt as if she had just recovered from a protracted illness. She was shaky and weak, depleted, as if her body were hurting from the ravages of an invasion by enemy microbes. Was Wolfson correct? Would she forgive Les? The drugs explained everything—and nothing. At least Les was innocent.

She threw her clothes off in her bedroom, wrapped herself in Greg's heavy bathrobe, and sipped the spiced tea she had made for herself in the kitchen. She had no energy left to build a fire in the living room. Her body ached, her temples were taut, on the verge of crashing pain.

She lowered the lights with the dimmer and ran the water for the tub, not daring to put any of the foreign substances she had used before she was pregnant into the water. After placing scented raspberry candles around the tub, she turned out the light in the bathroom and tuned the radio to WNCN. The very act of fussing with her bath, an old habit she used to unfocus from the prey of memory, relaxed her.

Oh, thank God, she thought with a sigh, Scarlatti sonatas, played by Rubinstein. She wouldn't have to hunt for a tape. The gods were with her. She dropped the robe on the carpet and slipped into the tub, heavily into the clear, warm water that caressed her like her mother's fingers.

Her tension seemed to evaporate with the rise of the heat waves off the surface of the water in the white tub. She closed her eyes in the flickering darkness, the candles beginning to emit their berry scent. Cradled by the soothing water, she felt the smooth, round bulb of her belly and looked at her full breasts, the round, brown nipples enlarged. Her fear about her baby momentarily abated.

For a few seconds she drifted off to sleep. She wavered in and out of consciousness. Oh, peaceful dark. This respite would renew her. She would sleep—only for a minute.

The house kept silent. All was silence.

18

The mirrors, clouded over with steam, barely reflected the dull light of the candles in the old-fashioned bathroom. The walls were covered with dark, tongue-in-groove wood, and the floor retained the original black-and-white tiles of the 1900s. The pale, transparent, and delicately etched glass window was oval like a ship's porthole, and the bathtub with its wonderful claw feet, where Julie dozed fitfully, was set high up off the floor.

She awoke with a start. Tiny beads of perspiration emerged on her neck, and she heard her heartbeat. She looked through the window at the half-moon cutting a shaft of cold light through the glass.

"Where is my baby?" she cried silently to the sky, where she could faintly detect dead stars still twinkling their spent lives, emitting rays light-years away through the universe. She put her hands on the hard, taut bulge of her belly. Fear plucked at her abdomen. She could feel the fear with the tips of her fingers. She paused her breath. The silence seemed to be listening.

Was that a sound outside? Greg was gone, and she hadn't waited for him to come home before stepping into her bath. The ritual of bathing was so sensual they often made love when she stepped out, the drops of water still clinging to her oiled and scented body when Greg embraced her. But she couldn't wait.

The doctor *was* right. He had warned her about hot baths. She was dizzy from the heat, too limp to rise from the tub. She hadn't realized how hot the water was. She pushed the bathroom door open a crack and heard the light tread of footsteps on the bedroom carpet, and memories of the past, of her baby being snatched from his crib, choked her, her struggle to catch her breath feeding her panic.

"Greg!" she cried with all the sound her vocal cords could muster. A male figure filled the half-light in the doorway.

"Help me," she whispered. She stretched her arms toward him, and he took her hands and slowly helped her from the tub.

"What happened?" Greg asked, alarmed.

"The doctor warned me," she said, feeling heavy and cumbersome. She grabbed a towel and wrapped it around her. "I guess it was too much for me. I felt I was passing out."

"I could sponge your back," he offered.

"You can do that in bed. Without the sponge. It will make up for my small sacrifice," she suggested, spontaneously hugging him around the neck. Her towel fell off, and his starched shirt was dampened by her wet, glistening body. He put his arms around her and drew her tightly to him, her natural odor, the subtle scent of pregnancy detectable on her skin. He kissed her neck and shoulders again and again, suspecting that lurking beneath her usually subdued exterior some blithe spirit tied to earth was trying to fly away. He wondered whether his mind was playing tricks on him, because now he felt such love and desire for her, and he believed so keenly that she was utterly sincere.

Everything was going right, Julie thought, lying in bed next to Greg. His love fortified her. He put his hand on her belly to feel the baby stir, and when he kissed the round tight drum of her skin he felt movement with his lips.

"It's a miracle!" he whispered, brushing her ear as she fell contentedly asleep.

Julie skimmed along Park Avenue, gliding down the clean, smooth, macadamized street the way she had roller-skated in Washington Heights when she was a young girl. Only this was in her dreams. And she was on her way, slipping and sliding. Yes, she was swiftly reaching her goal, past the elegant buildings, past the uniformed doormen, but this time in straw shoes.

Julie awoke. She had arrived. But was she on such fragile

footing—on straw shoes? The straw man! Of course. It was Les exonerated. He had been the scapegoat for the kidnapping. And now she knew the truth. He was innocent.

It was Saturday. Julie delayed her morning. She scooted over into the place Greg had left in bed, recalling the second tape she and Martha had heard—the urgency in Wolfson's voice and Les's harrowing responses.

"You have got to meet her—face her. Tell her why you're here. No more skulking around secretly. You have to be open and honest with her."

"She doesn't want to have anything to do with me. I'm part of a life she wants to bury. I've caused her enough grief."

"Are you still obsessing about your guilt?"

"She devoted her heart and soul to me, put up with my moods, my depressions, my erratic behavior. And when it was her turn to be happy, to have the baby she'd always wanted, I left the door open for the kidnapper. Yes, I feel responsible," he said bitterly.

"I've been so crazed I even imagined I harmed my own baby or wanted him harmed," Les said. "Junkies have been known to do horrible things and not remember."

"Tell me again why you left the door open."

"You know why I did it, Doc."

"Of course. Tell me again."

"Because I needed the drugs I stashed in the maid's room behind the drums."

"You're guilty for leaving the door open. If you had known what would happen, would you have done it?"

"You know the answer to that, too. I would never hurt Julie or the baby."

"So you *needed* the drugs. Did you take them?"

"No. I didn't have the chance.

"Why did you grab Julie?"

"I heard her scream and scream—sounds I had never heard from a human throat. Such naked screams of shock . . . and terror. I was afraid to see what she had seen. I grabbed her throat to stop her. Those sounds made me crack. They pierced me—they cracked me open. My fingers were ice cold. Julie looked at my face—she crumpled in my hands. It's all my fault! Everything. I'm guilty!"

Julie felt that Wolfson had been too generous in his assessment of her. Was she so forgiving? Drugs finally explained Les's strange behavior and the two-year lapse in his career. But he had nothing to do with the kidnapping. She had been right to trust her instincts, to protect him when the police abused him, to recall their marriage with sorrow rather than with anger or fear. He was the father of her baby. If she had abandoned him, he would have been totally alone; he wouldn't have had a chance for recovery. In bearing his burden of guilt, he had been punished enough. She couldn't condemn him. He had to live with himself.

Les had been a tortured man during their marriage, and now his confession had relieved some of her own guilt: it was drugs that had undermined their marriage, not anything she had done.

But then the realization that the kidnapper had been lying in wait, that one day it might have been she, not Les, who had slipped up and left the door unlocked, took her out of bed.

One night they fought, the next night they made love, Greg thought. Some nights they did both. Their life together lately was like a bottle on a wave. The crests they had always taken for granted. Now the troughs began to consume him. Instability frightened him.

Greg concentrated on one of those late-night talks with Julie as the cab skirted traffic in midtown. Some pillow talk, he thought. But he had expressed some of the feelings he had been harboring.

"I feel you are excluding me from a part of you," he had revealed to her. "As if I were a stranger, sometimes." It was a difficult admission. But her sudden happiness, the look of peace on her face, their ecstasy over her pregnancy allowed him to say it.

"As a matter of fact," he had continued, "sometimes I see a

side of you that I think I don't know at all."

She had tried to laugh it off, not wanting to spoil the closeness they felt. "One day I'll reveal all of my deep, dark secrets," she had said. And then from out of the blue he had remarked, "Maybe we all have something to hide, a Mister Hyde behind the Doctor Jekyll we show the world. Only some of us keep him in check better than others."

• • •

The winters were cruel in those years. On February 1st, almost eighteen years ago, a blizzard closed the schools, and the infamous hearing was postponed until the following day. His mother had arranged to take off work on the day of the blizzard, and she couldn't be spared a second day.

They were all seated at the rectangular oak table in the principal's office, he recalled, the image as vivid as the hour it happened. There was the principal, Oxley, Baumgarten, Frossard, and *her*, the only one left before the grand finale.

He had overheard Bobbie as he waited outside the office, angry and fearful, wondering whether his mother would show up, torn between hoping that at the last minute she would show and give him some moral support and being happy she wouldn't be there to see his disgrace. He heard Bummy talk about the proceedings.

"I'm not comfortable with this. It's like a tribunal," she had complained. Everyone else had been silent. When it was all over, he had looked up the word. "The seat of a judge, a court, or forum of justice, something that decides or determines, an inquisition." He looked up *inquisition.* "A severe investigation for discovery and punishment conducted with no regard for individual rights."

Even *they* knew how wrong it was. They had hit on him, ganged up on him, with no one there to defend him. After that, things got bad. It was the beginning of the end of his life.

But he had learned some things. Everyone in prison thought he was a pussycat. He had learned to put on a mask, to "defer gratification," as his bullshit psychiatrist called it. He had learned how easy it was to get away with murder if he was patient enough, if he planned. Then everything would fall into place.

It was the third summer after the tribunal had condemned him that he had executed Oxley. The police, of course, thought that Oxley had gotten dizzy and fallen in front of the train, overcome by the heat, the tension. Several people had fainted that day in the sweltering station, and the fumes from the fire infused the air. Everything had conspired to assist him in that killing. Oxley had recently been diagnosed as having a heart condition, his wife, Tanya, had reported to the *Post*. He had saved the clipping. Her husband was only months away from retirement, she had cried. Tough luck, sucker, he had thought when he read the paper.

And then he had waited on Frossard. For years he was patient. He finally discovered she had transferred to an elementary school, which turned out to be closer to his home. It was fate again, making it more convenient for him to do his investigation. But she had fucked him up and gotten married one summer, and the change of name had worked to confuse him. He couldn't find her name on the mailboxes in the office. But he had done some homework. Ha-ha, he laughed. He never did no homework when he was in school. But this kind of homework he enjoyed. On Open School Day he followed her into the school and up to her room. Then he cross-checked the list given out to parents. Room 218, Ms. Frossard.

That incident and the one on the subway platform taught him to be crafty. He had learned not to let his emotions and his need for revenge, or for saving face, get him into trouble. He had decided wisely to forgo the satisfaction of knifing his next luscious victim at home in her bath. He could afford to delay. Before he had been easy pickings for the law. Now he was invincible.

• • •

Les walked down Broadway toward the Church of the Holy Name, where the priest who had held out no hope for him waited to hear his news. Les had just had a session with Wolfson. A very satisfying session. And now, with the serious winter chill gone from the air and an occasional suggestion of that tender touch of warmth that would bring the migrating birds, sometimes darkening patches of New York sky, he felt relieved, as if a weight had been lifted from his back, as if he had left some heavy baggage behind.

"I'm freed from a memory that has been oppressing me," he had told his shrink. He described the figure of the woman in the hallway that had emerged when Eleanore's hypnotherapy had succeeded in releasing it from his brain.

"I love Eleanore," he had announced to Wolfson. "She's rational, she's beautiful, she's a nurse. She's just what the doctor ordered," he had said with a laugh. "Fourteen years ago I escaped to California to start afresh, and I went through some stages. California is filled with freaks and gurus and channels and every answer to a neurotic's prayers. Fads and faith healers at every turn, and I managed to find Eleanore. But Julie was different; she was so free, so open. Sex just isn't the same with anyone else," he admitted.

Les recalled the disapproving look on Wolfson's face. "In what way?" he had inquired suspiciously.

"Sex with Eleanore is more gymnastic, a physical release. With Julie it was more enthralling, spontaneous, and fraught with feeling. I was transported to another plane. It was orgiastic. With Eleanore it's orgasmic."

"Could it be that you're older?" asked Wolfson. "I didn't know you were such a romantic."

"You mean it's that simple? If I had met Eleanore first, I would have had that special feeling with her? It's all hormonal?"

Wolfson had shrugged and given him an odd look, a bit of gleam in his eye. "All I'm saying is to take into account that you are a certain age now."

Why had this remark released him, just as Wolfson's previous words had released him from his obsessive guilt, helping him shed the layers that had burdened him? Accepting reality, the reality of losing Julie, was liberating. He now understood what the shrink was trying to tell him. Grow up! was his message. She's out of your life for good, and you're strong enough to take it. A mature man could cope with the fact that he might never see her again, that their relationship was over, that she was married, *wanted* to be married to another man.

Wolfson was preparing him for this eventuality. There was nothing to connect Les to Julie any longer if he didn't succeed in the quest to find his son. The irony of all of this, Les thought happily, was that conquering this problem had made him stronger. It made him even more capable of carrying on the search and of actually finding their lost little boy.

• • •

He remembered the first time Robespierre came out. Even he hadn't known it then. Who he was became clear only later on, as he took shape gradually, assuming the form and name of the great Friend of the People, champion of the social revolution. He was called "The Incorruptible" in France after the revolution because of his fanatical devotion to virtue.

He raised his foot on a chair across from the full-length mirror on his bedroom door and observed himself in his long-sleeved white silk blouse with the frills that wound around the neck and wrists and along the buttons down the center. His tight black pants were stuffed into his calf-high boots. He brandished his stiletto and raised his chin up, readying himself to address the Revolutionary Tribunal, thinking again about Oxley, the first fallen.

It was on account of him that he had been kicked out of school. It had happened in Oxley's room. And Oxley had been present at the hearing, never saying nothing. It was too bad too, he thought to himself, because Oxley was a good guy. Never gave me no trouble, he thought. He was quiet, never screamed or gave me no shit. But Robespierre, he didn't make no exceptions, and Oxley had voted against him. Justice was justice, and Oxley had to pay along with the rest.

When he and his boys knifed a punk in Oxley's shop because the kid had done him dirt, broken the code, Oxley had turned him in. But he was only fifteen, still a JD in those days, so he hadn't done hard time. But it was the *last* time, he laughed, that he would be interned in the Bastille.

19

It seemed to Les that his thoughts, rather than his feet, were carrying him down the streets to the church. He looked up at the Jazz Club on Ninety-Ninth Street and Broadway, where he had agreed to play for an old singer friend who was now its owner. El would be happy. She was definitely into the Protestant work ethic, and it had saved him. The work would justify his stay in New York to hunt for his child, and he could earn some extra bread. It would be good for his head, keep things in perspective. He was looking forward to planning an interesting program. El would say it was a healthy decision, that it would build his self-esteem.

The elegant, flamboyant shops he passed, with their outrageously expensive and theatrical clothing, were the fashion that Julie would have enjoyed in the old days. The exotic displays featured styles she would have worn back then if she had been able to afford them. Eleanore would consider them outlandish, and now Julie was an East Side type, wearing pricey, conformist clothing. She was truly hiding her identity, he thought, even from herself.

Les was reminded of Wolfson's remark that Julie's salvation was to forget the pain and Les's salvation was to remember his. Drugs were to forget. Now he was strong enough to remember. Wolfson had suggested that Les was stuck in time, that he, an avant-garde composer, a cool modern, a radical, couldn't accept growth and change.

But he had truly given Julie up! He thought of Eleanore

with pleasure, laughing at the fact that he was still attracted to women who loved causes. El was into her cancer spa, regaling him on the phone last night with her alternative lifestyle cures for cancer patients.

"Repressed emotions depress your immune system," she had told him with her customary zeal. "People who vent their negative emotions conquer adversity," she explained. He would express himself on the stage, he thought, with his music. That was his way. He passed a health food store and heard El's admonitions about coffee, tea, preservatives, and a host of no-nos he had begun to eliminate from his diet. Fresh fruit and organic veggies were beginning to make him feel downright wholesome. And suddenly, imagining Eleanore—her healthy white teeth, her even, sunny smile, her light, young voice—made him optimistic about his mission, happy about his life, and hopeful about impressing the priest with his information. And he mounted the steps of the church feeling he was headed in the right direction. He pulled out the cross and mentally hung it around the neck of the old, bent woman of his recollection. Armed with these, freed of guilt, and with the help of the priest, he would find his son.

The priest held the cross, stretching his memory back. An old, bent woman with the initials E.L. Who? Who?

"We have no record of her, even if she was involved in church programs," he reported to Les unhappily. "There's no one currently registered in this church with those initials, and I've checked out all the churches." He pounded his head with his fist. "There is something, something there. A woman with a baby."

Les's heart pounded. Better not get my hopes up, he thought. But he had a strong feeling. So did the priest. Les could see it in his face, in his body language. His whole being was trying to remember.

Then Les had another idea. The atmosphere of the church, the serene surroundings, the beauty of the wooden pews, the latticework on the confessional with its deep purple velvet draping the opening all gave him a feeling of hope. And the strong sense of connection to the past, to the truth, opened toward the memory of Willie English drinking wine on the street. Les had seen him leaning in doorways for twenty years. Who would know better about the street life, the subculture of the shadowy figures living on the fringe? Les left the church and bore down on Riverside Drive with such fervor that one would think his life depended on it.

Something about Les's description worried DiFalco. He stirred his memory to emit recollections from that year, the year he began. He remembered how grim and characterless the neighborhood had been, how his worshipers were Spanish-speaking then, rather than the predominantly Haitian flock he had now. This group, which had immigrated recently, spoke patois, a form of French. Of course there were still Puerto Ricans, Dominicans, and a smattering of Irish and Italians among his parishioners. He recalled a woman dressed in black, graying black hair pulled back in a dignified bun, no makeup, praying at the altar on her knees, with a lovely silver cross dangling from her rosary. No, she couldn't be the one. He would have to think on this, shake out his memory.

"I'll think some more," he had promised. "I'll try my best. You can count on me to help," he had assured Les. And Les had been encouraged, more by the look of interest in the priest's eyes than by his modest words.

• • •

Les nearly fell over a young man curled up on the sidewalk, he was so intent on finding Willie English, hoping he hadn't moved from his SRO, praying that the building hadn't been turned into a condo. He could remember Willie's menacing bark and the curses he uttered under his breath, which had always frightened Julie. If only that old wino, who fancied himself a gentleman and effected a courtly bow in his delirium, were here now. A policeman had passed on the myth to an unbelieving Julie that Willie had once been a famous actor. Let the old wino still be holding up his corner, braying and laughing at the air.

The homeless had replaced the crazies, Les realized as he

watched a grizzled beggar with a matted, dirty beard hold out a plastic cup toward him. The man's jacket was filthy, and his hands were blackened with soot. A middle-aged man on the border of respectability, stroking a kitten, was sitting on the sidewalk, his new home. Julie must be emptying her pockets, Les imagined. There were street people on every corner, and she was too softhearted to resist a plea for help.

He turned the corner where the crack dealer was counting out a wad of bills. Dirt ball! Scum bag! Les cursed him mentally, his ire rocketing. But he controlled his silent tirade, saving the adrenaline rush, which started running high, for the task ahead. Mellow out, he told himself. And no more of that moralistic crap. Wolfson had warned him not to go overboard in his condemnation. It was amazing to Les how totally unappealing drugs were to him now. There's nothing like a reformed addict, he thought. The junkies on the corner were more repugnant to him than ever, and he condemned his respectable user friends with more vehemence because there was no glamour, no allure, nothing positive attached to that world anymore. His total rejection of the habit made it despicable and dirty to him.

"Never trust a fanatic," Wolfson had said once to Les. "It's a toss of the coin as to which extreme will come up."

Les reached the building next to his old apartment house, the building in which Willie had lived. It was still an SRO. He slowed his pace and breathed with relief. The clientele had improved, he could see from the stream of Asians and assorted lower-middle-class types pouring in and out of the mirrored lobby, but it was still a cheapo hotel. The prostitutes and addicts had cleared out, but, he hoped, not old Willie English.

Les hung around in the lobby under the glitzy chandelier, thinking about the change in the neighborhood, how the yuppies had replaced the minorities, how the bottles had come flying out of the window of the hotel when he and Julie had lived next door. The elderly were robbed and terrorized in their own apartments then, and the police were often pelted with dangerous objects when they came to make a bust.

Then Les's heartbeat nearly got away from him. Sashaying past the doorway was none other than Willie English, his peaked Robin Hood hat replaced with a new chapeau. Les raced after him, watching him list and sway, the bottle in brown bag in hand, sporting a cowboy hat with deep creases, the brim pointed up and complementing his long, narrow face. His goatee and sideburns were neatly trimmed. He wore an orange kerchief, leather-looped, western-style, around his collar. And of course he had donned his leather boots. He was headed to his old post on the corner, where, in spite of his condition, he affected a dapper look in his own lunatic way.

When Les approached him, Willie waved wildly and began to mumble incoherently, rolling his eyes and cursing. "Remember me?" Les tried unsuccessfully. "I lived here fourteen years ago." Willie looked away and drank from his bottle.

"He growls only at women and children," Julie had complained to Les, explaining her aversion to Willie. "He's crazy like a fox," she added whenever Les had defended him.

Les took a ten-dollar bill from his wallet and held it out to Willie. It caught his eye. "Sure I remember you," he slurred, eyeing Les slyly. "I know you live over there in that building." He accepted the bill and carefully folded it into his shirt pocket. "Your wife used to pass me by with the baby buggy, and I would . . ." Willie made a low growling-animal sound. Then he cackled happily. "I think she was afraid of me," he lisped proudly.

Les took out the cross and showed it to Willie. "Have you ever seen this?" he asked.

"Yeah," said Willie immediately. Too quickly for Les.

"Do you know who owned it?" he asked warily.

"Yeah. I know. She wore it on a long chain."

Les believed him. Willie had plucked it from his memory as if it were yesterday. Les was suddenly hot in his coat, in spite of the wind on the corner.

"Who is she?" he asked, hearing his voice waver.

"She used to call me *Poco Loco* because I cursed her when she went by," Willie whispered, his hand to his mouth.

"What's her name?" Les asked, his voice faltering.

Willie shrugged.

"Do you know where she is now?"

Willie's eyes narrowed suspiciously. "Hey, you a cop, man?"

"No, bro. You know me. I play bass at J.C. You can check me out." Les pulled another ten spot and held it away from Willie. "Come on now, Willie. This will buy you a couple of drinks. Do you know where she lived?"

"Yup, but she done moved."

"When?" asked Les, the fear finally hitting him full force.

"As soon as she come back with the baby," he said, delicately withdrawing the bill from Les's fingers.

20

Zach Eisner was the only damn teacher who had made school interesting, he thought. Zach told stories about the French Revolution that made you feel you was there in the middle of what was happening. It wasn't just facts he taught. And he wasn't afraid to tell, for example, how the pamphleteers drew pictures of royalty nude and performing scandalously, as the teach put it, in bedrooms. He described how the illegal books banned by royalty were interwoven with the sheets of legal books, and he passed around a replica of the letter Bergeret of Bordeaux sent to a printer, instructing him to "marry" sheets of pornography to an edition of the New Testament. That Eisner knew what kids liked. Eisner had a way of teaching that made you put things together, such as the word *marry*.

He remembered the tale all the kids loved, of the governor being beheaded, and especially that his head was displayed on a pike. Another interesting point he made about the times was that universal suffrage meant men only, and that the woman who wrote *The Rights of Woman* was guillotined. But most of all, he remembered vividly the Reign of Terror and the storming of the Bastille, "the embodiment of despotism," Eisner called it. And because it was a revolution against arbitrary arrest, against crimes of the court, against tyranny of the innocent, the era encapsulated his dissatisfactions.

Then he lay in that institution after the plane crash. He went off the deep end because he was so stirred up by the symbolism in the fact that Mrs. Anna Marietta Fontana, ex-principal of Catherine Dunbar Junior High School, had met her maker conveniently up near heaven. Ha-ha! But it wasn't so funny looking at the four walls in that narrow white room, knowing his own mother had him put there herself.

But it was in that crummy shit hole that he continued his reading about the republic, about the call to popular insurrection. And he had decided, slowly, without conscious deliberation—it was more like a revelation—that he would take on the role of Robespierre, as he had discovered that he and Robespierre had much in common. But of course he kept it to himself. The shrink thought it admirable that he steeped himself in history. He told that dunce, that spy, about his history teacher, Eisner, and the fool said it was good to have a "role model." Ha! *Robespierre* was his role model.

He regarded the framed copy of the *Declaration of the Rights of Man* hanging on the wall opposite his bed. Eisner had called it a revolution in print. He said the print shops reeked of ink, sweat, and piss and rang with the raucous noises of men eating, laughing, and working. Those were the kinds of details that kept the students from sleeping in Eisner's class. Now, when he got up each morning to look at the Declaration, he thought of Eisner's description of how his counterpart, Robespierre, denounced the aristocrats because the fucking queen, Marie Antoinette, who had her head chopped, told the starving population, which demanded bread, "Let them eat cake!" Eisner was right: words can kill. He thought of the suspension notice sent to his mother, by registered mail; of the profile each teacher had submitted to the principal, to help hang him at the hearing; and of the only positive comment, written by Eisner. "He's a diamond in the rough. Bright. He has a razor-sharp brain."

But where was Eisner when he needed him? He had gotten a job as assistant principal in another school right before the hearing. So he was alone, had to face the judges himself. He had memorized the letter of suspension they sent his mother.

"January 20, 1970. Dear Mrs. Gatreaux, I regret that it has become necessary to suspend your son, Jean-Claude, from school. I am setting up an appointment for a conference with you and your child in the principal's office, room 110. At that time you will have an opportunity to examine and discuss the relevant facts with all the parties concerned. If you wish, you may bring two persons with you. They may be attorneys, but may act in the capacity of advisers only. If you wish to appeal the determination, you should do so setting forth the grounds for the appeal and the relief requested."

Relief requested! He was too young and ignorant to think of redress then! Even though Eisner, the year before, when he found out that Jean-Claude had been caught with a knife, had the typical Eisner balls to tell him to become a doctor if he liked knives, that doctors were weird too. That year Eisner had him put in the biology honors class. In no time flat he memorized all the bones of the frog and started on memorizing the bones of Homo sapiens. But he shocked the class, especially the girls, when he bit the heart out of a dissected frog as they watched it palpitate on the lab table.

It was true that he and his boys had rushed the creep who had ratted on him in shop for some minor thing. That's what had stuck in his craw, that they didn't know who cut the creep, so they suspended only him. He couldn't stop reviewing it bitterly again and again in his mind. It was the moment of his downfall. Then the cops tricked him and told him the creep fingered him, and he was sent to JD detention in the Bronx. Boy, was he dumb in those days. Now he watched every step. "Think before you act" was his motto. Use the brain that Zach Eisner, his idol, taught him he had.

"Use that gray matter between your ears," Eisner told him more than once. "If you used that mind and energy on succeeding instead of on the dumb shit you do with those morons, you would be someone important." But after they threw him out and he was locked up, he spiraled down, instead of up as Zach had predicted. It took a couple of years to pull himself up after he was down and out, when there was no more Zach Eisner, when his mom thought he was a bum and he almost went down the tubes, hating, hating, feeling sorry for himself. The bottom came when he slept in an all-night theater on Forty-Second Street and a pimp tried to recruit him. He was too low to fight; he even thought he would jump off the roof of his building. But even his mother wouldn't have missed him. So he sank into his seat in the theater, immobilized by the loss of alternatives.

Then he saw Anna Marietta in his mind again, exploded in the air by a terrorist bomb over the Atlantic Ocean. He could see her in pieces, flying around, burst open by the explosive. And he felt happy for the first time in three years. He had something to look forward to every day when he woke up in the morning in that fleabag hotel across from Julie Layton's apartment building when he looked at the *Rights of Man* across from his bed, planning the next death, *executing*, he laughed happily at the pun, his clever plan.

He closed the bedroom closet door and could no longer see his reflection in the mirror on the inside. He took out the suspension notice, which he had photocopied, cut into a circle, mounted on a cardboard shaped to fit it, and hung on the hook on the outside of the door. There were two small slits in the paper where he had thrown the knife from twenty paces across the room. Each slice was labeled with a victim's name in red ink. "Bummy" and "Oxley" were side by side on the circles, drawn very close to the center.

He was practiced by now, and the hour had come for his next act of the blade, to take pride in the glory of his justice and revenge. He threw the knife. Clump. This time it was a bull's-eye.

• • •

Jesus had taken to daydreaming. Now not only did he attend Julie's class and Shop; he went to all his classes, Nilda suspected, only to catch a glimpse of *her*. He had a crush on her, mooned over her, found excuses to be in the hallway when he knew she would be there. Nilda couldn't say a bad word about her. She was the goddess. Nilda wouldn't have expected it of him, especially now that the teacher was losing her shape, becoming a mother. It only made him love her more. Hispanic boys all adored their mothers—except Jesus, up to now. Suddenly Nilda made the connection. Sometimes she was smarter than Jesus, saw what he was doing. She realized that instinctively she had made the right decision, had felt the proper anger when Jesus had asked her to cut her beautiful, long, wild hair.

He had brought her a picture from a magazine and demanded, "Take this to the beauty parlor and cut it!" She saw immediately that it was the same short, even cut that the teacher wore.

Nilda had been so hurt. Jesus had always loved her hair. It was one of the things she knew he admired. Now he paid attention to her only as an afterthought, to enhance his dreaming about *her*. Once she even thought he was thinking about her during sex. He hadn't been fucking Nilda. She knew it. And they had stopped screwing then, because when she pushed him away, he knew why. Now when they were together he was with someone else. *Her!*

And how could she compete with someone like Julie Greenwood—her clothes, her jewelry, her classy walk, the way she talked, the words she used. Nilda was pretty—she had a sexy figure and a pretty face—but the teacher was living in a different world, and Jesus knew it and wanted it. He no longer wanted cheap little Nilda, his old childhood friend, his girl. They had been through some shit together, and he was throwing her and crazy Esperanza away for Disneyland, make-believe.

She had heard from the other kids how Jesus bullied the troublemakers in her class, keeping them in line. And now they were laughing behind his back because everyone knew he was in love with *her*. And it made Nilda look stupid. She wished he would wake up, that some kid would confront him. But of course no one had the guts. Hiding behind his new face he still had his rep as a killer.

• • •

Julie was relieved when only fifteen of the twenty kids in her reading class showed up, even though you could hear a pin drop because of Jesus's efforts on her behalf. Today she suspected that it wasn't only for her benefit that he was keeping order as she watched him bent over the poem, poring over it with total absorption and interest. Naturally his reading required more concentration and effort than others', but his tunnel vision on the page, his excluding the outside world while he read, his brow furrowed, and his gaze, boring into the page, might mean something else, and it was touching.

Julie was struck by the sight of his dark head bent into the book. His cap was, miraculously, gone, and his hair was cut short. He had moved Jimmy Lopez to his seat in the back, and he himself sat right in front of her desk, where she could see clearly that his hair was chestnut brown, combed and shiny. She stared at him, and he was oblivious to her watching him because, while he read the poem, it was as if he were wearing blinders. The moment seemed to her the reward of years of teaching, and in the unaccustomed quiet—knowing how fleeting this sensation would be with Jesus—tears filled her eyes and her throat closed. She tried to dwell on the pleasure, to stem the surge of emotion, embarrassed that any kid might see her. And to control her sadness, though she knew it was a lie, she tried to pretend it was just another ordinary day.

How to Eat a Poem

by Eve Merriam

Don't be polite.
Bite in.
Pick it up with your fingers and lick the juices that
    may run down your chin.
It is ready and ripe now, whenever you are.

You do not need a knife or fork or spoon
or plate or napkin or tablecloth.

For there is no core
or stem
or rind
or pit
or seed
or skin
to throw away.

While Jesus carefully read the poem, he pictured his first words strung together. How mysterious that the letters cohered to make a word, to make a sentence, to make a poem, to make a something that spoke to him. He read the poem with emotion. Nothing mattered but the poem as he fixed his eyes on the lines, capturing their cadence when they fell unevenly across the page.

The poem was revealing its secret to him, just as she had promised him. "No one can read the poem the way Jesus reads it," she had said. The poem would say something to him and only him.

Words, like Julie, were beautiful. A poem, he thought—you could cut it, peel it away, love it, taste it, see what was inside. That's what love was. That's how he would like to love *her*. That's how she would love her baby. How lucky, how loved, how cared-for the baby would be. He would have her there every minute, not just for an hour on schedule, hoping to see her, grabbing odd extra moments to fill him with a fine sense of himself and more longing. He imagined how it would be for the baby, breast-fed and sated, her presence like a sun, warming him. He could almost feel it himself, and he suddenly loved the poem he was reading and loved living.

• • •

Julie was grateful for the spate of warm weather, because she could stroll arm in arm with Martha through Central Park to see the cherry blossoms in full bloom. Poor Greg! He had no opportunity to see Paris on the verge of spring; his business trips were all-consuming, shunting him from hotel to hotel. This time, at least, he had decided to take the train from Switzerland to Paris, a scenic change of pace from airplanes, which he was getting leery of.

Now that she was unable to enjoy the French wines they used to sample when he returned, she had collected enough perfume to last a decade. What would he bring home this month? It was hard buying presents for the woman who had everything . . . but her son. . . . She cut herself off, not allowing further thoughts to materialize, to ruin her pleasure in the morning. Instead she inhaled the fragrance of the magenta and snowy white flakes on the polished fruitwood boughs and thought of Greg and their baby.

"How is our little juvenile delinquent?" asked Martha after several minutes of silence as they crossed the Victorian bridge heading for the tennis courts.

"He clings to me. He's like a little boy. For the first time, he's open and vulnerable. What will happen to him when I leave?"

"He's not your problem. He has parents, remember?"

"Something doesn't add up there. Normal parents don't produce a Jesus."

"Are you the authority on nurture versus nature?"

Martha was surprised when she didn't get an argument from Julie. She was almost disappointed. "What, no tongue lashes? No more Lincoln–Douglas debate rounds?"

Julie smiled. She was eager to be convinced, especially now that Jesus was getting so attached to her, when she knew that her own baby came first and that she would ultimately be forced to make a choice. And she knew that the choice she would have to make would be to abandon Jesus.

• • •

Nilda was so shocked by his appearance it disoriented her. She was sure he enjoyed her reaction, but he looked so different she didn't bother to cover her confusion. She felt tricked, as if he had substituted another person for the old Jesus.

Meeting in front of the movie theater, in an impersonal setting away from home and familiar surroundings, made it worse. Surrounded by strangers, waiting in line, through the crowds milling around, she looked out for him. She was early as usual, he was late, and she didn't recognize him immediately, thinking she had made a mistake when she spotted him, identified him from a distance by his shape and his walk. His face was clean-shaven, and there was no trace of a mustache or facial hair—not on his chin, not on his cheeks, nowhere. No sideburns, nothing. And his hair was cut short! He was transformed.

She almost laughed. Who do you think you are? she almost yelled at him. He seemed uncovered, exposed. It occurred to her he had been hiding under the hair like an animal. And now he didn't look ferocious anymore. Maybe he didn't need to look tough—everyone knew not to mess with him. But what about the ones who didn't know?

Walking into the movie with him, Nilda didn't feel protected the way she always had before. She felt that something had been shaved off between them as well. Why was she so anxious about it? She knew why he was changing. It was to please *her*. She would find the right moment to tell him she was on to his tricks, on to his bullshitting himself, that he wouldn't impress Miss Rich Pussy who didn't give two fucks about a homeboy like Jesus. But not now. She knew when to keep her trap shut. If she opened it now, well, he was still Jesus.

• • •

When Jesus arrived in Julie's room for his private hour of tutoring, the hour where she locked them in so no one could disturb them, he realized that the old, clever demon was still there in his head, still ticking away like a clock. He looked around at the familiar clutter of her desk, of books piled up on the window ledge, and at all her plants. The atmosphere was almost familial, and he realized how intimate they had become, how he knew all the funny little habits she had, like leaving the radio on in her room when she was gone. He realized that he had been thinking all along of how to do it, noting opportunities, spotting weaknesses, and above all, waiting for the right time. It felt so right; it was what he wanted, not like the time he punched the kid and stole his watch. That was a fast fix, a spur-of-the-moment release of anger, rapid revenge. Or when he stole from a store—that gave him what he needed for the instant, but he would have to go back for more—for what? It was nothing!

But this. It was something better. He couldn't describe it. It was like the feelings he had when he was a baby, or a little kid—it must have been before Esperanza turned loco. It was something he had to do—was almost directed to do. Like Esperanza. He quickly disregarded that notion; it was just because he was ridding himself of the ways of Esperanza that he had to do this.

He thought of Julie, and he was filled with an inexpressible longing he couldn't identify or satisfy, a feeling he had never before experienced in his life. When he looked at her, it was with the kind of desire he didn't know existed; therefore he had no way of quenching the need. He tried to define it, but only the usual methods of getting what he wanted appeared in his lim-

21

A chill went through Les. He clutched Willie English by his frayed jacket, but he instantly released him when he saw Willie's wild-eyed look of paranoia. Then Willie clammed up, and Les couldn't abide it. He shook him like a mop, trying to extort the information as if it were dust that needed to come loose. He shouldn't have given him all that money. Now he had no way to bribe him, and Willie was scared. The drama had excited Willie's thirst, and he was probably itching to buy a bottle of booze. If he allowed that to happen, Willie would be drunk for a week and he might never recover the information from that disintegrating brain.

Les shook him convulsively, and babbling burst forth like bubbles from Willie's foul-smelling lips. The stench of alcohol and human body odors reminded Les of who Willie was, of his life condition. Willie's brain was pickled in wine and beer.

"Where is she now?" Les screamed. Willie's eyes darted around. He thinks I'm the fuzz, Les thought, backing off. Suddenly an idea that should have immediately broken through his thick skull occurred to him. "Does she speak Spanish?" he demanded angrily.

"She crazier than me now. Used to call *me* loco," Willie offered, looking fearful.

Les was so impatient that he was afraid he might beat Willie.

"She's a P.R., man," Willie added quickly.

Les moved toward him, his eyes narrowing on him, and

Willie knew he wouldn't get his drink unless he got rid of him. "You want me to show you where she lived?" he asked.

• • •

"You love her!" Nilda had confronted him, taunted him, embarrassed him. Last night, Jesus recalled, Nilda had gone home angry because he had ignored her, had been blotting her out of his mind. He heard Nilda's hurt voice in his head, needling him, when he returned to the lonely apartment where Esperanza was asleep (she was sleeping a lot these days), and he was torn.

But he had never felt so special before in his whole life, and it was because of Julie. It was as if he had been singled out for attention, was followed by a glowing spotlight wherever he went. He understood for once why people believed in God, why Esperanza had named him Jesus. God loves you, the Church said, and Esperanza believed. Now he knew how it felt when God loved you. He walked around in an aura of well-being, feeling he was in a bubble, protected, like the boy who needed to be kept away from germs. Jesus liked almost everything around him these days. Everything seemed soft as butter, and he wasn't even high. All was right, except for Esperanza, of course. She was a living reminder of the fucked-up way to live.

And Nilda, she was a thorn in his side. He didn't want to take the chance of losing her. That would be dumb. He still needed her. And she was almost like a part of him, he hated to admit. They had been together so long he couldn't really imagine life without her. But these days he wished he could. It was an old attachment. Maybe he was outgrowing Nilda. Whenever he thought about Julie Greenwood, about how she lived, how she looked, how she behaved, he wanted to know more, wanted to see more, to hear more, wanted, wanted, wanted . . . wanted the unattainable.

He knew he should begin concentrating on his questionable status in school. He had let things slide in the last month; Francisco was getting brave, getting up in his face, and Jesus hadn't taken it seriously, hadn't gotten uptight. He imagined the class whispering when he arrived. It could be that he was losing face, that he was moving down from number one. Maybe that's what Nilda was trying to tell him.

He had to prove to Nilda that she was wrong, that he wasn't getting soft, that he was the same inside. But he knew that he wasn't exactly the same anymore, and he never would be.

"You're nothin' to her," Nilda had mocked him contemptuously. That's why it was so easy to get Nilda's help. She wanted to hurt Julie. And this would satisfy both of them.

• • •

"What was her name?" Les asked over and over again as he followed Willie into the lobby of his hotel. Willie was in charge now, held all the aces.

"No names, no names," Willie insisted, putting his finger to his lips. "She in P.R."

"With the baby?" Les asked anxiously. "Tell me about the baby. A boy?"

There were doubles and triples of them in the lobby mirrors as they entered. Willie refused to answer. Les saw his own shape duplicated, beseeching several grimy Willies, as Willie marched unsteadily ahead of him, grinning at the desk manager, who openly scowled at him. Willie was one of the last remaining derelicts frightening upscale renters.

"Where did she live? Are we going to see her?" Les couldn't let up.

"I told you, man, she lit out. She above me, top floor," Willie said, annoyed.

When they stepped into the elevator, Les checked the numbered buttons. Eleven was the top floor!

"All the singles with no kitchens on this side," said Willie. "How she gonna keep a baby without a kitchen?"

Before Les could respond, the elevator stopped on six and Willie kicked open the stuck door to his room. He used no key, and Les saw why. There was nothing of value in the room. A few clothes were strewn about, and an unmade cot and a kitchen table with two painted, peeling chairs with broken cane seats stared from the run-down room. There were no lamps or accessories. Willie turned on the overhead light, and Les saw at once through the film, which was an accumulation of dust and pollution, fogging the windowpanes that he faced the side of his old building, the side opposite his baby's bedroom. Red curtains, faded in the spots exposed to the bit of sun that crept through the alley between the buildings, hung limply on either side of the narrow window.

Fear thumped against his breastbone at the surge of recognition. They were the same curtains Julie and he had stared into from their infant's nursery window. Willie's woman with the baby had lived on the top floor of this building, the eleventh floor. The room was just across the way! Les stuck his head out the window, and five floors above he could see the old nursery window. Fourteen years ago he had stared daily into the stranger's black abyss and she had stared back, at their baby!

Horrified by the sight, he knew he had found her, that living within inches of his infant, lying in wait, had been a stranger, a woman, hoping, watching, waiting for an opportunity, like a hawk circling. And he had provided her with the right moment to swoop down on her prey.

• • •

Nilda sat on the floor, her back against the wall opposite Julie Greenwood's classroom. The hall was deserted except for the guard, Rudy Ramirez, who sat on a chair at the other end listening to his Walkman, and the pudgy cop, Gordon, who glanced up and down the hall on his rounds and left. If he saw her, he would tell her to find a better place to wait next time, but he would leave her alone.

It was fifteen minutes until the end of lunch hour, and Jesus was inside Julie's room, twisting the combo on the narrow wooden wardrobe by her front door. He was on his knees to avoid being seen through the glass, and Nilda was his lookout. Nilda had stolen the master key to all the doors on the third floor from her homeroom teacher the first week of school, copying it before the woman even knew it was missing, in the same way Jesus had stolen Bummy's key, gaining access to all the fourth-floor rooms. Nilda had unlocked the door for Jesus, and she was trying to look as bored as possible waiting for the bell.

Julie had a free period and no homeroom, so she always came up a few minutes after the lunch bell.

A minute had passed, and Jesus was still inside. Nilda worried. She knew it took him sixteen seconds to crack a lock. But he wasn't out yet. He had to copy the keys in the next half hour and return them to Julie's bag before she returned. Nilda checked her watch. Three minutes had passed. Maybe she had taken her pocketbook with her this time, had gone out instead of bringing in her food. Maybe that's what was wrong! Should she get up and rap on the door? No, she sat tight. Jesus was smart. He knew what he was doing.

Jesus had turned the dial on the lock, by feeling the clicks, in record time. He felt he was taking a test and was passing with high marks in spite of the racing of his heart, which he hated to acknowledge. Julie's smooth gray leather pouchlike bag, sitting on a pile of books, was half open. When he touched it to open the zipper, it was like cream in his fingers. He put his hand inside, and he could smell the leather and powdery odors, flowery and musty, emanate. He pulled out a gold compact ornamented with little gold buds and a lace-edged handkerchief that he wanted desperately to pocket but forced himself to return. He groped around, and when he fingered the house keys he zipped the bag, with its tantalizing contents, closed to temptation.

He hurried now that he had what he wanted, replaced the lock, shut the front door, which was set on lock, and ran down the hallway to the nearest exit, leaving Nilda sitting there as planned. When he returned, he would have a fresh set of keys and he would be able to enter Julie's house whenever he desired.

• • •

Les hadn't had time to even think about Julie's call. What had prompted her change of heart, to ask him to reserve her a table at tomorrow's gig? Sure, she had read the reviews, knew where he was performing, but she had sounded so warm and friendly, eager to see him. Could it be that she didn't want to push him away anymore, to pretend he didn't exist? Why look a gift horse in the mouth? he thought. Perhaps she had changed.

Life was looking up for him; he had made a breakthrough. But there was still unfinished business between them. All in good time.

Now he was on the trail of his baby, following the bread crumbs left by his poor, lost babe in the tangled forest, and they were leading him closer. He dialed El in Monterey to tell her the news. He had begun to realize how very important to him she was, how much she meant to him. Now that his star was rising, his fortune almost made, his professional comeback a startling success, he could afford to make a stab at planning for the future, a permanent future with Eleanore.

• • •

Jesus snapped the combination lock shut and pushed Nilda up against Julie's closet. The hall had been quiet as Nilda watched Julie enter the English office. Forced to hide inside as he returned the keys after the hall was cleared at the late bell, Nilda saw that Jesus was animated, enlivened by the drama of his adventure.

The new set of keys was still clutched, dangerously visible, in his left hand. He rubbed the keys against his parted lips and poked them down Nilda's tight V-necked blouse, between her breasts. His right hand followed, and he squeezed her soft bare skin. Nilda felt a surge of sex rush from her panties up her body to her neck.

"You crazy," she said, struggling. "We'll get caught!" She saw Jesus closing his eyes, and she worried at how carried away he was. And he was getting hard, pressing her harder against the closet with his body. She could feel the lock poking her in the back.

"Later," she whispered. "When we get home," she told him, and she pushed free, afraid the door would open and Julie would catch them with the keys still in his fist.

It was an instantaneous reaction that preceded thinking. The flee-or-fight adrenaline pumped at the hint of danger, at the sight of Jesus out of class past the bell, closing her room door, dashing away, at Nilda scattering to her homeroom. Julie rushed to her room and frantically tested the doorknob. The door was locked. She fumbled with the key and opened the door, blood still rushing to her head.

Her face was red-hot, beads of perspiration dotting her brow. The room was sweltering, but she dove for her closet before opening the window for a rush of air, postponing the relief in order to quell her fear. She botched the combination, missing it once. Finally she released the metal from its cylinder. Her bag was where she had left it! Relief number one. She unzipped it. The wallet was there. She counted the bills: thirty-eight—correct! She rummaged madly through. Keys, makeup kit, change purse—everything intact. She peered through the closet. Books, sweater, Walkman, tapes, assorted possessions of little value, all untouched.

She replaced the lock. It was suddenly cool enough to leave the windows closed. The little emergency receded, and she looked forward to the evening ahead of her. But a tiny sense of unease lingered, and she knew it wouldn't be dispelled until 7:00 P.M., when she saw Greg, and she would feel hopeful again. For the first time, she looked forward to leaving the school for good. The terrible pang of fear had convinced her that Greg might be right about quitting. She took a deep breath. Greg was her real breath of fresh air. This school was becoming stifling.

22

"When are we goin' to rob her house?" Nilda asked Jesus.

"*We?* Who said *rob?*" Jesus goaded her.

Nilda felt she had been tricked, used. Then she had a bad thought. "What are you gonna do?" she asked.

Jesus was unpredictable, volatile. She should never have agreed to this. Jesus started to undress her, and she was afraid, too preoccupied with thoughts of what Jesus might do to Julie to be turned on. Jesus wasn't interested in waiting. He struggled with her, laughing. But it was over very fast this time. Horribly fast.

"Make up your mind!" he said, looking down at her, suddenly angered. "We shoulda fucked in her room. We never done that before." He grinned.

"You steal from everyone, don't you?" Nilda cried, feeling as if in a nightmare, that she was an inextricable part of something she had helped to unleash, that was out of control, something she would regret.

• • •

Julie was sorry she had taken the crosstown bus home today. She should have taken a cab. She wasn't up to the mass of marauding, screaming, cursing kids who descended on the buses at three o'clock when the schools let out. Old people avoiding the rush hour, when their half-fares were invalid, were also beset by teenagers, outraging their delicate constitutions. Sometimes the bus driver stopped the bus to throw off the characters who squeezed in the back door without paying. Today Julie was crammed in the back with smokers, and her ears were split by ghetto blasters. There was no one from any of her classes on board who would offer her a seat, and her feet hurt.

She couldn't stop thinking about Jesus. Was he trying to get into her classroom? It had been locked when she used her key. Maybe he was just hanging out. He liked to hang around her. He even eavesdropped when she talked to other kids. He was getting too involved with her, and when he looked at her he had that dreamlike quality on his face. It was better than the provocative, abusive looks he had given her before she taught him to read, though. His gaze was almost tender, childlike at times.

What had Jesus been up to if he wasn't trying her door? He hadn't really changed, she thought. He and Nilda were still up to no good together. She noticed that Nilda had been hostile to her recently. Adolescents! she thought as she was shoved to the rear door by a massive surge of kids. It was Lexington Avenue, her stop, anyway. She tried to step off the bus and onto the curb without tripping, looking forward to the walk alone down Lex. Shouldn't she attend to her instincts, which told her to be careful? Or was she paranoid? She looked over her shoulder automatically as she put the key into the wrought-iron gate and pushed it open with relief at being safely home.

• • •

Telling Eleanore about Julie coming to his gig had been a mistake. Why should Eleanore be happy? He realized what an ass he was, how Eleanore's voice showed hurt, and how immediate his need and love for her was. The meeting with Julie would wind up the threads of his past while he hunted down the kidnapper.

"I'm getting closer to my son, El. I can feel it in my bones." When Eleanore didn't answer, he felt for the first time what she had been through with him, got inside her skin and knew he always wanted her near, wanted to be touched by her physically and spiritually.

"Soon. I know it will be soon. Will you marry me then?" he surprised her.

"Are you serious?" she asked, delighted. "Is there a date?"

"How 'bout being corny and making it June?" proposed Les.

Eleanore had thought to ask him, "Are you sure this Willie didn't make up all these stories to get your money?" But she didn't say what was curled on her tongue. She couldn't upset his applecart. Or hers.

• • •

Father DiFalco had grave doubts about the Puerto Rican woman whose window faced the baby's bedroom. He tossed and turned in his bed, unable to make himself comfortable in the dark. It was past one o'clock, and he was too old to function on a few hours of sleep. But from the moment Les Layton told his story he had felt some complicity in Les's life, and as DiFalco thought about the problem every position in bed seemed more like lying on a bed of nails.

She could be a totally innocent person with a baby, he decided, lying on his side. But the cross! The cross was the unbreakable link. His arm fell asleep, and he lay on his back listening to the night sounds on the street. On the other hand, many Puerto Rican women wore crosses. An ambulance siren pulsed, screaming for attention, blocking out thought. When he began in the church thirteen years ago, he had slept like a baby every night. He turned over on his stomach wearily. Could such a coincidence happen? Could this lone woman in an SRO be innocent? E.L. could have been watching from her window, waiting for her chance, a schizo obsessed for some reason with getting a baby, a nut case whose baby had died. If she was, Les Layton might get lucky. A crazed woman like that didn't usually kill the baby; she was more likely than a pervert to keep it alive.

He closed his eyes. The initials E.L. swam in his head like electric eels in neon under his eyelids. He charged his brain to produce the answer. Let it come, he invoked his unconscious, allowing mysterious functions to overtake his thoughts, allowing sleep to descend.

Was it Elba? No. Was it Elena? No. Was it Evita? No. Eugenia? Emma? Elsie? No! No! No! Was it Esther . . . ?

DiFalco awoke with a start. It was pitch-black, and the name Clara came to him—it meant *clear* in Spanish. He knew it from his basic college Spanish, improved over the years in the neighborhood. But Clara began with *C*, not *E*. What was the meaning of this? He coaxed random names, with obvious meanings, from his memory. Innocencia? Lourdes? Luz? Felicita? He fell exhausted to sleep. Sometimes sleep would yield the answer.

• • •

Julie was thinking of Jesus as she walked by his house on Broadway on her way to the Jazz Club. She had made a mental note of his address and looked up at the building, to the eighteenth floor where his window might be. It was a solid building, the old-fashioned type, with large rooms that were built when architects designed for beauty and didn't cut corners. The bricks could use a sandblaster, and the building was aging, but it still bore the patina of its proud past. Gargoyles and ornamental ledges embellished the facade, and she noted that the top floors might have a river view over the tops of some of the low buildings on West End and Riverside Drive.

She quickened her step, jaunty because she felt gratified. Jesus was the boy in the happy family picture after all. He wasn't neglected or abused in a squalid tenement. She could rest easy and attend to her own life now. She looked forward to hearing Les and his trio play in the new room just a few blocks south. Some of her youthful feelings stirred within her, and Les, her old love, awaited her, she hoped, as a friend.

• • •

Dr. Wolfson had just closed the door of his Fifth Avenue office on the last patient of the night. No wonder his patient was depressed. Wolfson thought about the executive he was treating. It was hard to be a good person in an evil world. He compared the young man, who was a cocaine addict, to Les. He had just replayed a taped session with Les, trying to make a decision about whether to terminate him—a term that gave Wolfson the chills.

Heroin had been the drug of choice in Les's day, easier to kick. His yuppie patient charged his drugs on a credit card and deducted the expense from his taxes. Wolfson had heard of charging call girls, but this! How could his patients control their vices in a corrupt society?

Some of his patients felt no guilt, and some had a surplus, like Les, who appeared more neurotic than he actually was. "There is less here than meets the eye," the laser-tongued Dorothy Parker had once observed. Les's guilt had led him to believe for a moment that Les was psychotic, that he was crazy enough to kill his own baby. But it was a figment of Les's overwrought imagination. Les was a gentle man, and now he had discovered creative ways to defeat emptiness and he was free of drugs.

It was time for Les to strike out on his own. He was getting married, had coped with Julie's rejection reasonably, and was sensitive to her emotional needs. He recalled how Les had cried when he read a line from her letter: "I can see our baby's face in your face." It would be a heart-wrenching experience for Julie to see Les, yet they were meeting tonight at the Jazz Club. Their reunion was an integration of their lives, the mourning process over for them, he thought, closing his notebook.

Yes, it was time for Les to fly away alone. The empty-nest syndrome was a problem for therapists too. Les's last session had convinced Wolfson that it was the end of their relationship. As soon as therapy becomes enjoyable, it's time to quit, he'd always said. He would feel like Hamlet's father sending him away.

Wolfson, considering the new abstract painting he had acquired for his waiting room, got up to turn the lights out and shut the door behind him.

• • •

It was the perfect Upper West Side jazz scene. Instead of being in a dark, smoky cellar, the club was on top of one of the few remaining wooden houses in the city, in a slightly make-shift, homey room overlooking Broadway. The padded walls and ceiling, the brick wall behind the stage, and the chunky blond wood chairs—filled with intellectuals with rimless glasses and the mix of conservative black and white Columbia students around the triangular bar—were quite a change from the old days. The mustaches and the beards were gone, and the smokers and heavy drinkers had been replaced by sedate women in black dresses and men in turtlenecks and jackets.

Julie was seated at a table at the window, and she ordered a delicacy she hadn't thought about for over a decade, shad roe. She remembered the nets cast out on the Hudson, when the shad ran in the river past her window, and she wondered where the fish on her plate had come from. Were the waters of the Hudson clean enough now for the shad to survive?

The drummer, who looked like a salesman to Julie, came in and adjusted his instruments. Her heart hurried as she finished her meal, waiting for Les. The pianist, a replacement for Rus, was an old friend. He wore his hair down to his shoulders the way Julie remembered. He rambled over the keyboard of the grand piano, and when he searched the audience for her he threw her a kiss.

Finally Les took the mike. The tables were jammed, and the applause and commotion gave her shelter. But he looked directly at her table and smiled shyly, introduced the first number, and stood at the bass.

She could barely concentrate on the music, her emotions were so strong and positive. His voice was confident; his eyes were clear, vibrant, and alive, not like they had been at their last encounter. He was still slender and casual and sexy. His lean and hungry look was gone; age had deepened him, making him more appealing. She hadn't realized it in the West End Bar because she had been so afraid of him, too afraid to recognize that he was capable of growing apart from her.

Maybe she hadn't wanted to see it, in spite of her pushing him away. He had definitely changed. Immature people don't seem to age, she thought suddenly, lulled by the music, by Les's experimental composition, which she always found hard to follow. Was it an illusion that shallow people didn't reflect the inroads experience marked on their features?

Les looked up at her during a drum riff and caught her off guard, and he laughed knowing she was lost in thought, the way she always drifted off when he played his modern sound. And as he plucked the bass, the way he moved, the way his fingers arched, and the tilt of his head triggered a flash of Jesus's face, and Julie wondered what it was about Jesus that echoed in her being, vibrating like the tones of the tuning fork Les struck when he pitched his instruments. The feeling lingered long after the sound disappeared, singing in her spirit—there was something about Jesus she couldn't grasp in her two hands, something that eluded conventional reason but existed no matter how hard she tried to deny it or reject it. It was a breath of spring air, the smell of freedom wafting through time, a whisper, a hint of the haunts that she and Les wandered through in Greenwich Village, of the coffee shops of her college days. And it came over her when she saw Les and sometimes when she looked at Jesus. A gesture of Jesus's, a movement, an expression, brought back an instantaneous wash of connection to her past, like the subliminal blinking of a star from another universe.

It was probably wishful thinking. Jesus's learning to read was like a rebirth, a budding, a greening of his life. That's what she wished for him, hoped for him, a distinctly overly optimistic goal, she realized. She was merely overjoyed by success, captivated by Les and his music and the mood, drunk on the possibilities for Jesus.

But then the creepy feeling she had gotten when Jesus lingered in the hallway that day, when she checked her closet in a frenzy—and the suspicion, the unpleasant unknown—turned her stomach, soured her vision, and turned her mentally away from the sight of him.

There was no dressing room, and Les sat side by side with Julie in the hallway. "I know this is not the place to tell you," he began, and he told Julie his story. The buzzing of the crowd arriving for the next set and the noise of patrons leaving were backgrounds for their conversation.

Julie was grateful she wasn't hearing his tale for the first time, that she had had a chance to forgive him. She took his hand, realizing how strong he had become, stronger than she, wishing she had the courage to tell Greg the truth, wanting for the first time to tell him. Greg was in love with the inner Julie who hadn't broken through, and she had deceived him and Jesus. She was a sham, offering Jesus more than she was willing to deliver.

"I could have left the door open that day," Julie consoled Les. "If someone was watching us, they would have gotten in somehow. You can't always be alert. I had a feeling that day . . . Was I being followed? There's always that one mistake I might have made, like leaving the carriage for just a moment, because I wasn't on guard."

Julie tried to keep her emotions in check, but she wasn't successful. Tears came to Les's eyes as he squeezed her hand.

"I'll try to make it up to you," he promised, "by finding our son." But he stopped when he saw the glint of fear in Julie's eyes, and he knew she was thinking he was off the deep end again, bonkers. "Don't worry," he told her, and he dropped the subject like a lead weight. He had his head screwed on right, and he wanted her to know it. He looked into her eyes with a clarity of purpose, with a shining that couldn't be taken for anything but healthy optimism.

"I have some news," he announced, his voice bright. "I'm getting married! You would like her," he told Julie.

Julie was glad for him. Thank goodness I heard the tape, Julie thought, or I might not have come, might have hated Les forever.

"I want you to meet her in a couple of months, when I'm finished with my gigs here," he said. Julie got up to leave. People were crowding toward them for the next set. And when they embraced, she felt that complete happiness was just at the edge of her outstretched fingertips.

But as she held tightly to the railing, maneuvering down the narrow steps to the street, feeling the baby, a new guilt assailed her as she thought of her future, of leaving her job. Was it fair to seduce a kid like Jesus into believing that she cared for him in a deeply emotional way, the way a mother would, when she was only his teacher? Was it fair to bring out his tender feelings and tie him to her and then leave him behind?

23

Jean-Claude Gatreaux had his own apartment, so he had the privacy to plan the next murder. His mother, he thought bitterly, was relieved that he was on his own at long last, that she was freed of responsibility, rid of the jailbird who might scare away her new husband.

Jean-Claude hadn't dared kill his next victim in her bathtub the way he envisioned, but he rationalized his cowardice. I don't want to lose the war over a daring battle, he thought. Then he figured out how to get her. He had committed murder the last two times in broad daylight with witnesses everywhere. Now he began to understand that crowds were the perfect cover. He would slice her up with his persecutors swarming around him.

He remembered the night he feared the most as a student, the night when his mother got all the bad news and there was hell to pay: Parents' Night. "It's too bad," they always badgered his mother; "he's got such a high IQ." Bright and bad was the verdict. The mob scene of visitors in Catherine Dunbar Junior High School, his alma mater, would conceal him perfectly next week.

That's when he would give his next victim, one of the murderers of his life, *his* verdict, on Open School Night. Death by dagger. She would get her report card, but she wouldn't be alive to read it.

• • •

It was a quiet, tree-lined street. The leaves were rounded and even on each branch of the tree in front of her house. He knew they were ginkgo trees from the urban survivor's course in

biology that Bummy had given last year. The name of the yellow
flowering bush in front of the town house was one he couldn't
remember, but he noted that the ceramic boxes in the windows
had the same white flowers that were planted around the ginkgo
tree. The street was actually empty. It was 1:30 in the afternoon,
and the day seemed lazy to Jesus; her street lacked the tension
and bustle of Broadway. The very silence seemed luxurious, a
privilege of the wealthy. He unlocked the gate, his heart thumping in spite of his confidence. He climbed the steps, forcing
himself not to look behind, breathless not because of the danger
but because he was climbing her stairs, had been touching her
gate, and he was fitting the shiny key into her lock and peering
through her curtained glass. The house was empty. Any minute
he would have it all to himself. He had rushed directly from her
class, watched for signs of life, and called her number repeat-
edly. The phone had rung in a deserted house. He had exactly
one hour. He set his watch, the one he stole from the kid in the
park, to go off at exactly 2:30. That's when his time was up.

• • •

Sleepless nights had taken their toll on Father DiFalco. But
he put his mind to the task at hand, preparing to greet the new
people who were joining the congregation. He chose his favorite
prayer and sat in a pew watching the window washer who was
creeping along the stained-glass windows to the left of the altar,
only a rope visible as he seemingly hung, suspended in midair,
outlined in the light.

He opened his book to the Prayer of St. Francis, written in
Spanish, which by now he could translate easily to himself into
English. *"La Oration de San Francisco,"* he read, comforted by
its familiarity, preferring the lovely, almost frilly, ornate lilts of
the sounds in Spanish.

"Lord, make me an instrument of your peace. *Senor, hazme
un instrumento de Tu paz.* Where there is hatred let me sow love;
donde hay odio, dejame sembrar amor. Where there is injury,
pardon; *donde hay injuria, perdon.* Where there is doubt, faith;
donde hay duda, fe.

Where there is despair, hope; *donde hay desespero, esperanza.*"

24

"Shut the fuck up!" Jesus had screamed at the class. And there had been immediate silence. Julie didn't want to sanction his abuse, his threats on her behalf; she hated it. He put her in his debt, and it appealed to his machismo to keep order for her, unwittingly undermining her authority. He made her look bad. His eagerness to be her equal, to dominate, to be manly, blinded him, and her discomfort and the other kids' sniggering at the situation eluded him.

During their tutoring hour, when she had tried to hint at the problem, he had taken it as a slight, and she had chickened out instantly. But it made teaching even more difficult than before, and she began to dread the class, feeling more and more alienated from him and her job. Only one more to go, she thought, as her last class straggled in at the bell. This was the first time she had ever counted the minutes to dismissal.

It must be spring fever, the promise of giving birth, anticipation of life ahead of me, she thought, explaining away her disaffection with teaching, her waning interest. Nothing can compete with a momma and her cub, she thought. She tried not to dwell on Jesus and his future, because it spoiled her pleasure, made her feel responsible again, responsible for him, making her feel she had to sacrifice. And for once she wanted a little piece of the promise for herself.

• • •

Why had he lied to Nilda, sneaking off from school to break into Julie's house? His heart took off inside him as he walked into the living room, chock-full of her possessions, filled with her essence. He couldn't wait to see the objects that surrounded her, what she ate, where she slept. The room was awe-inspiring. It had a delicate crystal chandelier that tinkled in the breeze coming through the heavy windows, which were open a crack. The colors were deep and rich and muted just enough for elegance. The carpet, which covered most of the floor, had woven designs like the ones he remembered from the museum on Fifth Avenue, where his third-grade teacher had taken the class when they had studied old New York.

Jesus was beginning to feel so much at home that he played the CD that was lying next to the stereo. He looked at the face in the plastic CD case, the handsome, arresting face of Les Layton. He pressed all the right buttons and turned the volume dial down to one. The odd music came from two giant speakers six feet tall and only an inch thick, filling the room with a quality of sound he had never heard from an amplifier before. The red light on the sound meter danced quirkily with each note as his eyes roved about the room, and he would have liked to listen to more, but he had to learn to ration his hour.

There was a fireplace, he noted, a real one—he could tell because of the soot in the bottom, and above it on a ledge he saw at once two decoy ducks, just like the ones he had carved. Julie and he liked the same things. But he didn't stop; he had to see the rest. The dining room had large mirrors and a museum-type table and chairs. Not that interesting.

The bathroom was what he examined next, guiltily but curiously. It was odd, with its wooden walls and its oval window. The room was large enough for a dozen people to hang around. It had a big old tub and a chair. He looked at the wooden seat on the toilet bowl where she peed. He tore himself away and climbed the stairs, checking his watch.

He was glad he hadn't told Nilda. He wanted this all to himself. He didn't want to share it with anyone, especially Nilda. Hurry, hurry. Time was ticking by in sync with his heartbeat. Tick-tick-tick. He had reached her bedroom and his breath was short. He looked in, to her dark wooden bed, large enough for two, of course, but he imagined only her. A picture of a man stared at him accusingly from the dresser, and he slapped it down to continue his reverie.

The cover on the bed was a quilt of patches, brilliant in color. The bed had a funny shape, a sleigh, he realized after pondering it long and hard. He stared into it with pleasure, not wanting to leave its sight in spite of the speeding seconds his heart ticked away. Then the closet, the huge, dark wood, grainy, shiny closet, caught his fancy, delaying the inevitable departure. The hinge needed oiling; it squealed aloud in the quiet. She heard this sound every time she chose a dress or took a filmy gown from its hangers. He stroked a satin negligee covered with a matching peach-colored dressing gown. The white lace would rest on her breasts. Her blouses and skirts and dresses hung nearby, and he recognized those she wore to school. He touched them, making them his, making it real that he was there. He rubbed the satin of the nightgown to his lips, pretending it was her skin, feeling sure this is what it would feel like.

• • •

Julie fastened the straps on her new green sandals in the little curtained cubicle in Dr. Blum's examining room. Maybe she would have a girl this time, she thought happily, secretly wishing for a girl to start fresh memories. Her new flowered cotton dress was bold and original, the colors of a Georgia O'Keeffe painting, for the first time plainly a maternity dress.

She enjoyed the match she had made, and her canvas bag complemented her outfit. She knew Dr. Blum would congratulate her on her blooming health. She laughed to herself at the pun.

Suddenly she looked down at her shoes, and the real meaning of her dream, the one where she skated on straw shoes, came to her. She had been walking in someone else's shoes, trying to get through life on false pretenses. But the dissembling had put her on a flimsy foundation, and she was still not on firm footing. The meeting in the Jazz Club with Les had been an important reconciliation. Now more than ever she wanted to tell Greg the truth. And she cursed her cowardice.

• • •

Nilda had egged him on. But the longer he stayed in Julie's

room, the happier he was he had kept this from her. "What you waitin' for? Steal something from her house. She's rich. I wish I had her clothes, that green ring, her life. Get it for me," she had begged. "Get the ring."

Jesus opened the door to the other half of the heavy free-standing closet and shut it quickly. It contained a man's wardrobe, as he had suspected.

He jerked the top drawer of the bureau open recklessly. He almost yanked it out of its bed. Flimsy panties and bras were jumbled in the drawer. He ran his fingers through the pinks and mauves and beiges like a blind man. There was an apple scent, a scent like a witch's smell emitted to draw him toward her, to make him forget the hour, reality, to tangle his soul with the invisible waves wafting into his heart. He struggled to replace the drawer. His watch had gone off, and he had ignored its warning.

Then he saw it. The emerald ring was gleaming on her dresser. He tried so hard not to pounce on it, devour it, close his hand on it. But for a fleeting instant he felt he would have a piece of her; he would have the constancy, the wealth, and the care that went with it, like Aladdin's lamp. But he knew that if he took the ring he would never be able to return, so he wouldn't go near it, touch it, afraid of its allure.

But now, wherever he went, even if he turned his back, the emerald in the ring was like an eye following him around the room. It forced him out of the bedroom, to examine her possessions elsewhere, out of the accusing beacon of its gaze searching him out.

Jesus opened the door of the extra bedroom, and he was astounded. In the center of the room a white crib stood like a throne with a white lace canopy. The nursery was utterly complete, down to the picture of a clown performing on the back of an elephant painted brightly on wood. It hung on the wall facing the bed, which had sheets and covers and side bumpers with matching clowns. A night-light was a clown, and the toys dancing in a circle hanging over the crib were clowns. The furniture was white wicker. It was a fairy-tale room, but Jesus slowly realized that this fantasy room awaited a living, breathing baby that would be sleeping in the soft comfort of the crib.

Jesus felt like a flower closing up at dusk, but instead of experiencing anguish he visualized crashing down on the dainty white bars with a hammer, smashing to splinters the toy with its lullaby, which he hadn't been able to resist playing. He gave the leg of the crib a kick, making a dark spot of soot at the base, clinging to the white rail with his fingers clutched so tightly the skin was pale. He wanted revenge. He clenched himself and his rage until he was bursting, and then he remembered the ring.

He roared out of the room, crashing into furniture in his path. He snatched the ring from her dressing table, squeezing it roughly in his hand. He raced down the steps three at a time, slamming the door so angrily behind him that the glass almost shattered, locking it without even a glance at the street to see if he was being watched.

Nothing mattered to him anymore. He knew she wasn't coming back now, that he meant nothing to her, that he was but a temporary episode in her life. Soon she would have her baby and leave him. And then he would be forgotten.

25

Julie panicked when she saw her empty dressing table. She couldn't believe it. She pictured the ring right there, sitting right in front. She crawled under the table on her hands and knees. It could have rolled along the polished wood floor, but she couldn't find it!

She was scared now. "It's not here, it's not here!" she cried aloud, hysteria rising with her tears. But she stopped herself from losing control by an effort of will, forced herself to think rationally. She retraced her steps mentally to last night, when they had gone to the opera, when she had decided to wear her diamond ring instead. She pulled the false, hollow book, where her diamond ring and earrings were hidden, from the bookcase. *Treasure Island*, by R. L. Stevenson, was printed wryly on the cover. The diamonds were there! But no emerald ring.

It had to be in the house. When she was calmer, she reasoned, she would remember what she had done with it. When she wasn't looking for it, she would find it. It happened all the time. She would stop thinking about the ring. But her heart continued to express fear. And from nowhere she had a horrible recollection. Hadn't Bobbie's roommate at school had her house burglarized *just* before Bobbie was murdered?

She took her journal from the locked rolltop desk in the bedroom to calm herself before Greg came home for dinner. She didn't want to spoil their evening with her hysterics. She propped up the pillows on her bed and threw off her shoes, preparing to make her first entry with her green pen, noting that she hadn't written anything in three weeks.

She leaned back with her eyes closed, exhausted, dreaming of her baby for a moment. Her baby's eyes were also closed as he swam in her womb, she thought. At six months the baby could see if there were light. And he—or was it she?—could hear through the amniotic fluid. "This is the reason it recognizes its mother's voice so quickly," Bobbie had told her. "And the baby hears the beat of your heart." Julie listened to her heartbeat. It dimmed as she listened. But as soon as she was relaxed, almost asleep, the grotesque dream flashed in her mind, the dream of her baby, large, overgrown in his carriage. And Jesus's face grinned at her. The dream and Jesus seemed to her connected, like demons in a dream of death, and she opened her eyes and grabbed her pen.

She thought of her conversation with Martha the other day, when she had shown her the new crib.

"I'm beginning to dread seeing Jesus," she had told Martha. "I don't understand it; he's my biggest success."

"You can't like every kid. Some kids are unlikable," Martha had sympathized.

A wave of nausea overtook Julie as she pictured Jesus, his matted hair, his faint mustache, and the almost pleading look in his eyes. He wanted more from her than she could give.

"But if I can't like him, who will?" she had asked Martha.

• • •

Willie English was the only one who had seen Esperanza L. in the flesh, Les thought as he raced to Riverside Drive. But he had been too aggressive with Willie last time, and Willie had led him up and down the Drive, through side streets, and finally up West End Avenue looking for her apartment.

"Was it a brownstone?" Les asked as they stood on One Hundredth Street looking up at a conglomeration of assorted dwellings. "A big apartment building? Small?"

Willie didn't know what he was looking for. It was obvious he was trying to get Les off his back by leading him around. Maybe he once knew and couldn't remember. Willie would say anything when he was afraid. Today Les would be more circumspect.

Les had to look twice to be sure it was Willie he had spotted. Willie had strayed from the Drive to Broadway and was bowing deeply to oncoming traffic, as a matador would to a bull. He was wearing shorts and his old sharkskin boots and clutched in his hand the inevitable bottle in a brown bag. But in deference to the warm weather he had trimmed his beard, making him look younger, almost normal.

Les waved to him and waited for him to end his ballet, spying the cornered look that disrupted Willie's cackling performance. Willie's afraid of the cops, Les had realized when he first revealed Esperanza's name. He had never known it, Willie had sworn.

"What does she look like?" Les had asked.

"She small, bent over, dark. You know, man, like a P.R."

"Was she old?"

"Nah, somethin' wrong with her back."

It was the woman in the shadowy corridor. Les felt the hair on his neck tingle. *It was Esperanza.*

Les faced him across a dirty table in McDonald's on Broadway.

"Why you after her?" Willie asked.

Les chose his answer with care.

"I'm not after her. I would like to find . . . *her son.*"

Willie shook his head as if he understood. As if he should have known all along.

"She outta her gourd now. No wonder. Her boy is mean! Mean mothafucker."

• • •

Something was wrong with Jesus. When he finally admitted to her he had gone to Julie Greenwood's house, Nilda sat in Julie's class picturing Jesus unlocking Julie's door and roaming through her house. And it was thrilling. But he had come back with nothing, saying nothing.

He was going downhill. His face was unshaven, his hair in his face. She tried to engage him with her eyes because words were not working, but his eyes were inscrutable except for a faraway pensiveness uncommon for him.

Nilda was about to tease him about Julie, but she instinctively held back. She knew she couldn't ridicule the terrible longing Jesus had, the dream they all secretly had, if they cared to admit it, that the families they came from weren't really theirs; the dream that someone who loved them would appear one day and claim them as their own.

• • •

"Moral Dilemmas—The Me Generation," Julie wrote in her journal.

"Martha doesn't know if she can help anyone in trouble, be a good samaritan. She still hasn't gotten over her anger that her husband gave up his life for someone else, leaving her a widow.

"And I want my own life. I want to walk away from the school and leave its troubles behind. If you have a conscience, what do you do?"

She skipped a line and wrote, centered on the next line, "Strange Happenings."

"1. There was a crack in one of the ducks on the fireplace. Ella would have told me if she had dropped something while dusting. 2. A picture of Greg fell over. Was it the wind? I never leave the window open more than a crack. 3. MY RING IS MISSING!

"I've searched and searched. Yesterday I couldn't concentrate on my diary, so I searched the house until I nearly dropped, each time trying a new spot. Not left on the sink while I took a shower, not in the wastepaper basket, fallen from my dresser, nowhere, nowhere, nowhere to be found. I might as well admit it. It's gone. And I can't bear to tell Greg. It's not the money, though it's expensive!! But it's precious. Precious because Greg gave it to me—when I got pregnant, to celebrate the baby . . .

"Am I getting forgetful? It makes me so nervous. I'm always looking over my shoulder now, wondering. Last time I wasn't vigilant. I had a creepy feeling that day, didn't follow my instincts. I was naive then. My instincts must be telling me I'm in danger."

The next line seemed to write itself. "My instincts tell me to get away from Jesus."

She closed her journal. Am I crazy? she wondered.

• • •

Esperanza was awake and waiting for Jesus when he returned. She smiled at him, happy that he was home and that he had come in to see her. She was thin as a skeleton, and her gauntness frightened him. Her collarbone was beginning to protrude. He raised her right hand and placed the emerald ring on her finger. *"Para ti, Mamacita,"* he said and kissed her fingers. Her fingers were too thin; the ring hung limply. But she curled her fingers under and admired the stone.

He had been too busy to notice how bony she had become, and compassion ached in his chest when he looked at her brave, frail face. Then a terrible understanding closed in on him. Esperanza was dying!

His life darkened in an instant. And all light dropped like the sun from the horizon of his soul.

26

"I'll call the police!" Julie said aloud, just to hear her voice in the silence. "The morons," she said, surprising herself with her vindictiveness. They couldn't find my baby; how can they find my little ring? she thought. In her victims' group, mothers told how their murdered teenagers had never been reported missing by the local police. "In small towns they don't have the know-how; in big cities, where crack murders are commonplace, the work is shoddy," the group leader had told them. "The police don't have time for missing children."

Then Julie heard the key in the lock. She ran downstairs, her face puffed with fatigue.

"Greg!" she cried out unhappily. She threw her arms around him and blurted out what she had sworn she would keep to herself, did what she had promised herself she wouldn't do: overwhelm him with her problems the moment he walked through the door.

"I'm falling apart," she confessed when they sat together on the bed as he comforted her over the ring.

"You'll find the ring," he said, "and if not, Julie, a ring is replaceable." And then Julie burst into tears in his arms.

"I love you so much, Julie," Greg said. "Oh God, I do love you."

"I love you, Greg," Julie answered.

"I've arranged to cut down on travel. By the time the baby is born there will be no more trips," he said softly in her ear.

"Oh, yes!" she cried, her eyes shiny with tears, with relief. "I'll need you after the baby is born . . . so much." She sobbed again into his chest.

Greg was astounded by her grief. Then she looked into his face, and laughter bubbled up, through the catharsis of her tears.

Greg laughed with her. "Soon I'll be able to hug you both, one at a time," he said as they rocked together contentedly. And he pictured their baby with a rush of anticipation unmatched by any elation he had ever experienced before.

Julie confided one last fear to Greg that night.

"I was so happy about the baby, and now I'm worried," she whispered as she lay in his arms in bed. She was drained but calm.

"About what?" he asked.

"About whether the baby will turn out . . . healthy."

"What does the doctor say? Didn't your checkup . . ."

"Yes. Normal. Perfect!"

"Why should anything go wrong?" He caressed her hair, kissed her damp forehead. "This is just the normal jitters of a pregnant woman getting close to the end. Everything is going to be all right. Don't worry, my little lamb. Everything is okay."

• • •

Jean-Claude readied himself for Parents' Night. He had just finished a tragedy by his favorite writer, Will Shakespeare, whose works were stacked on the window ledge near his bed. Jean-Claude slapped his book shut and returned it to the pile with satisfaction.

It was time to leave, and he made a last-minute appraisal of himself in the mirror. In a necktie and jacket he could pass for a parent, especially if he waited with the early crowd eager to be among the first ones there. He looked closely into the mirror and patted his close-cropped woolly hair into place over his high forehead and his bony sculpture of a skull. His long face and cheekbones and wide mouth suited his tall, rangy, sinewy frame.

Most respectable, he judged, pleased at the effect. What he didn't see was the deranged rove of his eyes in the sleek, fleshless face when he wasn't focused, when his mind wandered and his discordant thoughts clanged against one another and were reflected in the frightening look that appeared spasmodically on his face.

He suddenly stepped back and grabbed his dagger from the wall. He thrust it into her imaginary body as she pleaded for mercy.

He treated himself to a cab, and as he cruised toward the school he recalled one of the lines he had read before he left his apartment. It was for her.

If you have tears, prepare to shed them now, he thought.

• • •

"It's my last obligation," Julie said with a sigh. "I don't want to go, but I can't disappoint the parents," she explained to Greg. "Most can't come during the day. Parents' Night is the one time they can see me." She put on a navy linen jacket over her white dress.

"Don't come," she pleaded. "None of the husbands or wives come. You'll just be in the way," she added, just as he was about to object. She pictured him arriving in his three-piece suit and with his Gucci briefcase.

"I'll pick you up. It's a dangerous neighborhood."

"David Carr will put me in a cab," she assured him. "It's not dangerous. The school will be filled with people."

Greg grabbed her and tried to kiss her neck as she giggled, pushing him away.

"You're going to have a very naughty boy if he's anything like you," she warned.

• • •

The school was ablaze with light, looking festive from afar. Jean-Claude approached with purposeful steps. Now he was on the other end of the stick. He clutched the switchblade in his pocket. The dagger was for show, useless to a modern assassin.

He stepped through the door as a Frenchman would into a palace ball. The comedy is over, he thought, not realizing that he was smiling. Tonight she would pay the price.

• • •

At the sound of the bell the parents rushed up the stairs like horses bolting the starting gate. There was a mad frenzy to reach all the teachers in the hour and a half before the final gong. Some parents were even given numbers on little slips of paper, to keep them in turn. And Julie's throat would be hoarse by the time she finished talking with dozens of parents about the accomplishments of their offspring.

"It's like a bakery, with all those numbers," said Andrea Pappas, reluctantly leaving Julie's room to return to her art room down the hall.

"Lucky you," said Julie. "You get to read the *Times* tonight."

"It's triage tonight," Andrea said with a laugh, "and art isn't essential to life. "At least to most people, she thought, unlocking her door. She sauntered to the storeroom in the rear of her classroom where her supplies and canvases were stored, unlocked the door, and dropped her belongings.

She checked the coffeepot with relief. She had turned it off, as she thought. But it was the third time she had worried about burning the school down, or at least having an embarrassing pot meltdown, which had happened once before.

Aha! A visitor. Of course, Mr. Flowers, her star artist's father, coming for the accolades. It would be a pleasure to congratulate him. She hated like hell to give bad news, but she had done it a thousand times. The room was actually filling up. Two parents were walking around inspecting the Andy Warhol-ish comic book characters, the abstract oils, and the pastel still lifes. She often regarded her kids' work more highly than the mystifying choices the museums made.

A young man sat in the rear, waiting for someone. He looked vaguely familiar. A brother of a student? She had taught whole families, generations, she realized after Mr. Flowers left. The thought depressed her.

When she looked up from her last parent, the young man was gone. She looked at her watch. Not long to go—just enough time to finish the crossword, she thought, reaching the storeroom.

She felt for the light. *She didn't remember turning off the light.*

An arm, a hideously strong arm, locked her neck in a stranglehold, crushing her throat from behind as she labored to scream. In an instant she would be choked to death if she didn't fight, sound the alarm through a scream. But her shriek was mutilated in her throat, muted in her mouth by a hand viciously clamped over her face. Excruciating pain in her mauled cheekbone and jawbone, damaged in the savage struggle, vied with her panic. He was squeezing her life out!

Life and breath and all the world dissolved into a meaningless black mass as she sank to her knees, dragging her murderer down, still detecting his presence, faintly, in the abyss, a second's worth of life left.

She had struggled like a man, bucked like a stallion, but he had broken her. He felt a sharp pain, and he had to release his elbow from her neck. But she was limp, and he supported her by holding her under her armpits to keep her from clumping to the floor, crashing into the stacks of canvases, toppling them noisily, attracting attention.

He heard gasps and guttural sounds coming from the body. She was taller and stronger than he imagined, and he had needed both hands, all his strength, to cut off the air to her windpipe. He reached for his knife to finish her off. He liked to see the ooze of blood; it gave him a sense of accomplishment.

Suddenly the bell clanged and his heart leapt forward at the impact.

"Andrea! Andrea!" It was a man's voice calling for her.

A voice boomed out over the speaker.

"The school is closed. All visitors must exit the building."
The lull of voices ceased abruptly.

He stepped over her body and out into the light. Two women hurried past the room on their way to the staircase. A man headed straight toward him! He froze. The stranger stared into his face. He was coming for him! But no, he continued past, into the art room, crossing his path, allowing him to escape.

He blended in with the parents descending the staircase.

It was only then that he noticed his bleeding hand. A small chunk of flesh had been clawed from his thumb.

27

Through the window of the main office Julie could see medics carrying Andrea Pappas on a stretcher and David Carr running beside it. A line of teachers who had been questioned by the police waited behind her to call out, and Julie had to talk fast.

"Get me out of here, Greg!" she pleaded. She didn't care that she was overheard. "Someone tried to kill Andrea. She may be dead already! I'm scared. Hurry!"

She could hear the scream of the receding siren as she dropped her keys on the principal's desk. Hurriedly she wrote a note and signed it. "I'm sorry. I can't come back. Tell the kids I'm sorry!"

• •

Jean-Claude was surprised when he heard the news flash on TV because he had felt the cartilage in her neck snap in his grip. But he was elated at the headline in the *Post*.

"REIGN OF TERROR IN THE SCHOOLS." He was a leader of the people, like Robespierre, like Toussaint L'Ouverture, the Haitian liberator who had defeated Napoléon. Recognized at last! He hadn't realized the sheer joy of notoriety, hadn't known what bliss was before. The killings were excitement enough, but this! Now he understood what Robespierre felt, what power, what exhilaration.

The headline in the *News* wasn't bad, either.

"KILLER STALKS PUBLIC SCHOOLS."

But the late edition of the *Post* was disturbing.

"BOYFRIEND SAVES LIFE OF TEACHER AFTER BRUTAL SECOND ATTACK IN PUBLIC SCHOOL." Jean-Claude experienced a trill of terror as he read the next line. "After the quick-thinking science teacher, David Carr, resuscitated Andrea Pappas, thereby saving her life, he sent a tissue sample he had dug from her fingernail for DNA tests.

"Determined to catch the madman, David Carr stated, 'Modern technology can determine who tried to kill my fiancée through genetic fingerprinting.

" 'It's fail-safe,' Carr explained to *Post* reporters yesterday at the hospital where Andrea Pappas was given a tracheotomy to assist her breathing and is recovering from extensive bruises to her face and neck."

So she was alive, he thought. And that science teacher was right. The skin Pappas had gouged from his finger would supply the police with a genetic blueprint that was his and only his. No one on the face of the earth had a complete set of genes—arrayed like beads in precise sequences along tiny, spiraling chemical strands called DNA—in his inimitable exact arrangement. Not unless he had an identical twin somewhere.

This David Carr was a worthy adversary, didn't trust the dummy police. Not to worry, Jean-Claude told himself, smiling broadly. It was a pity, though, that his brilliance, his uniqueness, wasn't recognized except in his DNA.

Jean-Claude decided to keep the game going. He couldn't live in obscurity after this taste of fame. He picked up his quill and dipped it into his antique inkwell.

"Death to the old regime," he wrote. "*Vive la liberté!*" he scrawled on the parchment he had squirreled away in his drawer. He addressed the envelope to the *New York Post* and carefully licked the flap before closing it.

That will give them another clue if they're bright enough to pick it up, he thought, knowing that saliva was excellent material for genetic analysis.

You may have my gene map to condemn me with, he thought, adding a stamp to the letter. But you'll have to catch me first.

• • •

The school was almost empty, and Jesus had ignored the parents picketing outside. Most students were all too willing to boycott the school. It was a hot day. The sound of fans whirring and the voices of teachers lazily chatting with small groups of students through open doors floated down the corridor. A security guard patrolled each floor, and Gordon, the policeman regularly assigned to the school, guarded Andrea Pappas's art room, where the attack had taken place.

A guard eyed Jesus as he tried Julie Greenwood's door. He rattled the knob, unbelieving when it wouldn't turn. It was his hour for tutoring. She had never missed a single day.

The guard ambled over to Jesus. "Didn't you hear the announcement? All Greenwood's classes travel with Mr. Davis, the shop teacher in 212."

"She absent?" asked Jesus.

"She quit! You ain't never gonna see her no more. I hear she's havin' a baby. Left her keys on the principal's desk and walked. Never even came back for her things . . ."

Jesus turned his back and walked away.

"Hey, can ya blame her? I'm not crazy to work here myself."

Jesus wasn't listening. He trudged down the stairs, heavily, like an old man. But he stopped at the bottom of the landing. There was something he had to do before leaving for good.

• • •

The odor of sickness enveloped Julie as the automated doors admitted her into the hospital corridor where Andrea Pappas was recovering in her room. David Carr was standing in her doorway talking to a reporter.

"I understand you sent it to a lab yourself. Why didn't you give it to the police?"

David indicated Julie. "Here's the person to ask. Hello, Julie," he greeted her.

"Not me!" she claimed. David was surprised. It was Julie who had begged him to send the tissue he had pried from Andrea's pointed fingernails to the lab instead of turning it over to the police. He had rushed it to the science room and secured it under a slide when the medics arrived. "Believe me," Julie had said, "the police will fuck it up." It was Bobbie talking, she had said, desperately trying to help them find her killer. He saw no harm in sending the tissue to Cell Codes, a professional lab, and Julie had offered to pay the fee for the DNA print.

David remembered Julie's reaction to Bobbie's display on designer genes; Julie could barely contain herself when Bobbie explained that minute samples of blood, semen, saliva, or even a strand of hair could be analyzed.

"He's an amateur detective," stammered Julie. "And he has a personal interest."

The reporter, a young woman trying to squeeze some new info from David, gave up and gathered her papers into her briefcase when Dixon arrived unexpectedly. "I'll catch you later," she promised as they moved into Andrea's room.

Andrea had a tube in her neck, and her face was black and blue, but she was sitting halfway up on the raised mechanical bed. The gray room was filled with flowers, and Julie handed her a box of marzipans, Andrea's favorite sweet.

Dixon wasted no time. "Did anyone have a grudge against her?" he asked, treating Andrea as if she were invisible.

"The only one everyone hated in the school was the Bitch of Buchenwald, our ex-principal," said David. "You had the good fortune not to know her."

"Oh, yeah."

"She ran the school like a gulag," Julie added.

"What happened to her?"

"She died," wheezed Andrea, talking slowly as she got air through the tube in her throat.

Dixon looked nervous. "What do you mean, she died?"

"She was killed by a terrorist bomb in an airplane."

"What?"

"Nine years ago," said David.

"Did anyone else in this school die a horrible death that I don't know about?" he asked sarcastically.

"Why, yes," said Andrea, her voice breathy. "That's how you got your job. The dean of boys, Sy Oxley, died suddenly of a heart attack. It was pretty gruesome . . ." She stopped herself and looked at David for confirmation that it was a heart attack.

"Shit!" said David.

"I never thought . . ." said Julie.

Dixon was angry. "What's going on?"

"He fell under a train," said Julie, barely whispering.

"Pushed," said Andrea, trembling, her voice failing.

"I'm next!" said Julie hysterically. "I knew it! I'm next!"

• • •

Esperanza refused to lean on Jesus, but she was too weak to stand in line in the clinic. Jesus sat her down on the bench and waited in her place to have the card stamped.

Next was the wait for the doctor, at least two hours. *"Dios mio,"* whispered Esperanza. "The pain, *mucho dolor,"* she cried. She clutched her stomach, her back. "God is punishing me," she murmured. Jesus jumped up from his seat next to her in the waiting room. How could he stand this anymore? He paced in the room, a lineup of poor people, depressed, waiting for the doctor.

But as Jesus was about to give up, Nilda arrived. The receptionist ushered them all into the hallway outside the doctor's office, where a nurse took Esperanza's blood pressure. "Very high, very high," the nurse advised the doctor, alarmed. The young doctor shook his head to quiet her. Jesus looked at the doctor, terrified. The doctor took Esperanza by the arm and led her into his examining room. Jesus and Nilda followed.

"What is it, Doctor Rodriguez?" Nilda asked when they were seated. Jesus was struck dumb. The doctor's eyes were sad. "I can't tell you for sure without tests. And she won't take tests, refuses to be admitted to a hospital."

"The crazy woman!" Jesus blurted out. "She's all I have." He buried his head in his hands.

"Does she have any other family?" he asked, looking at Esperanza. He had asked her before.

"A brother, Marcos, my uncle."

"No, don't tell him," whispered Esperanza, suddenly alert. "He has his family. Promise me! I don't die in the hospital." She clutched Jesus's hand. "I want to go home. Don't let them take me away."

Jesus held her papery hand to his cheek, and Esperanza felt a tear on her fingers.

• • •

After he gave Esperanza two of her painkillers, Jesus

climbed into bed and pulled the cover over his head. He imagined he could still hear her scissoring the babies from the ads in the magazines to put into the album she no longer thought to hide under her bed. The myriad cutouts, outlines only of tiny forms, of baby after baby, were piled helter-skelter in her album. Love and hate and misery, mingling like the pulverized human bones Esperanza bought in the *botanica* to save her soul, growled within Jesus in an unuttered howl of anguish. And he wondered, lulling himself to sleep, his tongue wrapped around his thumb, how could he hate her? She was so defenseless she needed him to protect her.

Esperanza rocked in her rocking chair, her paper dolls strewn about her on the floor. "I've got you back now, Marcos," she crooned in her delirium. The breeze from the open window gusted the paper dolls in swirls on the floor, and now that she imagined baby Marcos cradled in her arms she felt free. Pain and pills, pills and pain, she thought. She was no longer for this earth. She looked through the open window at the sun sinking in the sky. If she didn't go out now, the sun would soon be on the horizon and they wouldn't be able to see the angels.

A lightness began to buoy her. She hadn't been able to eat anything of dinner, and she was so light and thin the pills that Jesus gave her were speeding through her small body.

She couldn't even feel her feet as she started out of the window to climb to the ledge. Where was the baby? She had just held him in her arms. It was eighteen floors from the ground. Esperanza didn't think to look down.

Jesus awoke freezing cold. His light was still on. A blast of wind from Esperanza's room beckoned him.

"*Mamacita!*" he cried, lunging at her, dragging her in, fear and chill shocking him awake. He held her shivering body, warming her with his embrace, looking into her trusting eyes. She was totally unaware of what she had done.

He lay her head on the pillow of her bed, covering her wraithlike form with a blanket, and in minutes he watched her eyes close.

"You're not going to die!" he told the sleeping Esperanza as he slammed the open window shut, the sound, like a pistol shot, jolting him from his grief.

"Please don't die," he begged her unashamedly, hugging and kissing her frail form. "Please don't leave me alone."

• • •

"Here's a brilliant letter for our wastebasket," said May Chen, waving a letter she had just opened. It was addressed to the *Post*, city editor.

"Just drop it into the circular file," said her bored colleague without looking up from his work.

But she stuck the letter under his nose anyway. This one was different.

"What the fuck does this mean?" he asked, irritated. "It's signed, 'Robespierre'!"

Then it hit her. "The Reign of Terror." She would send it to the police. Let them figure out whether it was just another fruitcake.

• • •

Jesus had little to do with his days. He gave Esperanza her pills for the pain, and she was out of it more and more. Sometimes she didn't know him. She ate so little that he tried to find mushy food she could digest, to keep her alive. But he was losing the battle; she was getting thinner and thinner.

He had waited a week, until the police were out of the school, to break in at night. But security was tight. He had to do it from the inside. He hated to return, to see the other students, the teachers. But he forced himself to walk in the door. And no one paid attention. He was still a student. He climbed the stairs to the second floor reading lab and unlocked the door, knowing the room was empty, and stared into the mirrored wall. All the reading class kids knew it was a two-way mirror. Behind the wall was a narrow room where observers could watch through the mirror while teachers worked with students. Although it was designed for teacher training, it had never been used.

He locked the outer door. If anyone checked at three

o'clock, he would be safe. But just in case, he would hide in the room behind the mirror, because the guard didn't even know it existed.

• • •

"Did you get any threats?" asked Dixon. Andrea was up and around, and David and Julie sat with Dixon in the hospital lounge overlooking Morningside Park. Andrea's roommate was recovering from surgery.

"Are you kidding? Remember Velma? She threatened to kill me every week. And I wasn't laughing, either. She was two hundred pounds of mean blubber."

"It's gotta be a student who had a grudge against you, Bobbie, Oxley, and the principal who was killed."

Andrea shook her head. "We had so many kids together over the years."

"What about Ronald Doctor? Remember him? He was a scary kook. He murdered someone when he graduated," David said.

"I never had him. I don't know why; I get them all," Andrea said.

"What about that Haitian?"

"Jean-Claude!" cried Andrea. "Jean-Claude Gatreaux."

"He was a maniacal kid," said Julie. "But that was years ago. I remember him because it was my first year as a teacher and I had him in my class. He gave Bobbie some grief."

"The footprint on the staircase was a man's," said Dixon.

"He was a real sicko and a French Revolution buff," recalled Andrea.

Dixon looked blank.

"He was before your time," said Andrea.

"He stabbed a kid in Oxley's room . . ." said Julie.

"Wasn't Oxley the dean?" interrupted Dixon.

"In those days the dean taught classes," Julie explained.

"And we suspended him!" Andrea coughed, and her breathing became labored. "We were all there," she rasped.

"Bobbie was at the hearing," announced Julie. "And Oxley and the principal . . ."

"And 'Good, Better, Best.' Remember her?" Andrea asked, recovering her voice.

"I sure do." She joined Andrea in a mocking singsong. "Good, better, best. Never let it rest 'til your good is better and your better best."

"That was the motto of Bonnie Burns. She was at the suspension hearing too!" Andrea said to Dixon.

"I wonder what ever happened to her?" Julie said.

• • •

When he was sure the school was deserted, Jesus came out of his hiding place. He was walking through the hallway for the last time. He climbed to the third floor, to Julie's room, unlocked her door, and was unprepared for the rush of her presence. She had left the room exactly the same as he remembered.

He worked the combination lock on her closet from memory and saw that she had left all her possessions behind. He took the can of kerosene from his backpack and squirted it on the books in the bottom of the closet. Then he doused her clothes on their hangers. He lit a match to her sweater and closed the door.

Her wooden wardrobe would ignite in a minute. He dribbled kerosene as he ran along the front of the room and walked out, leaving a trail all the way to the bottom of the staircase, where the can ran dry. He tossed it aside and exited through the backyard just as he heard a whoosh and then the explosion. The science lab had contributed to the fireworks.

• • •

William Graham sat down, loosened his tie, and leaned back in his swivel chair. He looked across the desk at his visitor. He had heard about Dixon from his friend Bernie Frankel. The dean was only in his forties, Graham thought, yet the streaks of white in his hair gave him an older, more distinguished look than he deserved. But the five o'clock shadow on Dixon's face offset any improvement made by the gray at his temples, Graham noted sardonically. Graham rolled up his starched white sleeves. It was almost summer and the school year was winding down.

Dixon had sat patiently waiting for twenty minutes just to interview Grace Frossard's principal, taking the chance that he might find some connection to the murders in his school. True, Grace Frossard meant nothing to the teachers. But they hadn't connected the deaths right in front of their long noses. And his pal, Gordon, admitted that the police hadn't done any checking. They didn't have time!

"Had Frossard been teaching here long?" Dixon asked the tall, lanky black principal.

"As long as I can remember," the principal answered.

Dixon looked him over. He was still wet behind the ears.

"Eight years," he supplied.

"Have you received all her records?"

Graham laughed. "The board won't move their ass unless they're sued. Even for murder. But my secretary is working on some pension papers for poor Bonnie's heirs, if that will help."

"Bonnie? I thought her name was Grace!"

"Yes, Bonnie. That's what everyone called her. Most teachers never knew the poor soul's given name was Grace."

Dixon snatched the papers rudely from under Graham's fingers. He usually didn't antagonize principals that way, but he couldn't wait.

He shuffled through the papers quickly, his eyes racing down the pages until he found something that shocked even him. It appeared on the change-of-name or marital status form. "Maiden name," it read, "Grace Burns."

Dixon slammed his fist on the table. "Bonnie Burns worked at Catherine Dunbar Junior High School!" he shouted. "Her married name is Frossard, and the *Post* gave her legal name when she was killed. *Grace Frossard*. That's why no one connected her to the other murders," he announced to Graham, who up to that second had been imagining a left hook to Dixon's bulbous nose for his rudeness.

• • •

It was dark, and the blaze was more dramatic against the blue-black sky. Jesus watched from across the street with the crowd. His heart leapt in the flames engulfing the entrance and

died when the hoses extinguished their light. The excitement
was over. The crowd, formerly agitated, quietly dispersed with
Jesus among them, depressed at having to confront their diminished lives.

• • •

"Tragedy strikes again at Catherine Dunbar Junior High.
The scene of recent multiple murders is now in ashes, the result
of arson," announced WINS radio.

It's Jesus, thought Julie, crashing the stem of the wineglass
she was rinsing against the side of the kitchen sink. I know it as
well as I know I'm standing here, she thought. Jesus set that fire.

• • •

"Find me Jean-Claude Gatreaux," Dixon told Hank Gordon, the cop assigned to the school, "and you'll be a hero. You
have four to six weeks. The DNA print will be ready then, and
you can collar him and match him up with it."

"Why don't I tell my chief?" asked Gordon.

"I don't want the papers to scare this fucker off. He ain't
afraid of killing. He's done it four times—almost four. Five if he
planted the bomb on the airplane. And I don't want him on the
loose. Who's gonna protect me? You?"

"You got yourself a deal," said Gordon, slapping Dixon's
palm. He didn't care to be stuck by this loony tune while he was
patrolling the school, either. Nobody loved cops, he reminded
himself.

28

Greg strode into Julie's room in the maternity ward and joyfully threw the morning papers down on her bed.

"SCHOOL COP NABS SERIAL KILLER" was the *Post* headline.

"DNA TRAPS GENIUS KILLER," headlined the *News*.

"FORMER STUDENT SLAYS TEACHERS IN VENDETTA," Julie read.

"Jean-Claude Gatreaux was tracked down by clever cop Hank Gordon, assigned to Catherine Dunbar Junior High School, who realized that the murders were connected to the former student, suspended seventeen years ago by his teachers. With the information supplied by Mason Dixon, the dean of the school, Gordon was able to narrow down the suspects to Gatreaux, who had been a brilliant but troubled youth with a history of violence. Gatreaux admitted the crimes. 'My DNA print is unique,' Gatreaux stated. 'I bow to science.' He quoted Shakespeare as Gordon put the cuffs on.

" 'It is a vile thing to die, my gracious Lord, When men are unprepared and look not for it.'

"However, as Officer Gordon reminded him, in New York there is no death penalty to date."

Julie kissed and kissed her precious baby boy. She kissed his black hair, his flat newborn nose, his delicate fingers. She peered happily into Danny's wide-awake, contented eyes.

"We're home free!" she sang out and gleefully handed the infant to Greg. She and Andrea were Gatreaux's next victims, and her life had been spared. Greg was right. He always said the school was a dangerous place. He didn't know *how* happy she was; the murderer was not connected to her past as she had feared. Now no one was out to get her.

• • •

Jean-Claude could barely pace, his cell at Rikers Island was so narrow. And looking through the bars was worse than staring at the enclosed room of the mental ward. Here the noise of the other prisoners, from whom he was kept apart, maddened him, their roar irrelevant to him. He was not waiting to be judged. There was no doubt about him, no presumption of innocence. He had confessed. Confessed to everything. Everything but one crime, the crime that mattered the most, that was his ace-in-the-hole, his last revenge.

Yesterday when he was arrested he had arrogantly rejected his one call to the outside world. He had no need of anyone. But as he paced, as he slept, and finally when dawn jolted his inner clock, his heart began to beat in sync with his fear, with the realization that he had wasted precious hours! What if she saw his picture in *El Diario*, panicked when she discovered he was a murderer, was at this very moment at the police station babbling the truth. He knew too well how anyone who wanted could hold her heart in the palm of his hand, the way he did, and squeeze it.

He had memorized her new number because he always knew one day he would be making this call. When the guard passed the phone through the bars, he played the numbered buttons slowly, with faltering fingers, and then listened to the methodical rings with fear.

Answer the phone, Esperanza, he begged. Answer the phone.

Esperanza picked up the phone after the ninth ring, the number of letters in her name.

"*Aqui es Jean-Claude,*" he said.

Her heart fluttered in fear. It was a voice from the past, with its strangely accented Spanish, an unmistakable voice she would always recognize. It had the urgency, the same insistent rasp as a saw's teeth buzzing through the flesh of a tree. She was in awe of its vibration just as she had been fourteen years ago, when she first met him.

"Esperanza," he said, threatening, cajoling. "Have you kept our secret?"

Esperanza quaked with fear. It was the Messenger of God calling.

Jean-Claude smoked sitting on his cot, relaxed. A good morning's work. His stomach began to growl with hunger, responding to the smells of breakfast being cooked in the basement of the prison. The phone call to Esperanza stimulated recollections of revenge. The kidnapping, he thought, with grim satisfaction, had merely been the hors d'oeuvre on his morbid menu of revenge; it had been what he liked to think of as the tidbit that had whet his appetite for murder. And he had planned to crown the deadly meal—after Oxley, course number one, Bummy, course number two, Frossard, three, and Pappas, four, with his pièce de résistance, the juiciest morsel saved for dessert—the killing of Julie Layton. He had thought she was his friend, and then she kicked him when he was down.

He delighted in thinking of the kidnapping first, and her murder last, as bookends crushing the others between. But he could rest easy now. He would still have his revenge. She would never know who took her baby. And she would never get him back!

In Esperanza's reverie the old room she had on Riverside Drive returned with the clarity of only yesterday. And she remembered the day she had confided her voices to the Messenger of God, whom she had met in the *botanica*. He was the healer who sold her herbs and powders and potions. Only *he* knew how to release their powers, and he had taught her his secrets and they practiced voodoo in her room together.

It was he who had told her that *La Mala* was evil, that when he had been thrown out of his family's house because of the devil herself he had taken a room in the hotel next to *La Mala* to spy on her. And when he saw that Esperanza's room faced *La Mala*, he explained that there was a war between good and evil and that he, Jean-Claude Toussaint Gatreaux, named for a warrior, had been sent by God to do battle with evil. Esperanza's voices had convinced him that she was put in the room across from the Evil One by divine intent, to help him win the battle. He had given her the binoculars to watch *La Mala*. He was the Messenger of God. And he had used her to steal the baby.

But now Esperanza began to think he was real. She had seen his picture in the paper, had heard his voice terrifying her after all these years, after he had murdered innocent people.

"*Silencio, Esperanza*," he had warned her many years ago. "*Silencio*." And she had been silent. And now she knew who he really was. He wasn't the Messenger of God, as he claimed. He was the Messenger of Death.

• • •

Julie took contented peeks under the pram hood as she and Greg walked on the park side of Fifth Avenue where there were few streets to cross. Next weekend they would be in windy Cape May, but today—the warm sunny day, the puffs of white clouds in a bright blue sky, her baby with his perfect little fingers and toes squirming happily—she would remember forever.

The scene in the sky was like the one on her first baby's blanket, a thick velour blanket of baby blue with white clouds and white lambs. She dismissed the image. She had been through too much to spoil her bliss with tortured thoughts. But every time someone stopped to admire her baby, her heart stopped. And the expression on her face once prompted Greg to ask, "Are you okay?"

Greg put his arm around her; she had let go of his hand. His skin, his touch, closed the mental gap she had created with her memories, and the moment she would always remember lingered, like the sun on her arms.

Suddenly she spotted Jesus, about to enter the park. But he turned away, pretending not to see her. He was talking to a friend dressed just like him in dark trousers, a black sleeveless shirt, and a black leather spiked band on his wrist. He wore no hat, but Julie noticed he was growing a beard. Nilda had entered the park a few steps ahead of him.

As Greg caught her staring, Julie was about to say, "Look, Greg, there's one of my students." But she stopped herself. Jesus didn't look like the kind of child Greg would be eager to meet. They continued their walk.

Nilda could see the color rush to Jesus's face. He seemed turned to stone, a statue watching Julie as she walked uptown with her husband. They were pushing a baby carriage past the entrance. Jesus had stopped dead still as they walked past, their backs toward Nilda and Jesus, strolling slowly away. And Jesus was unaware of anything around him. Pedestrian traffic was moving in and out of the entrance, jostling him, trying to maneuver around him, but he was oblivious that he was an obstacle in the path of the bustling weekend crowd.

Nilda urged him along while Jesus watched fixedly, the scene becoming a tableau in his mind. And when he continued on his way, not even bothering to pretend that the words Nilda or her cousin spoke to him registered any sense, she began to suspect that there was something very wrong with him.

Jesus found Esperanza in her bedroom almost toppling over with the effort of pulling out her heavily laden bottom drawer. She extracted a bundle wrapped in tissue paper and laid it on her bed. She opened it reverently, revealing an unusual blue blanket of soft, thick cotton, with lambs and clouds sculpted into the deep, heavy material. Esperanza pressed it to her lips and smiled. A tiny infant's yellow nightgown and a delicately woven short, light sweater were still folded on the tissue paper. They were very fine, things Jesus had seen in store windows, things that Esperanza would never buy. She bought clothes from racks on the street at bargain outlets. The baby clothes were slightly old-fashioned.

"Where did you get these?" he asked her, irked but trying not to hurt her with his usual harsh tone.

"Yours! When you were born," she said, speaking as usual

in Spanish, offering them to Jesus. He held the minuscule clothing in his hand, noticing the B. Altman label inside. "It's time for you to have them," she added, taking a box from the drawer and opening it. Inside were a long gold chain, a ring, and the deed to the house in Puerto Rico, which Marcos had given her. "From my mother," she told him, holding the gold wedding band.

She was preparing to die, Jesus suddenly realized. She was giving away her treasures.

"No, *Mamacita*, no," he begged her, closing the box.

She looked alarmed. He was disorienting her with his objections. And today she wanted to think clearly, to follow her desires.

"I have no strength," she pleaded. "Listen to me," she whispered. She sat on her bed. She was so frail she was a shadow. She drew him down with a motion of her skeletal hand. "This is yours," she whispered in his ear. She put her finger to his lips. Her skin was still soft, had life coursing through, he thought.

"I'm dying. God's will. I'm being punished," she explained. "I did an evil thing, and now you will be alone."

Jesus wanted to jump up, to object. But she kept him near her with her eyes.

"Don't cry," she said when she saw Jesus's face, the face she knew as that of her baby, contorted with the effort of suppressing emotion. "*Pobrecito*," she crooned. Then she held his face in her hands. "I am not your mamma," she said, looking into his violet eyes. "Your real mother is beautiful, not like me. God put you in the school near *La Mala* to test me, to taunt me. I was so afraid she would steal you back. I wanted to take you from the school, but Marcos wouldn't let me."

Jesus jumped up. "You *are* crazy!" he shouted, disappointed. She was talking mumbo jumbo again. But he saw that her pills were still on the bureau, unopened. She had waited for him, as usual.

"I stole you away when you were an infant." Jesus saw that her eyes were clear and direct. "I went to the apartment of *La Mala*, and one day," she continued, speaking with conviction, "I folded you into this blanket." Jesus listened, mesmerized. "God wanted me to have you. Why else was the door left open for me?" When she saw the cloud of doubt in his eyes, she said, "I swear on my mother, on Marcos."

"I was born in Puerto Rico!" he shouted.

"I took you there. The Virgin told me. There is no father. God is your father," she said, in pain, clutching her stomach. She removed a yellowing, crumbling newspaper clipping from the box. It was a story from *El Diario*. "Read this," she implored. "I saved it for when my time came."

"Here, here," Jesus said, ignoring her, fumbling with the pills. He rushed to get her water. "Take this," he said, hoping to beat the terrible pain to come.

Esperanza crossed herself. "Believe me. On my mother's grave," she said, falling to her knees. The edges of the newspaper flaked off and fell to the floor as she clutched it.

"Take this," he said, watching her swallow the pill. "I believe you," he soothed her. "I believe you," he agreed, to calm her, reluctantly removing the clipping from her hand.

• • •

When Esperanza slept, a dreamy, drug-filled sleep, Jesus hoped her mind was wandering to better worlds, that her painkillers put her demons as well as her physical pain to sleep. He sat on her bed and listened to her snore. She looked like a little boy, she was so small and thin, yet her skin was young. And for the first time he felt her ugliness had slipped away with her lost pounds. He felt like caressing her soft arm, but he was afraid to awaken her.

Jesus lifted her leg gently and removed the baby clothes she had tried to thrust upon him. The garments were so soft to the touch that he wondered what the life of a child clothed in these might be. He pictured the little blond boy whose watch he wore as a spoil of war. He imagined the boy growing up in a house just like Julie's. He pictured the boy's family on a sailboat, vacationing the way the ads on TV depicted the wealthy at play. He pictured the polished dining room table in Julie's town house and placed the family members around it, the table set with silver and glistening platters heaped with steaming food. The little blond boy was in the center, surrounded by elegantly dressed people, his father smiling genially at him.

All he had was poor, crazy Esperanza. And soon there would be no one. He lay the clothing down next to her, wondering how these little clothes had come into her imaginings. He picked up the yellowed clipping he had discarded. It was cut from an old newspaper, dated 1973. His eyes darted to a news photo of a young man and a woman, and the sight struck him breathless.

Esperanza, the bedroom, the consciousness of his surroundings disappeared instantaneously as his focus narrowed, riveting him to the image in the article. The familiarity and then the recognition of the grieving couple seized and shook him. It took only seconds for him to realize that the woman was Julie. And the caption under the picture identified the couple as "*Julie y Les Layton.*" Les Layton was the man whose picture he had seen on the CD in Julie's house! He was not her husband, Greg, the man who had held her hand in the park.

He read the article, stumbling over the difficult Spanish words. "Kidnap, infant, apartment, Riverside Drive, reward" were all he needed to understand. Esperanza had once lived on Riverside Drive! It was all there as she had described. The clothing on the bed and the clothing worn by the kidnapped infant were identical.

Could the drugs have created this tale for her? But she hadn't taken her pills until just now! Esperanza talked to the Virgin, but she never made up stories or told lies. Where did she get these clothes?

He clutched the clothing, unbelieving, feeling them, turning them over and over to be sure they were real, to be sure that he wasn't going crazy like Esperanza, because if he was the kidnapped infant in this newspaper story, then he was Julie's son.

29

"Is this Julie *Layton?*"

Julie's heart dropped. The fear of her afflicted past came from deep down, and she knew that now it was all over. Her life was ruined.

"Who is this?" she asked, her voice steady and resigned.

"I know about your kidnapped baby," the voice answered.

Julie recognized the voice at once.

"Jesus? Is that *you?*"

"If you wan' your son back, I'll come to your home in an hour."

"What do you mean? Tell me . . ."

"Yes or no. I ain't talkin' on no phone."

"Yes! *Please*, tell me . . ."

The phone went blank.

• • •

Jesus ran through the park with the pretty box under his arm, the box Esperanza had used to save his baby clothing and his blanket. He was going to Julie to claim his parents. The article was fourteen years old, and he wondered where his father was now. He shivered, hoping he was still alive. Les Layton, jazz musician! Maybe he would teach him the drums. He didn't dare hope for too much. He had never had a father.

Jesus would have taken a cab, but each one drove on by. He didn't care. Soon he would have everything. Now he understood that he had never belonged with insane Esperanza, in that lonely apartment on Broadway, in that broken-down house in Puerto Rico, or that little room she told him about on Riverside Drive, where there was no heat or hot water and they had rats to keep them company.

He rounded the reservoir, beating the dirt track with his tennis shoes, rhythmically running, on a happy errand. For once he felt at ease with the joggers. I'm one of you, he thought with a sense of belonging.

Now he wouldn't have to break into Julie's house to see what it was like; he would be living there himself in the beautiful room with the Chinese vases, the velvet curtains, the beautiful ducks! He leaped across the track, exiting the park at Ninetieth Street on the East Side, hardly minding the distance. He had spoken to his real mother, and he was headed home.

• • •

Julie couldn't believe that Martha was refusing to bring her the gun. The calm that Julie had fought to maintain when she called Martha was now dissolving into terror. Why was Martha abandoning her? "Get out of the house," Martha said.

"I've got to reach Greg," Julie said.

"Just get in a cab. I'll try to reach Greg from here."

Shaking, Julie dialed Greg again. "Please try to find Greg," she implored his secretary, her voice warping with anxiety. "Tell him to come home. It's an emergency."

Julie waited too long.

• • •

Jesus twisted the handle on the wrought-iron gate, surprised to find it wouldn't respond. He twisted harder, looking up at the first-floor window. She had forgotten to unlock the gate for him.

He ignored the sinking feeling, a warning. How was he to get in? He rattled the gate, feeling foolish.

The street was empty, and he easily scaled the gate, his box in tow. He climbed the stairs to the curtained door and peered inside. There was no light, no shadow in the deep hall. He looked up expectantly at the window and pressed his thumb on the doorbell. As it shrilled in the house, his anxiety grew. Where was she? She knew he was coming!

Jesus banged on the door. Maybe she couldn't hear the bell! He knew she was home.

"Open up!" Jesus screamed. "I'm here, I'm here."

• • •

Julie watched from the window as Jesus approached, stepping back into the darkness. It was early dusk, and the street lamps blinked on. She could see him clearly.

If he thought she wasn't at home, he would leave her in peace.

Her heart made a jump. He was climbing the gate, climbing the stairs! She heard the doorbell, unrelenting, insistent. Go away! Jesus was the plague she had unleashed, the fear in her nightmare. Go away! she begged.

But Jesus was expected. He beat on the door, beating and beating, his forehead pressed to the glass. The glass trembled on the door.

Julie covered her ears.

"Let me in!" he cried.

But Julie couldn't hear his voice, only the threatening thump of his fist on the door and not his despair.

And then, thank God, there was silence. Jesus had left.

30

Julie opened the front door and looked up and down the street. She had watched Jesus through the window until he walked away and had bounded down the steps after he finally gave up.

Julie's heart was heavy as her infant's shiny, trusting eyes peered up at her from the Snugli she wore. She kissed the top of his sweet head, his wispy, fine hair soft against her lips, noticing the rain clouds. No time to get an umbrella, she thought, when she kicked something with her toe.

She looked down and saw it, the box that Jesus had carried when he jumped over the gate. The long, yellow box had been sitting on the doorstep waiting for her, like an abandoned orphan.

Julie's heart beat uncontrollably as she opened the box. She clutched the baby clothing to her, pressing it against her infant.

"Is this your brother's?" she asked in agony. "Or is this a hoax to torture me?"

Oh, Jesus. What do you want from me? she thought. Her nightmare kept pursuing her. Jesus was sent by the kidnapper to get money from her! Or were heartless people, like the ones who had called her for ransom money when her baby was kidnapped, trying to suck her blood again? She had to call Les. But first she had to protect herself. Her heart skipped away out of control for fear of the possibilities. Her past was rising from its burial ground.

Julie's cab raced to Martha's apartment.

"I would feel safer if I had your gun," Julie pleaded.

"You don't know how to use it," Martha said.

"Just show me!"

"Julie," Martha said, putting her arms around her, "just stay *here*. Stay until we reach Greg."

"I can't. I left a message for him to come home. He'll panic if we're not there."

"Julie—oh, God, I don't know what to do."

Even through her hysteria, Julie now noticed two packed suitcases on the floor of the living room. "Are you going somewhere?"

"Yes. I didn't have time to tell you." Martha paced the floor. "I won't go. I'm staying here with you."

"No," Julie insisted. "Just give me your gun."

• • •

Jesus sat on a bench in Central Park facing the pond on One Hundred Second Street near the spot where the news reports said a jogger had been attacked. It was still light, and the few dog walkers and lovers who had dared to enter the park were thinning out. He stared vacantly at the debris floating at the edge of the water, which was catching the shimmer of the waning light.

Jesus put his head in his hands. He thought about Julie's quiet block; the sense of well-being that the houses, huddled like friendly families, gave a person; how hacked down he was, cut out of that world he had hoped to be a part of.

He wasn't good enough for Julie. He was nothing, a bum. She had her baby, her new husband, her money. She didn't want him busting in on her. When he thought of the baby, his anger coiled like an asp.

Jesus was in another world these days, Nilda thought as she spotted him sitting on the bench, oblivious to the world around him. She couldn't stop bugging him about breaking into Julie's house. Especially after seeing him go ape over Julie in the park and the cruel way he ignored her. She came after him to remind him of his promise to her, but she could see he was depressed. And she didn't want to say anything or admit she had been looking for him. He looked like total shit, she thought. He would never listen to her today.

But when he saw her, he sat up, surprising her by looking straight into her face.

"You want her jewelry?" he asked, spitting his anger, challenging her. "That's bullshit!" he said, a sneer snaking his mouth. "We'll take her fuckin' baby."

31

Jesus turned to see if anyone was watching as he entered the dark house. The rumble of thunder pounded with his pulse as he hid behind the pitch-black stairs. He waited, his heart fluttering like the beating of wings because he knew he was in flight now and nothing could stop him.

• • •

A light, warm rain fell like a lace curtain, and Julie protected her baby's head with her hands snuggling him tightly against her and crouching over him as she ran from the cab. Misery and foreboding overwhelmed her. She felt for the gun in her bag.

She went into the house and turned on the light, sensing a denseness in the air, a difference in the house, as if the molecules in the atmosphere enveloping her were rubbing, clashing against one another. Her skin was picking up a message, the hair follicles on her body intercepting vibrations. Like a blind person, she sensed a presence or an object by intuitive vision.

She pricked up her attention, cocked her ear to every nuance. She tensed to the creak of her step, attuned to the house itself as if it were speaking to her. She listened to the spaces between the molecules, tried to see the very air. This time she would trust her sixth sense.

She slowed her inner functions, her heart, her pulse, her breath, in order to be alert to the slightest sound outside herself. She clutched her tender babe and heard a contented, delicate gurgle.

She looked behind her through the curtained window to

the outside. No one there. She was too frightened to check the velvet of dark behind the stairs. She advanced to the hall, then went back and flung open the front door for an avenue of escape and rushed to the back of the stairway, despite her fear. Her heart boomed like a drum. Boom, boom, boom.

She almost screamed with relief. Empty! She slammed the front door shut and raced up the stairs, out of breath, still squeezing her baby, her heart palpitating wildly against his soft body.

Jesus had watched through a slat of the closed blinds as Julie clattered the gate behind her. She had rushed up the stairs in the rain, forgetting to lock it, leaving him only the front door to open for Nilda.

He moved through the rooms, looking for the best place to hide. The screen in the living room, the velvet drapes, the wooden wardrobe in her bedroom? He crept into the bathroom, the one Julie never used, and hid behind the opaque glass that slid closed in front of the tub. He spread a towel over the glass. He would grab the baby when Julie put the baby in the crib, and while she was in the living room or kitchen he would rush past her. She might not even miss the little fucker if he didn't cry. If he did, Nilda would be waiting at the door for him to hand her the baby, and they would be gone before Julie could see him or call the cops. He wished he could look out of the window to see if the old green Plymouth Duster was still there with Nilda at the wheel. No matter what, he was leaving with the baby.

Ten minutes passed before the telephone rang and he heard Julie's footsteps. He stepped out of the shower, hearing that the phone had been picked up as he ran nimbly into the baby's room. He was stunned. The crib was empty!

She had taken the baby with her. Listening for Julie's voice, he looked for Nilda on the street. The street was silent, and he saw the same parked cars. But no Nilda!

He closed the slat and took a terrible chance. He opened one of the closets and hid himself where the blankets and boxes were stored. With the blinds drawn, dark descended like death. Minutes passed. His anxiety rose.

About to bolt from his crouch, Jesus froze in the sudden

light as Julie entered the room. He was so close to her he steadied his breath.

Julie lay the baby on his back to undress him and put on his soft nightie. He was so exquisite, his skin so new, like a tender new shoot of a green plant, so rosy it was like the petal of a flower. It was time for a long nap. This newly arrived being had need for deep sleeps, thirsted for the refreshment of new-born dreams. Julie smelled his savory skin, an odor unlike any other in the universe, as she rubbed her lips gently over his forehead, his tiny chin.

But she sensed something. Again the prickle of a hair on the back of her neck, the disturbance in the ions of the air, told her of a presence, her awareness coming from years of fear, from years of knowing there was so safe place for her. She turned her head.

A hand grasping a heavy, gleaming object came down on her, consuming her vision. Then a sickly crack, a sticky, violent pain, and she reached for her baby, thumping to the floor, smashing him under her with a giant thud, splattering blood from the gash in her head everywhere. She fought to stay conscious, not allowing the blackness to overwhelm her.

She felt for her baby's body with her bloody fingers. His cries focused her brain. Hang on to reality; save yourself. She struggled to get up, grasped the crib bar for support, and felt a throb, an excruciating, shattering pain in her ankle as she twisted it on the foot of the crib in her fall.

A thickening flow of blood covered her hair. She was afraid to move to the window, to scream for help. Maybe he would hit her again. Where was he? She had her baby; that's all that mattered. He was comforted now, and all she had to do was hold on to her baby. And get to her gun!

He wondered if he had killed Julie. He usually knew how hard to hit someone to split his skull without killing him. But he had never hit a woman, and the heavy brass base of the lamp he had brained her with had been hard to control.

He had hit her from behind so that she couldn't see him. But she had grabbed her baby. The shock should have stunned her, but she was still thinking and was able to protect her baby instinctively, like an animal, even as she was being attacked, maybe killed. And she would have seen him if he hadn't run for cover when she crashed! He could see that he had fucked up the job. He stood numb, wondering what to do.

Julie crawled to the baby's dresser and removed the gun from the drawer. She turned out the light. Still, the street lamps' yellow lights would illuminate anyone entering the room. It was getting darker. She could see lights from the occasional car splashing through the rain come and go, headlights interrupting the quiet glow of her side street.

She was afraid to scream, afraid of enraging her attacker, afraid she wouldn't be heard anyway, afraid to try to get up, afraid to relinquish her position. She pointed her gun at the darkness. She would kill if necessary to save her baby.

Nilda sat in the car and waited. The thunder and downpour would make it easy for them to get away with the kidnapping. Nilda wanted the money, the jewelry, even the excitement, but as the rain pummeled the car and night fell on the deserted street her nerves twitched and jumped. She wouldn't wait a second longer; she didn't have the stomach for helping him steal a baby. She turned on the ignition, afraid to think of what Jesus would do when he discovered she was gone, and she drove headlong into the sheets of water.

Jesus's voice pelted her eardrum along with the hollow din of the raindrops on the car roof. Before he had slammed the car door shut he had tried to frighten her, making her wonder if he was crazier than Esperanza.

"I don't wan' no money," he had snarled. "Money don't mean shit to me. After the kidnap she ain't gettin' the baby back," he had warned. "I hate the fuckin' baby."

She had tried to fend off his anger with silence, her heart drumming with fear as he told her, his voice sounding dead, "I have a more better plan." She pressed harder on the accelerator, blocking out his voice, glad she had driven off without him, her heart getting lighter the faster she drove.

"I'll kill the baby," Jesus had sworn.

32

Nilda double-parked the car in front of Esperanza's apartment house. She could barely keep her feet from running. She was game for anything, but not murder.

There was a glistening quiet in the washed streets. She had to warn Esperanza. Jesus was way in over his head, and Nilda wanted out. He was talking about an innocent baby.

She ran from the car, straining her heart, thanking God she was young, that she could run as fast as a deer. In four minutes flat she was pounding on the door and Esperanza opened it.

"Jesus will bring a baby," she said, panting. "Hide the baby. Do you understand? Jesus will hurt the baby." The baby's only chance was to make Esperanza understand.

"I'm hurting, my little Nilda," Esperanza said. Tears were forming in her eyes. She sat on her bed holding her stomach and rubbing her back. She beckoned with her fingers weakly. Nilda twisted the cap on the plastic pill container. Esperanza gulped the two pills down before Nilda brought her the water.

"Esperanza, I can't keep the baby." I'm leaving Jesus, and he doesn't know it yet, she thought. She had to disappear before Jesus came home with the baby.

"After I make confession," Esperanza entreated. "Let me find my little priest, the young priest, before I die, to die in peace. Jesus won't let me," she cried.

Nilda helped Esperanza to the door, into the elevator, and out to the street. She was so light when she leaned on Nilda that

Nilda wondered how she would make it. Nilda pressed a bill into Esperanza's hand, put her in a cab, gave the driver the address, and took off.

Esperanza wondered whether she had the strength to continue. When the cab dropped her at the steps of Holy Name, she crossed herself, realizing she would never reach the top without help. She beckoned to a woman hurrying by. But it was no use. She was ignored. *"Por favor,"* she asked a workman strolling past on his way to the subway. He tried to avoid her eyes and moved on, thinking she was a beggar.

A teenager cautiously approached, and Esperanza pointed up the steep steps. He walked her slowly, supporting her until they reached the top. She walked into the cool, dark church alone after looking up at the sky. She stepped up to the deserted altar and entered the beautifully carved wooden confessional box. The pills had done their work. She felt no pain stabbing her innards, burning her back like an iron. She gave thanks that the waves of euphoria and peace were mercifully descending on her. She was surprised when the purple velvet curtains parted.

"Come back Saturday," the young deacon urged her. *"No hoy,"* he explained, indicating the confessional to her uncomprehending eyes. She grasped his arm. "DiFalco," she whispered, his name flying magically through the years to her tongue. She slipped to her knees, crying.

The deacon lifted her and shook his head. *"Esper aqui,"* he told her. And he ran to get DiFalco. This poor woman looked dreadfully ill. He would make an exception.

"The Virgin gave me a baby," Esperanza confessed.

Father DiFalco listened, believing her to be raving.

"But now I know it was wrong, because God has punished me. I'm dying a horrible death like my mother. I want to be forgiven. I've caused *La Mala* to be hurt the way I was hurt. But I beg forgiveness before I die."

The priest waited. He wondered if she was still breathing. No sound came for a while.

"Go on," he coaxed nervously.

"I named him Jesus. I meant no sacrilege. He was baptized. I gave him new life on Christmas Day."

DiFalco's thoughts were confused. The way she spoke of this son, Jesus, a common Spanish name, had a bizarre, other-worldly quality.

"I will have a new baby," she promised, her speech becoming more slurred and rambling. She rose from the box without a word.

A schizo, he thought. Then the voice, the crazy way she talked prompted him to ask a question. "Tell me your name," he asked, following her, helping her down the stairs.

"Esperanza," she answered. His heart skipped. "Lebron," she added, suddenly fearful. The priest's skin shivered, fear covering him like a sheet. He followed close behind. He must find out where she lived. E.L., *Esperanza Lebron*, the woman he was searching for!

God had handed him a gift, and he would hand it to Les, if only she would lead him home. Then he would find a phone, call Les, and tell him he had found his son!

• • •

Jesus waited until he realized that Nilda was not coming back for him. His usual decisiveness eluded him now. For a second he felt played out, his will exhausted. He hated Julie, hated the baby, but saying he would kill it and doing it were different. Why should that baby have everything, the easy life, love, a mother and a father? It was his house, not this baby's house. Conflict churned his guts as he stood behind the curtained door staring into the shining, rain-swept street. Nilda had deserted him; he would never see her again. No hope left, he thought. What was the point of getting up in the morning? Poor Esperanza would be dead soon. Even if Julie saw him now, he decided, he had nothing to lose.

33

Nothing moved. There was no sound in the house. Why was he waiting? The longer he waited, the better the chance that Greg would come.

She couldn't risk crawling to the phone. She was dizzy when she moved her head, and blood trickled down her neck, spilled onto her shirt. She didn't dare touch her head to feel the opening, the horrible crack, or she would faint.

Was he gone? She heard only night noises from the street. The house was dense with silence. But she knew he was there from the feel of the quiet. He was waiting to take her baby away.

The phone rang throughout the house, breaking her trance. She had waited and waited, interminably, ready to shoot. If he wanted the baby, he would have attacked her again, she thought. Her head was clear now; only the pain in her ankle slowed her.

She crawled out of her corner into the darkened hallway, slowly toward her bedroom—slowly to be quiet, slowly because she held her baby, slowly because she held the gun.

The phone kept ringing. Someone knew she was home.

Jesus crept to the front door, leaving it ajar for Nilda, hoping she would come. He climbed the stairs noiselessly and entered the nursery. Julie had picked up the phone.

"It's Les," Julie heard. "I've found our son! His name is Jesus."

The blood drained from her face. *Jesus had told her the truth!* And she had turned him away. Her body trembled. She could *feel* the truth of it now. Jesus *was* her child.

"He's here!" she cried out.

"The police," Jesus thought, yanking the phone wire from the wall. He stepped out into the hallway, looking for Julie.

Julie dropped the phone and backed into the corner, cowering at the sound of footsteps clumping down the hallway. Her heart raced. He stepped into the doorway. The light silhouetted Jesus's familiar frame.

Fear throbbed in her throat. She sat on the floor, her feet straight out, cradling her baby, the gun in her lap.

"*Jesus!*" she sobbed.

"Shoot me!" he said, stepping out of the light of the doorway into the dark of the room. He flipped on the light. "Go ahead, shoot me!" he repeated, advancing. "I'm nothin'. I'm not human."

"You don't *understand.* . . ." Julie reached for the gun. Her hand shook violently.

"Go ahead!" he shrieked. "See if I bleed. See if my blood is red like yours." He took a step menacingly toward her.

She released the safety. If he moved one more inch toward her he would be close enough to hurt the baby. If he took one more step. . . .

Jesus took one step, daring her. He laughed.

"I wan' something from you," he said.

Julie felt fear spread in her stomach. She knew she couldn't shoot. She knew her finger would never move the trigger, and she knew he wanted the baby. Her heart beat wildly.

How could she tell Jesus she loved him? Why would he believe her now?

She was desperate to play for time. "Do you want me to tell you," she began, imagining him as she had every year of his life, as a little boy sitting on her lap each night before he went to bed as she read him to sleep, crooning in his ear, "to tell you the story of when you were little and how I loved you?"

"Tell me," he pleaded. "Yes."

And she began to tell him . . .

• • •

Les crept up the stairs and into the room where they were.

"It's Jesus!" Julie blurted out.

Les was rooted to the spot. He saw the anger in Jesus's face, the toughness, the mean eyes as Jesus turned to him.

An intruder, a mugger, but not his son!

But suddenly Jesus recognized Les, from the article in the paper, from the picture on the CD. He took a step toward him to look into his face.

The anger on Jesus's face collapsed. Julie lowered the gun into her lap, holding her infant to her.

Jesus looked into Les's eyes, struggling with the momentary flicker of disgust he had detected, probing deeply for a sign that he was wanted as a son.

Les searched for his baby in Jesus's face. Fourteen years of loneliness peeled away, years his son had spent without him, fourteen years when he hadn't shielded him from harm, held him when he was sick, loved him. He put his arms around his son, pitying them both, crying as he held him.

34

The wailing in Les's ears terrified him. For a moment he couldn't tell where it was coming from. And when he finally understood, he really didn't want to know. The sounds were primal, from a place so deep inside her she hardly knew it existed. Julie was expelling years of fear and anger. Then, sobbing hysterically, she clung to her baby.

Jesus knelt down beside Julie. Her heart jumped in spite of herself. He put his hand out to touch her wet cheek, to wash away the blood with his hand, but he was afraid.

"Don't cry," he begged. "I wanted to hurt you . . ." His chest heaved with the emotion he had lost control of. "Because you closed the door on me!"

He faced the wall, unable to look at Julie's eyes. "When I brung my baby clothes to you, you turned your back on me even though you was my own mother." For a frightening moment he began to bang his head into the wall. Les grabbed him, hugging him, turning him around. Jesus's tears were streaming down Les's shoulder, his face now buried in Les's neck. "I ain't so bad," Jesus cried. "I just wanted to love her," he said.

Julie reached over and touched Jesus's hair as Les cried with him, still hugging him, rocking him, comforting him. And Julie's heart filled with pain and sorrow at the sight of them, emotion filling her up like water rising, dammed up with the cruelty life had visited upon Jesus, on all of them. She reached for Les's outstretched hand. He pulled her close. She put her arms around Jesus, too. "My baby," she cried. "Oh God, yes," she whispered. "You're just my own little boy."

She cried, seeing the look in his eyes, remembering his eyes when his ducks were smashed, how her heart had broken at the sight of his soul in pain. Now his eyes revealed ten times the pain, a hundred times the pain, so she cried for him until she had no tears left. And when the cold and the dark and their drained emotions left nothing more for them to do but to rise wearily from the floor together, she wished that their newfound hope was not just another illusion.

• •

Jesus sat numbly between Les and Julie in Wolfson's Fifth Avenue office, oblivious to the paintings, the leather furniture, the muted colors of the upholstery, focusing on his fear. His warrior heart, the heart that thrived on fear, now drummed a dirge. He knew his fate would be decided here.

Wolfson eyed Jesus, with his sullen look, his gaze downcast to avoid confrontation, a look that couldn't mask boiling turmoil, resentment. How Wolfson hated to convey to them the unbearable truth. He watched Les, happy and eager, watching Jesus, hardly able to take his eyes from his son. A former addict with a seriously troubled child. The blind leading the blind.

And Julie, vulnerable, confused, emotional, on the edge. How could he even begin to understand her array of feelings? And then Eleanore, who had flown in the day before, brought into this room by fate. And choice. She sat apart as if to deliberately separate herself from Les and Julie. Resolute and composed, thought Wolfson. He knew that with training as a psychiatric nurse she would be sympathetic to his judgment.

Throughout the meeting Julie watched Wolfson. She remembered his gentle voice from the tape, could see the distress in his face, could sense the awful news he was trying to give them.

"In my opinion," Wolfson said sadly, "the best place for this boy—" and now he looked directly into Jesus's eyes—"would be in a halfway house."

Jesus's heart stirred. Fear rose in his throat. He had lost everything!

Julie saw the look of fright on Jesus's face.

"An institution?" Les burst out. "I can't believe what you're saying!"

"Yes," Wolfson confirmed. He turned to Jesus again, addressing him directly. "If you were my own son, I would tell you it's the best place for you, at least for now."

Jesus crushed the urge to jump out of his seat to yell, "You ain't God! You can't take them away from me now!" But sitting between Julie and Les, he tamed his instinct to fend for himself and calmed the storm inside him, remembering Julie's fingers in his hair, the way she held him close.

Tears brimmed in his eyes. And Julie couldn't bear it.

"You're not prepared to handle a crisis situation like this," Wolfson told Julie and Les. "You're both too emotionally involved. Serious crimes have been committed. Can you deal with these problems? Honestly, you must think of getting help for Jesus."

"I have the training," announced Eleanore, speaking up for the first time. "I have more emotional distance, and I believe I have an understanding of this situation," she stated simply. "I have the motivation too," she added, looking over at Les.

Les swallowed hard. He didn't have the right words to convince Wolfson. His Eleanore, his brave, strong Eleanore was his voice of reason.

"Les has very deep feelings for Jesus," Eleanore continued. "No institution can give him love. Jesus needs a father. And I have resources available to me where we live. I know competent therapists. We want him. That counts for a lot. And we can take care of him. We understand the risks."

Wolfson was impressed with Eleanore. She was a levelheaded person. He imagined that she would be a good therapist.

"You know what institutions are like," Eleanore reminded him, drawing on their mutual experience.

Wolfson knew it was not his time to speak.

Eleanore saw the expression in Julie's eyes, seeing how torn she was. "I can be the bridge between you and Jesus," she promised.

Julie gripped Jesus's arms tightly and looked into his face. "Is that what you want? Would you want to live with . . . your father . . ." her voice broke, "and Eleanore?"

Jesus nodded. Julie embraced Jesus with full force for the first time, clinging to him, not wanting to lose him, knowing this was the only way she could have him forever.

Epilogue

Summer 1987

Jesus watched the Manhattan skyline curve away as the jet lifted over the city, headed for the West Coast.

"You can live with us as long as you like," Les said.

"Esperanza . . ."

"She'll be taken care of," Les assured Jesus. "In a hospice near Marcos. El will arrange everything, make sure she gets excellent care. You can visit her," he promised.

"Do you like the beach?" Les asked, trying to distract Jesus.

"Sure, man," Jesus said.

"You'll love our house in Monterey," Les said.

Jesus felt a heavy curtain being raised, giving him a feeling of weightlessness. It was a new feeling, being taken care of. Maybe it was the plane lifting off. But there was some fear too. He thought of Esperanza wasting away, of his new life without her. He looked out through the small window at the glare of the sky. The clouds were below him now.

He had waited to open the letter Julie had handed him when she left the terminal, waited for Les to open his book, embarrassed that his heart was pounding.

Dear Jesus,

I always knew you were my son. I know it's hard to believe, but I searched for you for so long my brain told me it was a lie when we found each other. But my heart told me the truth. Maybe we can make up for all the lost years when we weren't together.

Les has waited for you for so long. He will be a good father to you. He loves you. You can rely on Greg. He will love you too. And Eleanore is ready to open her arms to you.

And I have never stopped loving you, even when I didn't know where you were, when I imagined you far away from me somewhere on this cruel earth.

Jesus turned to look at the clouds. He couldn't bear to let anyone see his face when he read, "All my love, your mother, Julie," because he was afraid he would cry.

• • •

Julie stopped as she and Greg reached the walkway along the East River. They were headed for the River's Edge, the restaurant Martha had chosen for their meeting.

"I'm so sorry," she whispered to Greg. "After all you've been through—my lies, my presenting you with a new, difficult son, who may never be . . ."

Greg didn't let her finish. "We've been up nights for a week talking this through. I've told you it will be okay. But I still don't understand why you didn't tell me.

"I was *afraid* to tell you. I wanted everything perfect for the baby. And then when he was born I loved him too much to tell you. You live such a measured life, everything under control, no messes."

"I may like order, but I love you, Julie."

"Be honest. Wouldn't it have scared you away to know that my former husband was a junkie, that my baby was kidnapped and that the kidnapper was never found, that the police suspected Les and even me?"

"I hope not, I don't know. It's pretty scary stuff."

Greg saw Julie's face crumble.

"I can deal with Jesus. Now that it's all out in the open, we can work it out," Greg assured her, taking her hands. "He has four good people working on his case."

The tugboats on the river suddenly took on a new sound. They tooted hopefully, she thought, as she and Greg arrived at the restaurant.

"You were right, I could have killed him," Julie said to

Martha as they sat at their table, the river at their feet. She
slipped Martha the Beretta. The sky was dark blue. They sat
watching the barges slide along silently, illuminated by strings
of lights. There was a sliver of a moon. Each was lost in
thought.

"That demented Esperanza might not have taken your baby
if it weren't for Gatreaux," Greg said at last. "The police would
never have put it together if she hadn't told Jesus she saw him in
the newspaper."

Julie and Martha were silent.

"Toasts are in order tonight," Greg said, looking at Julie.
He ordered a bottle of wine. When it arrived, he raised his glass.
"To our new family," said Greg.

"To Jesus. Les, Junior," Julie said. "To the life I once
dreamed for you."

Martha raised her glass. They watched as she let the Beretta
slip from her fingers into the deep waters of the river.